LOVE OF THE BLOOD

LOIS SLATER

Gotham Books

30 N Gould St.
Ste. 20820, Sheridan, WY 82801
https://gothambooksinc.com/

Phone: 1 (307) 464-7800

© 2023 *Lois Slater*. All rights reserved.

No part of this book may be reproduced, stored in a retrieval system, or transmitted by any means without the written permission of the author.

Published by Gotham Books (November 14, 2023)

ISBN: **979-8-88775-566-3** (H)
ISBN: **979-8-88775-564-9** (P)
ISBN: **979-8-88775-565-6** (E)

Because of the dynamic nature of the Internet, any web addresses or links contained in this book may have changed since publication and may no longer be valid.

The views expressed in this work are solely those of the author and do not necessarily reflect the views of the publisher, and the publisher hereby disclaims any responsibility for them.

The Baxter Saga: featuring Liza and Lizzie Baxter
Stem of the Wildflower

Aspyn: whose love and devotion is unending

…….. always Chanda……..

PROLOGUE
SECRETS

Luke hurried like a madman as he put Willie and Becky's lifeless bodies in the back of the wagon and covered them with loose straw. There was no reason for anyone to know the about the failed escape that happened here in the shelter of the quiet barn. If Abe had any idea that Becky had been alive all these years—that she had been the one who had tried to kill the twins and kidnap Sarah, why it would simply push the man over the edge of reason.

The hired horse wrangler and devoted cook would see to it personally that no one would ever know about this travesty. That he and dear sweet Maria would take it to their graves. "Killer's!" he hollered. "You don't deserve burying!"

The salty cowhand gave Maria a knowing look as he rolled the wagon behind the back side of the majestic barn and headed toward the Old Willow pasture. That cursed piece of ground that seemed to cling to the Lazy AB Ranch like a festered boil. He would dump these two liars down that lightless cavern in that old ghastly place where they belonged. Vermin lived there. In his eyes these two were no better. When Luke thought of the horrible double-cross Abe's so-called brother-in-law Willie had done it made him want to shoot him again! All those years of nothing but lies! For his own benefit! "Jackal!" he yelled aloud through angry lips as he pounded the backsides of the hurrying team. He couldn't get rid of these blood-sucking killers fast enough

CHAPTER 1

Several years had come and gone as the Baxter ranch continued to prosper at an accelerated rate. The Lazy AB ranch was the largest parcel of settled ground in the Western valley. The notorious family had guarded the boundaries of their hard-fisted dynasty with the ultimate sacrifice, their own blood.

Abe had turned the horse and cattle duties of the ranch over to his twin daughter's Liza and Lizzie. Even though they were young they were seasoned cattle women and masters at their trade. They kept a tight rein on the business and a steady stream of livestock coming and going. It seemed they couldn't keep enough green broke horses or cattle available to trail or ship back to the army or their Eastern buyers. No one came out unscathed that tried to pull a high- jink's over on Liza and Lizzie Baxter. On this ranch their word was law!

The lumber business kept Abe going at a steady pace between the ranch and the established camp. Three things a man needed in settling a territory, lumber, dry goods, and water which he shared graciously with the drovers and settlers that trailed through.

For years this beautiful terrain had been barren of folks. Well with the exception of the hired hands that seemed to stagger through then disappeared like dry grass. But the explosion of restless people wanting a better life for themselves and their families seemed to get larger every day. Several smaller ranches seemed to pop up overnight pressing the serenity of the Lazy AB Ranch, crowding the perimeter of their sanctioned home.

It was awkward having neighbors on the outer limits of their protected boundaries and Liza and Lizzie didn't like it one bit! They rode the high-lying plateaus like two mighty warriors ready to do battle if a portion of their sacred savanna became disturbed. And, the outliers respected their space. Not only because of their constant patrol but also because they knew the identical women wouldn't hesitate to do exactly what they said. Trespass, and you'd be wearing a bullet! They had their own kind of justice riding right on the side of their hips.

Abe was proud of how quickly Liza's twin boys, Matthew and Jeffrey had caught on to the trade of the whole ranching business. Although lately, Jeffery seemed to be more interested in what was going on in the small scant looking place called Crocker that had sprung up out of nowhere, than he did for doing chores on the ranch. Suddenly, he'd become important. A ladies man enjoying his pride-filled ride to fame on the shirttail of his family's name. Not that he actually did any of the work.

His twin brother Matthew on the other hand was interested in every aspect of the ranch from the cattle, to the horses, to the lumber camp. It saturated his blood like a lifeline just like his mother's. Abe had a feeling after he was long gone and his bones turned to dust, that Matthew would be the one running things. He had the head and the heart for it.

Then there was sweet Naomi. Little Feather. She had grown to be a beautiful young woman. Wild as a blowing tumbleweed. Just like the one she called mother. She too had made it a point to learn the ranching business inside out. Lizzie wouldn't have settled for anything less. But deep down in her soul the girl loved it anyway. It was like the sweet prairie air filled her hungry lungs the way a single drop of sweat clings to a horse's frothy neck. She had a born spirit that boiled deep within her soul and a natural light that shined like a star around her.

It was unnerving at times how much she had grown to look like her dead mother, Sarah, and her grandmother Becky. Her long berry colored hair grew like wild grass as it hung to her thin waist like satin. And, she had the most startling eyes! They had a way of grasping your attention only to toss you aside when she blinked her distain. Her actions, however, were anything but those of her mother's. No, she was one hundred percent Lizzie Baxter's daughter. As though the wild child had been carried in the very womb of the cagey twin.

It had remained a mystery as to which twin actually gave birth to the beautiful child. As far as Liza and Lizzie were concerned it wasn't anyone else's business to know which of them was the birth mother to the little girl, and they dared anyone to ask. No one to date had been brave enough. When one of the snooty women would sullenly hide behind their wrist fans, whispering their distaste, one or the other twin would pull their horse to a stop, turn, look directly at them, and watch them scurry down the wooded walk like a fleeing rat.

Liza and Lizzie didn't give a hoot about becoming outcasts of society! They welcomed it! Raising their dead sister's mystery child was an honor they took seriously. A shared responsibility they carried equally.

Only those who were there for Naomi's rebirth knew Chief Flying Eagle and Sarah Baxter were her real father and mother. And, no one outside of the Baxter family needed to know. The penalty for any member revealing Naomi's true birthright would be death.

CHAPTER 2

Together the small group routinely made their way on a monthly basis into the small place which had exploded into thriving businesses for the settlers and drifters to buy supplies. At first it was suffocating seeing so many people that carried odd scents in one place. But now it had become a ritual of necessity that sure beat having to go all the way to Cheyenne, which took a good week coming and going.

Abe had declined their invitation to come to town on this beautiful summer day. He had more pleasant business he'd told them with a twinkle in his warm caring eyes. After all the years their father's heart had laid dormant it was good to see some kind of life make its way back into his hollow shell. The loneliness in his tired face had tortured Liza and Lizzie for too long.

The twins both knew that the other business was a beautiful Indian Princess named Dancing Bear. She was the only living member of Chief Mad Dogs or Chief Flying Eagles' tribe that had survived the horrendous ordeal of death. Naomi's only living blood relative from her father's tribe. And, although she was very vague about the first months of Little Feathers' existence it was obvious that the child meant more to the woman than life itself.

Still Dancing Bear never overstepped her bounds when Lizzie was involved in Little Feather's disciplining. No one over stepped Lizzie's boundaries! She was the ramrod of the outfit! What Lizzie said was law! It didn't have to be written, it didn't have to be explained, it was just a given. Not once did anyone see the tempered twin abuse her title, she was always fair when it came to the children. Everyone knew what Lizzie said is how it would be and if her instructions weren't convincing enough, they dealt with Liza. One tornado was enough!

The twin's didn't mind the match. They loved Dancing Bear. After her long black hair fell out like loose straw from a broom. After her face healed from the hideous blisters that ravaged her sick body. After the poison that had killed her entire tribe had left the pores of her plagued skin. After months of healing with the help of the ones who loved her, a miracle happened. She became the epitome of health. Her distinguished maidan feature's came back tenfold. She was stunning as she bloomed like a beautiful prairie flower. She became stronger every day as she helped Maria with little effort in the large old kitchen learning broken English. A simple, affectionate attraction had innocently wound itself like a sweet bouquet between the estranged Indian Princess and the stately Cattle Baron.

"Never thought we'd be within a hundred miles of someplace to buy our goods," Liza said from out of nowhere as she clucked at the moving team.

"Yeah, me neither. And look," Lizzie proudly smiled at her sister, "don't we just have the best company in the world?"

"Why, yes we do, sister. I'd say that someone did a pretty good job in raising them."

"Honestly, I can't take all the credit," Lizzie stated seriously.

Irritated at her sister's selfish remark Liza gave Lizzie a frown as she spoke, "Who said you get all of the credit?"

"Well," Lizzie spit back insulted at her sister's offhanded remark, "I did put in a lot of sleepless nights you know."

"Sleepless nights! You might have put in a few whining nights. I'm not so sure about sleepless!"

"What are you saying? That I didn't work as hard as you did? That I didn't put in as many hours a night as you did listening to those three yowling coyotes?" she snapped back.

"I'm not saying that!" Liza said disgusted at how her identical sibling had turned her words around. "Now, don't go putting words in my mouth!"

"Why not! You seem to have enough of everything else in there!" she stated hotly.

"What in the world does that mean?" Liza argued right back.

"You know what it means!" she challenged.

"Don't make me stop this wagon, Lizzie!" Liza threatened.

"Or what?" she dared her.

"Mother," Matthew said interrupting the battling duo with a huge grin on his handsome face, "I don't think any of us are any worse for the wear."

The three cousins grinned at each other. The behavior of the identical sisters never ceased to amaze them. They had a built in competition that was like a constant inner battle, always pitting one against the other on a daily basis.

"True," the twins grinned as Liza clucked the horses up a notch.

"Mother," Naomi asked, "can I buy some of that delicious looking blue cloth that I saw the last time we came in to town? I'd love to have a bonnet that color. And maybe a new dress for—you know the harvest dance."

"A bonnet!" Jeffrey piped up. "Good Lord, Naomi! What, you gonna wear that out gathering cattle?"

"I think that's a great idea," Matthew interrupted. "Besides, what difference does it make to you if she wants a bonnet? You're not wearing it." Matthew gave his brother an irritated look. It seemed like his twin sibling was always trying to start something with their petite cousin. Always finding ways to disrespect her.

"How do you know I won't wear it, brother?" Jeffrey said in a challenging tone.

"Because if I catch you anywhere near one of my bonnets," Naomi said in a threatening voice, "I will disassemble something near and dear to your heart!"

"Mother," Jeffrey whined, completely put off at his cousins underhanded remark, "did you hear what that little heathen said? Where do you think she learned that? Where's her bar of soap!"

"What did you call me?" Naomi snapped. Shocked that he would use her native heritage in such a derogatory way. "You'd better take that back, you horn toad!"

"Yeah," Matthew said completely taken aback at his brother's rude remark. "She's not a heathen; she's the daughter of a mighty Indian Chief. He was the heathen."

Naomi gave her cousin an odd look. "What?"

"Sorry," he said kindly, "that didn't come out like I meant it." Once again he looked into his brothers angry eyes. "You take that back!"

"See, mother, I told you, it's always two against one!" Jeffrey whined.

"Reap what you sow, Jeffrey," Liza said in an offended tone. "And I don't want to hear you refer to Naomi or anyone else on this ranch in that manner again." Her dark eyes showed that she meant it. "If I do, you and I will be taking a trip to the wood shed. Is that understood?"

The defiant young man rode along the side the wagon with no response ignoring his mother completely. He had turned out to be a stubborn boy with an ugly disposition.

"I believe that your mother is talking to you young man," Lizzie countered without looking up. "Don't make her repeat it or you and I will go to the woodshed—now."

"All right, mother!" he said almost immediately through angry lips. "I'm sorry. I didn't mean anything by it. Sorry, Naomi," he added in a flippant manner.

"Well," Naomi teased, "if you would really like a bonnet of your own I'd be glad to make you one."

"Naomi!" Lizzie knew the little snot would come up with something. "I think that's enough!"

"See! It's fine when she does it!" Jeffrey whined.

"No, it's not fine!" Lizzie gave her daughter a warning look. "Naomi you apologize to your cousin…Now!"

"I will not!" she said defiantly. "He started it!"

"Well, he might have started it young lady, but I will finish it in about two seconds if you don't do what I ask." Her tone held a definite warning.

"Yes, Mother Lizzie," she said stubbornly. "I'm sorry, Jeffrey."

The small party traveled for several minutes before anyone spoke. "I don't think blue is his color anyway, Aunt Lizzie," Matthew said from out of nowhere. Completely taken aback at his candid remark the small party broke into a round of laughter.

"I think I'll get papa something special, if that's all right with you, Mother Lizzie," Naomi said. "I have a few extra dollars I've saved."

"I'm sure he would like that," Liza answered. "He loves surprises." She gave her sister a knowing grin as she countered her last statement. "From his grandchildren!"

"I'm going to get him some of that candy he likes so well. You know, those long pink sticks," Jeffery added.

"Me, too," Matthew said. "And let's don't forget Maria, Luke, and Dancing Bear. They might like something, too."

Lizzie and Liza were proud of their children. And, for the most part they were goodhearted and compassionate. Naomi had turned out to be a beautiful flower just like her mother had been. She was a rare gem with a presentation that said she could hold her own. She didn't take any crap from either one of her cousins even though they towered over her like an old oak. She had a quick snappy temper and she was fearless in most situations. The boys knew better than to make her too mad because they never really knew what she would do. She might look petite and fragile but she fought like a grizzly, both, physically and verbally. When Naomi walked into a room—she filled it up with a presence that said, 'she was there'.

Matthew was the living replica of Abe Baxter. He was a tall sturdy built young man with wide broad shoulders. He had black curly hair that he wore at the nap of his tanned muscled neck. He had kind blue eyes that teased his aunt and mother on a constant basis. His disposition was warm, affectionate, and giving. He treated everyone the same, young, and old. He loved the ranch and everything that went with it. He was extremely bright as far as numbers and figures were concerned, which had helped Abe tremendously. Matthew had a heart of gold and a soul like an angel. There wasn't a young lady in the valley that didn't want to drag Matthew Jones Baxter to the altar of matrimony.

Jeffrey on the other hand was the spit-n-image of his father, Jacob. A tall, stout looking boy with sea green eyes that expelled his arrogance and self proclaimed importance. His hair was as yellow as the suns golden rays and sat in a curly heap at the nap of his neck. Somewhere along the line he had grown quite fond of himself. He had a big head and mouth to match it. He had an unkind, overbearing personality. If trouble didn't find Jeffrey he would surely find it.

He was a troubled boy that always seemed to be looking for something just past where he was. That elusive dream of greener pastures just waiting on the other side of nothing that had a way of slipping through his greedy grasp. He stood on the breaking point of right and wrong. Wrong bordering the fine line of justice. The older Jeffrey became the lazier and more arrogant he got. And the more arrogant he became the less interest he showed in the ranch. He'd caused his mother many sleepless nights and worrisome days.

He would argue endlessly over anything and everything. He always had to be right. Whether it made any sense or not. That is until Lizzie stepped into the picture and chastised his behavior. He was afraid of Lizzie. And with good cause. She never believed any of his deranged explanations and he knew it.

"Mother?" Matthew asked. "What do you suppose papa had to do today that was so important? I mean not coming with us and all?" His sky blue eyes twinkled against the summer sun. "He loves going to town."

Liza looked to her sister for help before she kiddingly answered, "Well, I don't know for sure but I think maybe he's takin quite a liking to Dancing Bear. At least I think that's who the picnic basket was for." Teasingly, they hit each other in the ribs.

"Mother!" Jeffrey exclaimed in a vexed tone. "He's not interested in her like that! Not her!"

"And what is wrong with her?" Liza asked, surprised at her son's critical assessment.

"She's an Indian for one thing! Nothing but a dirty old squaw!" he answered in an offended state. "More-n-likely she's been tossed around from one brave to another! She should be with someone of her own kind, not my papa!"

With that searing remark coming out of his mean-spirited mouth, Naomi let out a piercing yowl that deafened everyone within fifty feet! Like a lion she jumped from the back of her horse onto the back of Jeffrey's saddle. The terrified animal let out a loud squeal as it recklessly jumped into the walking team. It was all Liza could do to hang on to the set of startled horses as they bolted off of the well-trodden trail.

"Whoa!" she ordered the heaving beasts just as both riders hit the dirt with a loud thud. Jeffrey of course was on the bottom.

There was no missing the heated profanity coming out of sweet Naomi's typically innocent mouth as she clung to Jeffrey's back like a burr. She was hell bent on destruction, pounding her cousin's head into the dirt when Lizzie pulled her off. "Shut up!" she screamed. "Shut your filthy mouth! You don't know what she went through! You weren't there!"

"I know she's a stinkin Injun!" he hissed back. "She shouldn't even be on our ranch! Nothing more than dirt!"

"I'll show you dirt you piece of dog dung! Here eat this!" Purposely, she slammed her cousin's face into the dusty road.

"Naomi!" Lizzie yelled as she grabbed her by the back of the pants. "Stop it right now!"

Liza walked to where her insubordinate son lay face down in the sandy dirt sputtering like a floundering bird. She shook her head as she stared at the young man. "You my son are going to learn life the hard way." She let out a disgruntled sigh. "Have you any idea what it is that you just said? Do you not realize that you have insulted your cousin? Our Naomi. Not to say me and your Aunt. Have you forgotten who her father is? The sacrifice that we have made as a family? You cannot be my son. My son would never say anything so hurtful!"

In one quick motion, Lizzie literally threw Naomi up into the seat of the waiting wagon. She was fighting mad and no one, not even Liza said a word. "You stay there young lady!" she demanded.

With tears running down her dirty furious face Naomi answered, "Yes, ma'am."

Lovingly, Lizzie ran her work-worn finger down Naomi's soft wet cheek. Jeffery had crossed the line today. He had been acting like a little shit since early morning. He unfortunately had Jacobs ugly disposition and a little of his mothers. The kind of disposition that guilted Liza into believing that life wasn't his fault and made it hard for her to control him. But not Lizzie. She knew all about Mr. Jeffery and if learning the hard way was his destiny in life then far be it from her to keep him from getting there. Every day that passed he reminded Lizzie more and more of Jacob with his rude cutting remarks and self-important disposition. Now there would be a punishment for it. "Get on your horse you little scab!" she hissed like a snake. Her eyes were black as coal.

"Mother," Jeffrey whined in a terrified tone.

Lizzie never asked him again. She simply picked him up by the back of the pants and the nap of the shirt and like a sack of grain threw him onto the back of his skittish pony. With one quick movement she mounted Naomi's horse holding the other's rein. Then like a burst of thunder the two of them tore off into the distance. As they disappeared Jeffery was holding on for dear life.

"Don't kill him, Lizzie," Liza hollered faintly in a motherly tone. "I bet he thinks twice about what comes out of that mouth of his next time. He rubs her raw just like father did." Liza looked at Naomi's broken face, "I'm sorry, baby, he's just got a lot of anger."

"I'm sorry too, Naomi," Matthew said in a concerned tone although he played no part in his brothers actions. "I love you no matter what you are." The handsome man gave her an apologetic look, no matter what he said it didn't seem to come out right.

"Thanks," Naomi said sweetly to her cousin. "I think." Then she added, "Mother, she won't hurt him will she?"

Naomi gave Matthew a weak smile. She loved Matthew. He was so kind and caring. But that blasted Jeffery, he was going to get someone killed. "I'm sorry, Aunt Liza, it's my fault. I shouldn't have provoked him."

"You just hush about it, Naomi," she sighed. "It doesn't seem to take much to provoke your cousin. Besides, I have a feeling we'll see them both before we get to town," Liza thought about her father's warning earlier. 'You keep an eye on that boy, Liza. He behaves when I'm around, but with you, well, that's a different story'. "I hear you, father," she whispered to herself. Now, she wished he would have come along.

CHAPTER 3

Several of the hands saw the two strangers ride into the yard of the Baxter ranch. When they finally came to a stop, one of the Baxter men went into the old log house. "Abe, someone outside."

"Where are the twins?"

"Supply day. They all went to town about an hour ago. Want me to tell em ta come back another time?"

"I plumb forgot they left."

"Want me to tell em to come back?"

"No, tell em I'll be out in a minute."

"Yes, sir."

As Abe stepped onto the wooded porch he got an uneasy feeling in the pit of his gut. It was the same feeling he always got when something bad was about to happen. There were two men in freshly starched suits sitting on two worn out looking horses. The heavier set one had that look of authority on his smug face. He reminded Abe of a stuffed bull frog. "I'm Abe Baxter," he said politely. "What you fellas need?"

The tall heavier set man stepped down from his horse as he nodded for the other to do the same. The latter of the two hesitated for a brief moment. As though he was watching for Abe's approval. "Ben Parks, this is my associate, Clinton Small." Purposely, the gentlemen exchanged handshakes. "Beautiful place you got here," he said as he wiped the sweat from his thick forehead.

"We like it," Abe answered with pride in his voice. By now Luke stood on the porch directly to the side of Abe with his shotgun in his hand. He wouldn't miss trouble with a shotgun.

"No reason for that," Ben stated as he glanced at the waiting gun. "We don't want no trouble. We're here on behalf of Mattie Brown." They waited for some kind of recognition from the man in front of them. When there was none Ben continued, "I am to the understanding that Mattie owns a certain piece of property that somehow has gotten tangled up with a part of your property."

"My property. I don't understand," Abe stated plainly. "No one owns a part of my property."

Within minutes the man dug out a piece of paper as he put on a small round pair of spectacles. The magnified glass made his eyes bug out like an old toad. "Um, let me see, yes, thirty five acres called the Old Willow Pasture. Something to do with an old white house?"

There was no missing the pain that etched itself across Abe's scruffy face like a toothache. He hadn't given that place much thought in years. In fact, it was never spoken of on the ranch.

"So, you do know the property that I'm talking about," he stated firmly.

"I know about a lot of property on this ranch. That's not a part of what's mine. What does that have to do with me?" he questioned plainly.

It was plain to see that the heavyset man didn't like the vague answer that Abe had given to him. "A lot actually, you see, Mrs. Brown is going to be bringing her family out here and occupying that particular piece of ground."

"And the problem is what?" Abe asked. He knew what the stiff shirted man was asking about but he'd get no information from him.

"That she is going to have to cross a chunk of your land to get to it," the man answered astonished at his illusive remark. "We've been told that there might be some problem with that right of way. I've been hired by the family to straighten that out, you know, before they get here." He looked at the stocky built man. "That's where Clinton here comes in, he's a map maker."

"Sir," Clinton said politely. There was something about Abe Baxter that he liked immediately. He was a man's man and if he'd learned anything in his short life it was to always expect the unexpected from his breed. Respect was the only thing they tolerated.

Abe acknowledged the younger man's presence with a slight nod as he turned his gaze back to the stuffy shirted fellow. "I've only known one person who held title to that particular piece of ground, and he's dead."

"Well, she's not dead. According to this, she owns it." His tone was sharp.

"Then it's only fair you know that right of way is going to be the least of your problems."

The heavier set man gave him an odd look. "How so?"

"The man that owned it worked on this ranch for a lot of years. I didn't realize that he had living relatives. But it's not me that you will be dealing with on this particular matter. My daughter's take care of the ranch business. You'll have to come back another day when they're here. You will be more than welcome to address this issue with them."

"Your daughter's!" the man scoffed aloud, astonished at the confession. "I believe that there has been some kind of a mistake here! I was told that Abe Baxter was the owner of this ranch. Not his daughters. I don't deal with women on matters of such importance!"

Abe had dealt with men just like this for years. Men that were pumped up with self made pride. Men that usually wound up lying dead on the prairie with a bullet in their gut because of it. "Well," Abe said knowing that the man was expecting a rise out of him, "you heard wrong. My two daughters, Liza and Lizzie Baxter run this place. And you will deal with them directly." Underneath, Abe felt a little sorry for the puffed-up man. With an attitude like this he'd surely be in for a big surprise having to deal with the twins.

"Do you know who it is that we are talking about here?" he injected once again.

"I guess I don't." Abe didn't want to do business with the rude man. "But it doesn't matter any way. I just told you that my daughter's will be taking care of that business."

The heavier set man plunged on. "You see, Mattie is the wife of Tad Brown." There was no immediate reaction. "Or maybe better known as Billy Watkins. I believe that Willie Dark deeded those acres over to him sometime before his death. Mattie is Billy's wife," he said as though Abe were daft or something. "I don't believe that your daughter's have precedence over that."

The very sound of Billy Watkins name cut through Abe like a heated knife cuts through cold butter. The heartache that the man had inflicted on his heart after all of these years was still very fresh. "Believe what you want, my daughter's will still have the final say on that."

"So, what you're saying is that Mattie is right. There is going to be a problem with this exchange."

"Mister," Abe said in an authoritative voice through dark intimidating eyes. "I'm standing here trying to figure out if you're being difficult on purpose or just deaf." The typically cool headed rancher's heart had been pricked like a fork in a sizzling steak and it was time for these city slickers to leave. "Like I said before you have no idea what the word problem is. Liza and Lizzie will chew you up and spit you out like a dried twig. You'd better have more than a flimsy piece of paper for them cause they don't cotton to stuff-shirted, loud mouthed, rude land crossers. Now, I think it's time for you to be leaving." There was no missing the sound of cocked rifles.

"I see," the man said arrogantly disappointed. "I guess we'll have to see what the Sheriff has to say about that." Like an old lizard he walked back and climbed onto his horse. "Clinton!"

"Sir," the stocky built man questioned Abe, "you don't happen to have any kind of written score to your ranch? You know to scale?" He asked with the utmost respect.

"Son," Abe said compassionately, "I built this ranch with these two hands. I know every tree, creek bed, canyon, rock, and field. I've never needed a map to distinguish my property."

"Of course, well, thank you, sir," Clinton said in a distant tone as he tapped his horses side.

There was something about Abe Baxter that Clinton liked. The self-made man was intriguing as he felt an implused draw. Now he was sorry he'd gotten mixed up in this mess at all. Purposely, he tipped his hat to the two men standing on the wooded porch as he headed his horse toward the gate of the Baxter ranch. Something told him nothing good was going to come out of this so-called charade no matter how much he hoped there'd be some way they could all come to a settled understanding without anyone getting killed. His uncle had met his match on this one. As the two men rode toward the small town Clinton Small hoped that they wouldn't run into the two lady outlaws that he'd heard so much about.

CHAPTER 4

Liza clucked the horses as the small party got closer to the two hanging trees that criss-crossed the shaded road. For a brief moment they swore that they could see something dangling like a swinging bat in the middle. Liza took in a regretful sigh as she recognized the swaying object. Naomi put her hand over her mouth in shock as the wagon came closer and closer. Matthew hurried ahead as he waited for the wagon to arrive.

"Hey, brother," he said seemingly unaffected by his siblings foolhardy situation.

"Shut up!" Jeffrey hollered in an angered tone. It was obvious that he was mad about his uncomfortable predicament.

"Where's Aunt Lizzie?" Matthew asked curiously as his eyes scanned the immediate area.

"How should I know?" he snapped. "Probably finding some rattlesnake to kill me with! Cut me down, brother," he begged pathetically. "Please, before she gets back, cut me down! I won't tell! I won't! She'll never know!"

Matthew leaned against the horn of his saddle as he studied the self-inflicted situation for several minutes. He didn't feel sorry for his brother in the least. "Sorry, she'd just put me up there instead. Sides, you got to learn to shut that big mouth of yours, Jeffrey. Naomi's our cousin. What you said was mean."

"I know," he whined in a convincingly dreadful tone. "I just get so mad! I don't know why I say stuff like that!"

"Well, maybe you'd better figure it out cause here comes mother," he said quietly. "She's hopping mad! And besides, you made Naomi cry."

"Don't upset the princess," he hissed sarcastically.

"See, there you go again." Matthew remarked.

Liza pulled the wagon just past her hanging son as she coaxed the horses to a slow stop. She spotted Lizzie right away hidden within the leafy branches of the thick heavy tree. "Are you done now, Jeffrey?" Liza asked in a distraught tone. "Making a fool of yourself. Are you quite done?"

"Yes," he said pitifully just as Lizzie cut the rope. The startled young man fell into the back of the wagon with a loud thud. "Ouch!" he hollered, but he never said any more than that. There was no denying the wild look in his mother's stormy eyes. It was one that he'd never experienced before.

Naomi was shocked as she watched Lizzie appear from out of nowhere. One minute there was nothing but the mourning sound of the silent wispy wind and the next her mother was completely visible. Like the breeze had hidden her slender silhouette within the safety of its invisible arms.

Jeffrey gave the crafty woman an apprehensive look. He'd had enough of his aunt Lizzie for one day. She was like the devil to him and he'd been pricked enough by her unforgiving hand. Like a well minded pup he climbed onto the back of his horse and took his place next to his brother. Lizzie climbed back in the wagon and Naomi climbed to the back of her own horse. Like a child Lizzie reached into her pocket and handed Liza a piece of honeycomb. They exchanged knowing glances as Liza clucked the team forward.

CHAPTER 5

When they arrived in the small town it was busy as usual. The twin's knew most of the curious faces that followed their wagon as they nodded their pretty heads with acknowledgement. It was an odd feeling seeing so many jabbering people gathered on one chunk of dirt. They'd yet to figure out how anyone could actually enjoy living right on top of one another. All of the bustling faces gave the twin women a choking feeling like being enclosed in a tight cage. It was a concept that they were still getting used to.

Within minutes they pulled up in front of the general store. "You kids get what you want, Lizzie and I have some business at the land office, when we're done we'll be back. Jeffrey and Matthew you two get the wagon loaded," Liza commanded. "That means you will help, Jeffrey," Liza warned.

"Yes, ma'am." Together the three of them walked into the small general store with the list of supplies that Liza had given them.

"Mornin'," the clerk smiled in a friendly fashion. "I'll take that." Automatically, he reached for the neatly written note and started filling their order.

"Oh, Matthew, look," Naomi remarked in a happy tone, "there's some of that blue cloth that I wanted! And yellow!" Her voice was so excited.

Behind her Jeffrey rolled his eyes to the back of his head and mumbled something that she couldn't hear as he reached for a handful of red striped candy. In a huff he placed it on the counter as he impatiently waited for the clerk to come and wait on him. "Look," Jeffrey said in a mocking tone as he glanced out the large, glassed storefront, "that old man is pathetic. Standing there begging. They should throw him in jail. It's getting to where a person can't walk down the street!"

"So what?" Matthew countered, "You scared?"

"No!" he stated in an indignant manner.

"He doesn't look like he's begging to me," Matthew countered in a compassionate tone. "Sides, maybe he doesn't have what we have." For several minutes he stood and watched as the older gentleman sat down on the wooden step. He acted as though he was hurting. "He's an older man, Jeffrey, don't be so coldhearted."

Jeffrey gave his twin a high-toned glare. "Look at him," he stated coldly, "he's disgusting. Dirty and disgusting! Land grubbers! The Sheriff should throw their sorry carcasses out of town!"

"Don't let Aunt Lizzie hear you say that," Matthew said, "she's quite taken with the old fellow. He's supposed to know quite a bit about horses."

"Aunt Lizzie is taken with any old stray dog that comes along! That's her problem," he said in a know-it-all tone, "she's always putting her nose in where it doesn't belong!"

The storekeeper gave the young man a strange look before he spoke, "What cha got there, Jeff some candy?"

"Jeffery to you," he snapped back.

"Jeffery!" Naomi scolded in a hot tone. "Didn't you learn anything riding in here today? You'd better shut that big mouth of yours and be nice! Mr. Dott didn't mean anything by that. I'm sorry for my cousin's behavior Mr. Dott. He appears to think being rude is better than being hospitable."

The clerk gave the pleasing young woman a loving look. "Surely." But underneath the storekeeper knew that the young Baxter was nothing but trouble. That his patrons were tired of listening to his loud obnoxious mouth and someday someone was going to put a bullet in his chest.

"Mr. Dott, can I have some of those peaches over there. The ones in the glass jar. They're the best," Naomi asked in a polite manner.

"Certainly, young lady," the gracious clerk said as he handed Naomi the glass jar.

"Thanks," she smiled warmly. "Just put it on our bill."

Like a ballerina she stepped outside the small store and walked to where the older man sat. Jeffrey's assessment was right, he was dirty. His silver beard needed an overdue trimming and a good dunking in a hot bath wouldn't have hurt him any either. But there was something about him that drew Naomi to where he sat. "Here," she offered sweetly as she squatted down and handed the poor looking rounder the peaches.

"Why, thank you little lady," the man said completely set aback at her generosity.

"They're really good, I had some just like it this morning," she grinned. "What cha doing sitting out here?" Naomi questioned in a friendly fashion as she invited herself to sit. "It's kinda hot."

"Just watching time go by," he smiled through a mouth full of teeth that looked like they needed a good cleaning too as he stared at the old mule across the street.

"How bout you?"

"Just waiting on my mother and my aunt," she said sweetly. "Supply day."

"I remember those days," he said with a sense of knowing in his voice.

"Really, are you from around here?"

"I'm from a little of everywhere, little lady. Been here and there so many times I'm supposing someday I'll be meetin' myself coming back." He gave Naomi a crooked smile.

"I've not been anywhere yet," she confessed. "Don't know that I really want to. I love my mother and the ranch. I'm not sure I could leave."

"No hurry in the leaving," he said sincerely, "but there's always hurry in the coming back." He looked at Naomi for several minutes. "So which one do you belong to? You're not really the same lookin of sorts." Then he hurriedly tried to cover his tracks. "No offense."

Naomi threw her head back and let out a child-like giggle that sounded like a sweet lullaby in his ears. "None taken. I'm Lizzie Baxter's daughter."

"Oh, that one." His tone was very respectful.

"I must have taken after my grandmother's side. At least that's what everyone says," she smiled as she fiddled with her strawberry colored hair.

"That explains your good heart," he said sweetly as he held up the jar of peaches. "Lizzie is a fine woman. If I was only thirty years younger why I'd…" He gave Sarah a sweet smile. "Nah, that's only a foolish old man talkin' nonsense little sister. But when I was a younger man, I'd have swept that woman off'n of her feet."

"Really," she laughed. "I would have loved to have seen someone come and sweep her off'n her feet," she teased. "All I've ever seen mother interested in is horses." She continued her giggle. "And me." Naomi was totally intrigued with the older man's sweet spirit. It had a way of pulling you in.

REDBONE

"When I was a young man," the old cowpoke said from out of no where, "I used to have this old rangy horse called, Redbone. When he was a colt he was the orneriest critter what you'd ever come in contact with. Stomp a mud hole right through the middle of ya if'n he could. Well, some of the boys thought the best place for the hairy devil was at the end of a gun barrel. I said he'd be 'one-back-bustin' critter if'n you could ever get close to him. I had a few extra coins back then," he smiled at the lovely redheaded woman sitting next to him. "So I bought the scroungy critter. It didn't take much. The old trader was glad to get rid of him. Too much trouble for any typical man."

"But you're not typical are you, Charlie?" Naomi said in the most adoring tone.

"I'm darn sure a lot of things little Missy, but typical ain't one of em." He gave her a crooked smile and continued. "So, I cleaned him up by puttin' him in the river. Godly animal! Proud, determined, and beautiful!" With laughter in his voice he said to no one in particular, "That rascal tried to buck even in the water." He shook his gray flecked head as Matthew and Jeffrey walked out onto the sidewalk.

"You alright, Naomi?" Matthew asked.

"Oh yes!" she exclaimed. "Come, listen to this story. It's gonna be great."

The two of them joined the rangy looking outlaw on the wooded platform. Matthew took a seat next to the wily horse wrangler and began to listen. Soon, they became as engrossed in the story as Naomi.

"Anyways, I finally got to the point where he'd stand and let me put the saddle on. He was a monster of a horse that one. Seventeen hands if he stood a foot. Red to the bone! Long sleek neck, full wide chest and a back you could sit on till the sun went down. I'd led him for miles behind one of the other horses coming up the Powder River. So, I thought I'd give it a try. See if I couldn't slide onto that long sleek looking back. I figured he should have been good and tired by then. Led him right into the water I did, climbed on his back, and held on." He looked into Naomi's wildflower eyes. "Honey, it was like sitting on top of a mountain.

You could see forever on that animal's back. I waited; you know for the explosion. But there weren't none. The scrappy varmint didn't do a thing. He just swam around in a big circle like a hooked fish trying to figure out what in the world I was doing up there. When the recognition hit him, and those gigantic clod hoppers he called feet hit the dirt, well let me tell ya it was a rodeo start to finish. I'd climb on, he'd throw me off. I'd climb on, he'd throw me off. He was the most amazing animal. After a few weeks of pulling an undisclosed amount of cactus out of my as—behind, he finally started to settle down a bit." The old cowhand took in a remembering breath. "But God forbid if'n a tumbleweed, or a piece of grass or even a butterfly would blow past him, that critter just came uncorked and I," he looked from one to the other, "would wind up in a brush pile someplace. Like he'd never been bridled. Never been saddled. Never been rode. Most irritating thing in the world when you got a calf tied on behind."

"What a magnificent sounding animal," Naomi whispered completely enthralled in the older man's story.

"Magnificent might be an understatement, cousin," Matthew said thoughtfully. "He sounds like a horse that knows his own mind. Like a Baxter animal. You don't find breeding like that just anywhere."

"Breeding, nothing!" Jeffrey scoffed as his boot kicked at the wooden platform. "I'd a thrown on a pair of sharp spurs and let him know who the boss really was!" he popped off in an arrogant high-handed fashion. "No four legged hairball would get the best of me!"

Matthew snapped at his brother for his arrogant remark. "Like the one you're riding now?"

"Shut up!" Jeffrey snapped back at his twin. "You don't know! "I know enough that if mom catches you bloodying him again with those spurs you're so proud of you'll be walking!"

Jeffrey gave his brother a threatening look. "How I handle my livestock is none of your business!"

"Really? Should I tell Aunt Lizzie that? I'm sure she'd like to know!"

"Shut up!" Jeffrey demanded.

"Both of you stop it!" Naomi demanded. "You're ruining the story!"

The tired looking cowpoke gave Jeffrey an irked look as he continued, "Well one afternoon, the dang'dist thing happened. It'd been an odd type of day. Hot one minute, chilly the next. Them ole dark rain clouds would hang all round us, spit a little water in our eye," he gave Naomi a quick wink, "then disappear into nothing. Then, in one breath out would come the sun. Sure was the dang dist' thing I'd ever seen." He paused for a brief moment as though he was lost in the memory of his own tale. "Ole Redbone had been exceptionally quiet all day and I had a sneaking suspicion that he was just waiting for the perfect time to put me in a pile of cactus. But he kept watching the horizon, cocking those velvet looking ears forwards and back as though he were looking for something. Listening for somethin' I couldn't see." Then, as though an after thought hit him he said, "If'n I'd been in Crow Territory, I'd been a follow'n that ole bag of bones' lead. But it weren't like that. It weren't nothin like that. So, after a bit I done forgot all about his little playin' games and started pushing him hard gathering cattle. He was gettin hard to handle, fighting my lead and I'd just given him a good over and under when it hit." The old man had the most memorable look on his weathered face. "Just like that, out of no where's the wind started howling like the voice of a brokenhearted woman! Screaming in this high-pitched yowl. Why, it was so loud that I covered my ears! Sagebrush started flyin under ole Redbones feet faster than he could kick at it. Little pieces of sand picked at his nose till it was raw. And me clinging to an exploding freight train. There weren't no place to duck out of the open for cover and there weren't no time for the doin' it!" He said it in such a matter-of-factly voice that the three of them felt his confusion. "That nasty ole cold-hearted wind whipped around that knot headed horse like it had some kind of score to settle. Tormentin' him somethin' fierce. Scoldin' him on every turn." He looked into Naomi's brilliant circles as he spoke, "That snot-thrower started tossin' his head like the dern'd idiot that he was. But I held tight. Ta' be honest and if"n the truth was know'd, I was a bit skittish myself. Ain't see'd nothin' like it afore or sense! From out of nowhere's I swear that ole moan'n wind grew fingers and picked that ole pony up with one swift yank with me sitting right in the middle of that there wet saddle stuck like an ole thick tick on his back." He let out a soft laugh. "That danged knothead tried bucking right up there in blue wide sky! If'n you can believe that!"

"Hump!" Jeffrey scoffed. "Sounds like an old man's fib story to me!"

"Why, I could only imagine the look in his ornery eyes when he looked down and there weren't nothin under them oversized hard hittin' clodhoppers of his but the air God gave us to breath." The old man let out a loud laugh. "Well, anyways it twirled us round and round what seemed like forever."

Naomi was completely engrossed in the wonderful story. "What did you do?" Her voice had a mixture of concern and excitement.

"I'd have done what you did," Matthew said in a knowing tone, "hold on and enjoy the ride. Not many men have rode a steam-rolling bronc' beneath the hand of the Mighty One."

Jeffrey on the other hand jumped in and spouted off. "You're such a sucker, Matthew! The Mighty One didn't have anything to do with it. It was a wild wind hollow! We've seen em before! Why, I'd have dug my spurs so deep into his red defiant hide they'd of been dripping blood when we hit the ground! Obstinate hairball!"

"Just ignore him," Naomi whispered. "He's puffed up like an old toad that's fixin' to get popped!"

Jeff's statement had a way of pricking the old man's good disposition as he continued, "I don't know how long we was a flyin' in that there black sky. Ridin' the wind like the falling leaves on a cool autumn morin'. Watchin' the lightning snap at us like the frayed end of a bull whip. Hearin', the howling thunder as it roared through our ears like boulders dropping into a hollow canyon. I don't rightly recollect if'n I was even breathin'. But I remember seein' the misty steam rollin' off that there ole red bronc's hairy hide like smoke from a green-lit campfire. I remember hearing his panicked squeal. It matched the squalling wind as it whistled through his pink nostrils. I remember sitting on a mountain of red flesh that day—tamed by God's own hand." He looked into Matthews' mesmerized face. "It was the most amazing adventure I've ever experienced. Why, it would have been the most unbelievable sight to see if'n you'd a been watchin' from the ground." The older man let out a knowing sigh. "It's one I'll never experience again I reckon."

"Then what happened?" Naomi questioned breathlessly.

"Then—that same ole howlin wind what picked us up with its ghostly fingers put us right back down like they were lit on fire. Anxious to get rid of the both of us. Safe as a kitten about fifty feet from where we started."

"What a pile of bunk!" Jeffrey stated.

"Then what happened?" Matthew asked completely enthralled in the old man's story.

"I'll tell ya son. Me and ole Redbone, why we just stood there. Him on the ground. Me on his back. The both of us, soaking wet. Shiverin' like some ole grizzly had us cornered in a box canyon with no way out." He paused for a brief moment. "The two of us we stood there just lookin' in no particular direction. Why, I wasn't even sure what had just happened had happened at all."

"It probably didn't," Jeffrey said in a dry tone. "Just an old man's fairytale."

"Interrupt one more time, Jeffrey," Naomi hissed, "and I'll show you what will happen!"

The old man gave the lovely woman a warm smile. "With God as my witness it did. And as far as my eyes could see there was nothing but rolling hills of white. Why the sight nearly blinded ya. The ground that had been brown as a loaf of over-baked bread why it looked like someone had rubbed a knife-full of white frosting all over it."

"Snow?" breathed Naomi?

"Hail. Even some of the cattle what had piled up under a poor excuse of a small, lipped dangling ledge were white. All I could see was dark questioning eyes askin' what in the devil had happened. I patted that old horse's long red neck and waited until we both stopped shiverin' then I gave him a gentle nudge."

"Oh my, what did he do?" Naomi's voice was so full of excitement.

"I bet he bucked you off right in a pile of cactus!" Jeffrey laughed, hoping that is exactly what happened.

The old man looked at his captive audience with a bit of a mist in his old cloudy eyes. "I think that ole bag of red bones thought I played some kinda trick on him. That what had happened to us was my fault. That I did it." he laughed wholeheartedly. "I don't know. I couldn't read his cagey mind. But, whatever the reason for what happened that day, however the logic of the situation had sunk'd into his ornery head, it made that ole red boned horse dog gentle. He never one time offered to throw me off again."

"Never?" Naomi breathed through stifled fingers.

"Not one more time?" Matthew said in a disbelieving tone.

"Ah, that's a bunch of bunk! I don't believe that!" Jeff said in a haughty highhanded tone. "Not for one minute!"

With a prideful spirit the old man continued, "You could have rode that horse through the deepest darkest hole in the earth and back. He was calm, steady, dependable, and true. Why he was the most honest being that I think I've ever had the pleasure of coming in contact with. Animal or human," he said as he gave Naomi a huge grin.

"That is a most wonderful story," Naomi stated breathlessly.

"People only dream about owning a horse like that," Matthew stated in a far off tone. "I know I'd love to have an animal just like it someday."

"I'd of broke him long before I admitted that any ole storm did!" Jeffrey scolded in a loud voice. "It doesn't take much of a wrangler to do that!"

The old man didn't like the loud mouthed Baxter and it showed in his scruffy face. "There was only one catch to that crafty critter after all of that."

"What was it?" Naomi breathed.

"I was the only one what could ride him."

"No way!" Jeffrey boasted as he kicked the wooden plank in disgust. "That's not sounding right! Why, I could have rode that old horse any day of the week!"

"Other's tried, believe me. They did. But with little success. It was just a matter of minutes before they landed head first on the ground. I guess the hairy devil figured if I could ride him across't of God's darkened blue sky, I could ride his sorry carcass across God's green earth."

"Where is he now?" Naomi asked with a mist in her multi-colored eyes.

"Yeah," Matthew said sincerely, "what happened to him?"

The older man stared into the different faces of his young audience. "I buried that old horse at the age of thirty. No one believed for a minute that he would have ever lived that long but he did. Buried him with my own two hands," he stated as he let out a deep sigh. "But you have to remember that was when I was a young man. Much younger than I am now." He smiled adoringly at Naomi. "There's been a lot of years go by these old eyes since then." He gave Naomi an adoring smile. "I think of that story when I see your mother."

"A horse!" Jeffrey laughed aloud. "Did you hear that, Matthew! He called Aunt Lizzie a horse! I bet she'll love hearing that!"

"No, what I said was she's a wild spirit just like ole Redbone. Be proud that you're a part of that," he said sincerely.

"I am," Naomi said breathlessly. She didn't know how, but the older cowboy had told the story of her mother's life without even knowing her.

CHAPTER 6

"Hello, Charlie," Liza and Lizzie said in unison as all eyes faced the two approaching women. "You feeding these children of ours full of stories?"

"No, ma'am," he said in self-defense, "just tellin' them bout ole Redbone."

"Ah ha, I see. Well, you given much more thought about comin out to the ranch and lendin' us a hand? We could sure use the help right now. Bringing about fifty or so head of greens off'n the mountain. I'm sure Luke would appreciate the help. He ain't getting no younger," Lizzie said with a hidden twinkle in her eye.

It wasn't that the ranch really needed another working hand it was just that Lizzie had grown quite attached to the older man. She loved his stories and she loved the respect that crossed his kind steely eyes whenever he spoke of the beautiful beast that he affectionately referred to as Redbone. And, she respected the way the warmth of his mouth curled ever so slightly upward when he smirked. Lizzie didn't understand why every time they came to town and he had nothing more to show for his lowly existence than the last time they'd seen him. Was he hiding something perhaps? She wasn't sure. Still there was no doubt in her mind that the man had been quite a character in his younger days. She just didn't believe that because he had a few years of age on him that he was ready to be put out to pasture.

"I told you a' fore little Miss, I'm an old man, don't know how much work these crippled old fingers can do anymore," he stated sincerely as he held up his bent arthritic hands. "Don't seem right expect'n to get paid good money for somethin that I might not be able to do."

"How do you know you can't do it?" Lizzie countered, not wanting to take no for an answer. "You haven't tried yet."

"Sides," Liza added, "we might be able to help out with those old, crippled hands if you give us a chance."

"Don't know that I'm worth the trouble," he said honestly as his old eyes went from one lovely twin to the other. Danged if'n he knowed who was which by just lookin'.

"Gotta horse?" Lizzie inquired.

"Nope, just that ole broken down mule over there."

"She make it to the ranch?" Liza asked. "She looks pretty worn out."

"Just like me," he said with compassion as he looked at the dusty old mule that stood alone on the opposite side of the street swatting flies.

"Jeffery, go fetch that mule over there," Liza said in a motherly fashion.

"Ah, why do I have to do it?" he sulked.

Lizzie gave the young man a crass look when she spoke, "Because your mother asked you to."

There was no denying the surprised looks on the faces of the waiting party. Especially, Charlie. Now he definitely knew who ran what.

Begrudgingly, the boy did as he was told. "I always have to do the dirty work!" he grumbled.

"Charlie, you climb right up on the back of that buckskin over there and we'll see about getting you hired," Lizzie said matter-of-factly.

The old man's face lit up like the full moon on a warm summer night when he sat in the saddle of the finely bred horse. "Thank you," his voice was full of pride. Jeffrey's typically jittery horse was calm under the hand of the stranger. "Man, it's been awhile," he whispered as he gently patted the horse's long sleek neck when he noticed the deep bloody marks from a jagged set of spurs on the horse's yellow side.

"Hey!" Jeffrey hollered from across the crowded street. "That's my horse! Get off you filthy old goat!"

"Jeffrey!" Liza scolded. "That is quite enough!"

"What am I supposed to ride?" he snapped back at his mother.

"You're holding it," Lizzie said annoyed with the young man.

"What! I'm not riding this bag of bones!" he yowled like a wounded cat.

The disappointment showed in the older man's face as he started to step down from the buckskins back. Lizzie gave him a look that said he'd better stay put.

"You know, Jeffery," Lizzie stated in a warning tone, "humility is going to be the death of you yet. I'd have thought you'd figured that out once today already."

"You can't tell me what to do, Aunt Lizzie!" he challenged.

"Then I will tell you," Liza said in a dark threatening tone, "after all, I am your mother."

"Barely!" Jeffrey snapped.

"Sister?" Liza stated as she looked at Lizzies heated face.

"Yup."

"That young man is your mount for the ride home." Liza stated.

"I wouldn't be caught dead on that piece of dying carcass!" he yelled at his mother. Humiliated that they would even expect such a thing. "I want my horse!"

"Your horse is occupied at this moment," Liza said in a cool fashion. Embarrassed that her son was being so disrespectful. "Please except my apology, Charlie. He's young," she said, "and has many years of learning yet to come."

"Yes, ma'am," the old cowpoke answered in an understanding tone, knowing that the only learning this boy was going to get was at the end of a rifle.

Not wanting to see this ugly scene escalate to the next level Naomi said, "He can ride my horse, mother Lizzie, I can ride in the wagon. I don't mind."

"We still have several more stops to make. By the time we are done here today the wagon will be heavy enough." Liza said without taking her eyes off of her hardheaded son.

"Yes, ma'am," she said softly as she gave her cousin a weak smile that said she tried.

"We Baxter's don't ride such disgraceful looking animals!" Jeffrey hollered defiantly at his mother as he spit on the ground.

"Stop it, Jeffrey!" Matthew said in an irritated tone," that's our mother you're talking to. Show some respect brother!" His tone was threatening.

"We Baxter's ride what is available to us at the time," Lizzie said, furious with the smart mouthed young man.

"Fine!" he stated defiantly. "I'll walk!"

"I was hoping you were going to say that," Lizzie said with a devilish smile as she took the reins from the wooden railing and wrapped it around the horn of Naomi's saddle. "Liza, we best get our business done and move out."

"Yep, father will be expecting us before dark."

With that being said, the wagon moaned as it headed for the other end of the busy street as they continued to conclude their business. Several hours had come and gone and it had gotten much later than the party had expected by the time all of the goods were bought and loaded.

Liza and Lizzie looked at each other with a knowing glance. "He's not ready," Their faces said.

CHAPTER 7

Once again as the Baxter party made their way out of the busy place called Crocker, there was no missing the hidden smiles from the passerby's. The townsfolk didn't seem to judge the two rough shod twins and their unladylike past like they had in the beginning. No, somewhere between right and wrong they had developed an unconditional amount of respect for these two wily, identically clad sisters and they had come to agree with their hard schooled ways.

The two women did what they wanted, when they wanted, and how they wanted. Their generosity was genuine. Their rules were the law and today didn't seem to be any different. Not many had missed the loud-mouthed Baxter's temper tantrum. And, they seemed to agree with his punishment as they watched the disrespectful, hotheaded son of Liza Baxter trail behind the moving wagon—red faced.

As the wagon slowly rolled away from the hustle and bustle of the busy town the single ladies smiled shyly and the young men tipped their hats. There was no question in anyone's mind that the handsome dark haired son of Liza Baxter and his beautiful redheaded cousin were the catch of the valley. Any unattached man or woman knew whoever married into that dynasty would never want for anything. Sadly though, no one expected that Jeffrey would live long enough to make it to the altar.

Naomi jabbered like a light hearted bird as she talked about the beautiful bolt of blue and yellow fabric that she had purchased. She let everyone know that she couldn't wait to get back to the ranch so she could start sewing on her new dress. Swearing on her life that she would pay her mother back for every extra penny that she had spent. Lizzie expected nothing less.

Matthew was anxious to get home as well and give out the little tokens that he had bought for each family member. Peppermint candies for Abe, a new fang-dangled spoon for Maria, new checker pieces for Luke and a brown beaded bag for Dancing Bear that he bought from an old worn out woman standing alone on the corner of the wooded landing.

Liza and Lizzie in the meantime were hard pressed on discussing what kind of a salary they would be paying the older man riding to the back of the loaded wagon when they noticed the two men riding toward them.

"Afternoon," they said as they tipped their hats.

Neither woman acknowledged them but they never took their eyes off of the duo. "Never seen the likes of them before," Liza stated as she watched them ride past.

"Me neither," Lizzie stated in a distrusting tone. "But I know one thing for sure, they're trouble. I can smell it." With eyes as cold as ice she watched the men as they passed. Keeping a close eye on the straggler behind them. "Come on, Jeffrey. You can run your mouth faster than your walking," she taunted.

Bringing up the rear of the small party was one angry young man. His put-out face was beat red as he kicked at the clumps of dirt on the busy street. Defiantly, he gave his aunt a dirty look. It was plain to see that he was fighting mad. He never took the time to look anyone directly in the face because for the most part he was humiliated. Not because of his tactless behavior but the harsh punishment that his mother and aunt had handed down to him. He hated his Aunt Lizzie, always bossing him around and it never seemed to matter where! "I'll get you someday!" he seethed beneath his breath.

The two men didn't miss the troubled face of the young man trailing the wagon as they gave him a sympathetic look when they rode past. Telling him that if he needed a hand to just say the word.

Jeffrey gave them a highhanded glare as he tried to jump onto the back of the wagon only to land face first in the dirt as Liza clucked the team forward. "Mother!" he hollered in a huff as they exited the town.

The team had traveled a good mile at a nice slow pace. "What'd ya think?" Lizzie asked. "He had enough? His face is awful red."

"Oh, I don't know, maybe another mile."

"We don't want to kill him, Liza."

"One more mile, then you can offer the mule to him again. Not that he will take it. I'm not going to give into him this time. I'm not. He's got to get over this grudge or whatever it is that he has going on in that thick head of his."

"I know, remind you of anyone?"

Liza gave her sister a knowledgeable look. "Honestly, no. We might have caused trouble from time to time, got into things we probably didn't need to Lizzie, but we were never intentionally mean. Father would have never allowed that. What Jeffrey did today and the way that he treated that old man, that was down right mean. We've never taught our children to act like that."

"I don't think…" Lizzie said quietly.

"Don't think what?" Liza questioned in a testy tone. "Don't hide your feelings from me now, Lizzie. I'm falling down hard with this boy. If I ever needed you, I need you now."

"I think that he is dealing with something else. Fighting some kind of demon even he can't control. Like someone stuck a burr under his saddle that he don't know how to dig out. I mean, why he would say such terrible things about Dancing Bear. And Naomi. It's just not like him."

"It's just like him lately," Liza stated in a distraught tone.

"No, sister, I think there's something else bothering that boy. It…almost," Lizzie hesitated for a mere second, "feels like…black magic and if we don't get to the bottom of it soon someone is going to get hurt. Maybe killed."

"Black magic? We took care of that. Didn't we?"

"I thought so, but, something's not right."

"We should have told him the truth you know. We should have told all of them the truth." Liza sighed quietly.

"Why would you say such an odd thing?" Lizzie asked completely baffled at her sister's comment. "We agreed a long time ago that I would take the blame. Has something happened?"

"I dreamed about dying the other night," Liza said in a far off tone. "It was awful. You and me. I died and you died within me. What do you suppose that meant?"

"I don't know," she answered her sister honestly, not liking the condition of her mood.

"I haven't dreamed about them in years." Liza said sincerely.

"Who?" Lizzie questioned.

"But they were all there. Mad Dog, Flying Eagle, Dancing Bear, Sarah, you, me."

"Liza," Lizzie said in a concerned tone, "I don't like the sound of that."

"How do you think I felt? It was like drinking muddy water!" Liza stated matter-of-factly.

"Well, we have to stand together on this one if we plan on saving that boy's idiot hide. He's his own worst enemy!"

The rag-tag group had traveled for several miles when Lizzie turned and asked, "Jeffrey would you like a mount now?"

The young man completely ignored his aunt.

"Stubborn." Liza said.

"Jeffrey," Liza said in an annoyed tone, "are you tired of walking yet?"

"I'm not riding that maggot-filled old mule!" he hollered defiantly as he wiped the sweat from his forehead.

"Guess not," Lizzie said. "Naomi, trade me places for a bit."

"Yes, ma'am, she answered without hesitation.

"Liza cluck those horses up a bit, when you get to the double trees stop, and we'll give them a rest and give that arrogant prideful fool a following us a chance to catch up!"

Liza nodded at her sister.

"I'm gonna see if we can't help those old, crippled hands a bit. I'll be back shortly." Within minutes Lizzie loped off in the opposite direction.

"Where you going?" Jeffrey mumbled to himself as he trailed along behind the wagon, feeling sorry for himself. "To get something else to humiliate me with!"

Nonchalantly, Liza and Naomi busied themselves with conversation of gathering the small herd of horses from the highline. "Charlie," Liza asked, "you up to gathering a few horses in a day or two?"

"I'll give it my best little lady but don't expect too much," he said honestly. "My old hands are aching pretty badly these days."

"I'm sure we can help with that," she smiled.

"Matthew, you ready to help gather a few, too?" Liza asked.

"Yes, ma'am!" he said excitedly. Then as if he had an after thought, "That is if papa doesn't need me."

"I'm sure he can spare you for a day for two," she concluded.

"Thanks, mother," he said lovingly.

"And you young lady," Liza said as she looked into the colored circles of the beautiful young woman sitting next to her. "I know I don't even have to ask you."

"No, ma'am," she giggled.

Naomi was a natural. Her seat was perfection when she rode. It was as though she became a part of the animal itself. She had a quiet gentle hand and soothing yet controlling touch. But then, Lizzie insisted that she learn to ride before she walked. What choice did the child have? She'd went everywhere with Lizzie whether she wanted to or not.

Liza could see the double trees in the distance. Half way home. She didn't mind the monthly journey to town but she was always glad when they were headed back toward the safety of the ranch. Hopelessly, she looked behind her. Jeffrey had walked a lot farther than she had expected. She was sure that he would have feet full of blisters.

When they arrived at their designated spot Lizzie was there waiting. "Matthew, give your mother your horse," she said without as much as a hello.

"Yes, ma'am." Instantly he climbed down as he and his mother traded places. He saw the worry lines etch themselves across her stern face.

"Matthew, you take the wagon on towards home, we'll catch up in a bit," Lizzie instructed. "Jeffrey, you get your sorry ass up on that there mule and don't you get down till you see me coming, ya hear!" Her voice was full of warning.

"Yes, ma'am," he said quietly with no resistance. From the way he hobbled toward the waiting animal it was plain to that his stubbornness hadn't benefited his tantrum at all.

Then she rode to where the older man sat on the beautiful buckskin and handed him her son's rifle. "You use this if you have to," her blue eyes said all that needed to be said.

"A different kind of pride washed across Charlie's scruffy face. "For the brand, ma'am."

"Matthew, you know the rules," Liza gave him a knowing look.

"Yes, mother," he said in a worried tone as he looked into the startled eyes of his beautiful redheaded cousin. She was to be protected at all costs. That's why no one knew that she wasn't the real daughter of Lizzie Baxter. For fear that someone would try and take her life. "Naomi, put this pistol under that there blanket,"

Matthew instructed. "Just in case." Naomi and Matthew had a close relationship and immediately she did as she was told.

Liza and Lizzie headed south at a fast pace with nothing but a cloud of dust trailing behind them.

"What's up," Liza questioned.

"Company," Lizzie answered as they crested the hill.

"Now who do you suppose that is?"

"Don't rightly know." Like two stalking ghosts the women sat and watched from a safe distance. "But I'll bet you money those two men we saw in town do."

In the beginning there was only two riders taking their time coming across the open flats at a slow pace. Then from out of one of the ravines two more joined them then two more. They were headed in the same direction that the wagon would be crossing the widened creek. Liza and Lizzie were well ahead of the wagon and the small party of men. They knew the two would meet as they headed at a fast pace in that direction. The twins were well hidden when the small parties came in contact one with the other.

"Afternoon," the older heavyset man said in a friendly fashion as he pulled his horse to a stop directly in front of the moving wagon. He had an air of authority as he gave the older man on the buckskin a warning look. From the disdainful look on Charlie's face he knew them as well. Then the cagey outlaw stared at Matthew and Jeffrey. The other riders came to either side of their ring leader.

"Afternoon," Matthew pulled the team to a slow stop.

The older looking man gave Matthew a suspicious look. "Been to town?"

"Maybe."

"Looks like your wagon is pretty loaded." The man's eyes reminded him of a rat.

"Maybe." Matthew didn't give the man any more information than he needed.

"You got business way out here?" the intruder asked.

"I might ask you the same." Matthew answered with no fear in his deep voice.

"Yeah about that, we had business earlier this morning, just headed back to town. But you know we could sure use a little grub for later. Can you spare any?" It was plain to see that the older man was toying with the younger group. Thinking that he had them cornered. "Just a bag of coffee will do."

"Listen, Mr. we ain't got no coffee or nothing else you think you need. So, you best be on your way," Matthew said in a levelheaded but determined tone. Then he looked at Naomi and spoke to her in her native tongue. Like clockwork she cocked the waiting pistol beneath the blanket.

There was no missing the shocked look on the older man's face. "How bout that boys, pretty, and spirited." His men laughed like hyenas behind him.

Matthew never took his finger off of the trigger of the double-barreled shotgun as he picked it up and aimed it directly at the heavy set man blocking the road. It was obvious that he didn't like the way he was looking at Naomi. "Mr.," Matthew said in a threatening tone. "I'm going to give you three seconds to get out of the way. Then you're going to have a whole new set of worries to contend with."

"Ben," Clinton said in a worried tone as he rode his sweating horse up along side the older man's, "this is not our affair. We have business in town. Not with these folks."

"Well, from what I can tell we have business right here," Ben said smartly ignoring the younger man.

"No, we don't," Clinton said again louder and in a more demanding tone. "Leave them pass."

Then like a weasel Ben turned and threatened Charlie, "You want another lesson or two in stickin' your nose where it don't belong old man? Just cock that there rifle and I'll finish what I started a month ago. Sides, I don't think those bent fingers are gonna do you much good now." Ben let out a heinous laugh.

The young man sitting beside him gave his Uncle an odd look. "What are you talking about?"

Charlie never took his cold calculating eyes off of his large target. He just stared at him with a face full of contempt.

"What, you gonna shoot me, old man? Now that a set of skirts done picked up your stinking drunken hide. What, you've decided to grow some backbone?" he said dryly.

"I'll ride for the brand," he answered with no emotion. His finger never left the metal trigger.

"Ain't no one gonna do no shootin' out here," Matthew said in a controlled tone. "Besides, I believe it is you who are trespassing."

The older man gave Matthew a cocky look. "What, you think you own all of this land!"

"The land owns itself," Matthew stated in an irritated tone, "we just tend to it." About that time Naomi lifted her blanket as the small party looked down the barrel of her pistol. "She's a very good shot," Matthew said honestly, "from this distance she won't miss."

"Who do you think you are?" Ben scoffed as his men backed up their horses. "Why you're nothing more than a fool-hearted kid!"

"Ben," Clinton stated angrily, "this kind of behavior is ridiculous. These people haven't done nothing to us. Besides, we can buy our own goods in town. This needs to stop!" he demanded. "Now!"

"Shut up!" Ben hollered. "No one tells me what to do, especially no punk kid!"

"I assure you, I'm no punk kid. I'm Matthew Baxter and you're trespassing on Baxter land. So, I think it's time that you and your little war party here had best be on your way." There was no doubt that Matthew was scared. Although it never showed in his mannerism or his tone of voice, but he was scared just the same. These were men he'd never seen before. Trouble makers. He couldn't help but wonder where in the world his mother and Aunt were.

It was a standoff! But, just as Matthew was ready to pull the trigger on the shotgun Jeffrey kicked the old mule up to where the riders stood, stopping right in front of Matthew's aim. "We don't want any trouble," Jeffrey said in a cowardly tone, "just let us pass and we'll give you all the coffee that you need. We have plenty of food."

"Jeffrey," Matthew threatened, "get out of the way you horses ass! What are you doing?"

"I'm helping," he said angrily, "you're going to get us killed over a bag of coffee!"

"Jeffrey," Naomi injected angrily, "move that mule or I'm going to move her for you."

Ben started laughing as he stared into the dark eyes of the lovely young woman. "Boys, I think she means it."

"Ah, she won't shoot me," Jeffrey boasted, "she's my cousin."

The older man gave Naomi a look that undressed her top to bottom as he started to dismount from his horse but within a blink of an eye his destination was cut short. In an instant everything around them changed. It was as though some kind of blistering storm erupted from the very depths of the dusty earth. The howling wind picked up and the feathered beasts above them squawked so loud it was deafening. Matthew looked at Naomi and smiled. He should have known that they weren't alone. Matthew took in a deep sigh of relief as Jeffrey put his hands over his ears.

But the arrogant man on the tired looking horse that was determined to cause trouble was too stupid to know the difference. He was so caught up in his own selfish pride he missed the whole nasty event that was about to unfold. Determined to prove his superiority he continued his descent from the back of his standing horse. Just as he was nearly to the ground Lizzie placed a bullet at the bottom of his boot blowing the heel plumb off.

"Egg sucking b…" the older man hollered as he scrambled back into the saddle like a hurrying centipede. Completely taken aback at what had just happened.

Liza shot one of the pistols out of one of the other men's hand as he howled like a stepped on dog. Charlie fired a shot directly under his old mule's feet. The loud bang of the gun scared the mule as Jeffrey held on for all he was worth as the two of them bucked out of sight. The tides had turned and now the marauding bandits were sinking in quicksand.

From out of nowhere stood two identically clad women with guns drawn, ready to do battle. There was no fear in those dark blue eyes as they spoke in unison, "Step down from that glue-bag again and my sister will put the next one right in the middle of your foot."

The older man was so taken by surprise that all he could do was stare. They were a frightening sight. Like two black-eyed vipers ready to strike. But he was so angry at being treated in such a disrespectful manner that he man didn't listen. "Let me guess!" he said in a disrespectful tone. "You must be Liza and Lizzie Baxter!" Furious with the two hot-headed women he started to step down from the horse. When he did, Lizzie shot him square in the foot. He let out a yowl loud enough to be heard in town. "Witch!" he hollered. "You shot me!"

"Get back on your horse, Mr.," Lizzie said in a cold calculated tone.

"Or what, "he seethed, "you gonna shoot me in the other foot!"

"She won't," Liza stated matter-of-factly through thin icy lips, "but, I will." She put a bullet directly in front of where the arrogant man was standing. "It seems to me that you men are either deaf or just plain stupid. I believe that my son told you this is Baxter land. You best have permission before you cross it again." There was no missing the warning in Liza's voice.

"Cross it, I can't wait to get off of it!" he seethed. "You're crazy! Both of you! You're nuts! Just like they said!"

So this was Liza and Lizzie Baxter Clinton thought to himself. The two tyrants that so many people had told him to beware of. They were exactly as he had pictured. "I told you!" Clinton yelled as he helped the older man. "You always have to start something!" He didn't feel one bit sorry for his Uncle's disorderly actions. In fact it was rather refreshing to see someone actually call his bluff and stand up to the old goat. The younger fellow turned and faced Liza and Lizzie with a half smirk on his face. "I'm sorry, ma'am, ma'am's, I don't cotton to any of this!" It was plain to see that he was furious. "Uncle," he seethed, "you're going to get us killed one of these days!"

"Shut up!" Ben yelled. "And get me to town before I bleed to death!" Then he purposely turned and faced the twin's once again. "I could have you put in jail for this!"

"We don't need no lawman to take care of Baxter business Mr. But you go right ahead and do that. You bring that ole Sheriff right on out here and we'll explain to him how you been trespassing and given these youngin's a hard time. But meanwhile let me explain something to you!" Lizzie seethed. "You've got just about five seconds to move this here slug of vermin off our property or we're gonna just start shootin' at random," Lizzie warned in a threatening tone.

"And you will hit the dirt first!" Liza stated. Her face looked like stone.

Now Ben knew just what he was dealing with. The stories that he had heard about these two hellions were true. They wouldn't hesitate to kill him right where he sat. No, he was going to have to find another way in. So, like a king on his throne he grabbed the reins to his horse and headed toward town. As he rode away he could see the other young son in the distance as he lay flat on his back on the prairie. "I'll be talking to you later," he mumbled under his breath.

"Matthew," Lizzie motioned, "go fetch your gutless brother. Charlie, I'm sorry, that ole mule's probably back to town by now."

"Nah," he smiled as he let out a long whistle. Within minutes the old bag of bones came loping to where he sat. "She don't got no one either. Just me."

Lizzie gave him a respectful smile. "Good enough." Then just like that she gave her horse back to Naomi and Liza gave hers back to Matthew. "Did you happen to get any honeycomb while you were up in that there tree?" Lizzie asked.

"I'd nearly forgotten," Liza handed her sister a chunk of honey. Lizzie noticed the welt on the top of her hand. "I'm not as fast I use to be," she giggled.

"Yep, I hear ya talking." Like a well schooled doctor Lizzie took a can of salve out of her pocket and rubbed it gently on her sisters wound. "That'll hold till we get to the ranch."

CHAPTER 8

Several weeks had come and gone as the hands prepared for the gathering that would take place on the highline of the Red Shale Ridge. Liza and Lizzie had accepted a contract for fifty head of green broke horses. It wasn't so much the number of horses that the twin she-devils would be bringing down it was where they were going to go to get them. Slippery cliffs that wandered into deep brushy draws, that opened up into soft green meadows full of marshy pools. Why the four legged critters always seemed to congregate on that particular piece of ground on the opposite end of the ranch no one knew, but they did and gathering their doggy hides was quite an undertaking.

Naomi had been up for hours helping in the kitchen, preparing the food that they would be taking along. She made sure that there were several jars of the sweet, canned peaches that Charlie liked so well. He was a wonderfully kind man and she had grown quite an attachment to him. Meat for a good beefy stew, potatoes, and the likes. She had been in the kitchen most of the day baking golden loaves of bread and several hard cakes that her mother and Liza were so fond of.

In the meantime, Liza and Lizzie were busy outside getting the men lined out loading the wagon that they'd be taking. It was obvious to both women that several of the hired hands were more than grateful that they wouldn't be making the trip. They shrugged their shoulders as though they didn't understand their dilemma. But, underneath they both knew exactly why. "Cowards!" mumbled Liza.

Matthew was in the office with Abe taking care of any last minute issues that might come up with the lumber company. "Now, papa," he said in a much older tone than his years, "don't sign any of these papers till I get back. I'm not sure we want to do business with Mr. Martín. I'm not so sure I trust the man. So, until I have a chance to read them over, don't sign anything." He gave his grandfather a knowing smile. "No matter how hard he presses the issue."

"All right, Matthew," Abe conceded, "but it's an awful big contract."

"We've had bigger, papa," Matthew stated matter-of-factly. "The man can wait."

Jeffrey on the other hand hadn't made it back until the wee hours of the morning and he was sleeping one off up in his room. When Dancing Bear gave him a holler all he did was moan. No one had spoken a word about the incident that had taken place on the way back to the ranch but Jeffrey knew it was in the back of their minds. He knew at some point the whole ugly incident would come around full circle and it would all be his fault. And to make matters worse the buckskin that he'd been riding for the past several months, the one that he called his own, wouldn't let him near him without throwing a fit. The hairy hard-headed beast had taken quite a shine to the older man. "We'll see about that in the next couple of days!" he mumbled. "Any lying imposter can get their neck broke on the highline."

There was no doubt that young Jeffrey had a grudge against the older man that had recently been hired. And he hated the old mule for bucking him off in the middle of a pile of cactus in front of the very men that he was trying to impress. But more than that he couldn't forget how humiliated he'd been when his mother and aunt had to pull the long silvery bands of cactus out of his butt and upper thigh. "Why is **she** in here?" he asked in a belligerent tone. He knew that his aunt enjoyed every moan that he made.

"Am I here?" Liza questioned her son, surprised at his remark.

"Unless you're some kind of hallucination, I'm pretty sure that you're here." He snapped like a spoiled brat.

Lizzie hadn't spoken more than ten words to the insolent scoundrel since they'd gotten home and she didn't like the way he addressed his mother. Purposely, she twisted the long barb as she pulled it out.

Jeffrey yowled like a stepped on cat. "You did that on purpose!"

"Maybe you should keep your butt in the saddle next time instead of trying to impress vermin!" she hissed. "I've told you how to address your mother! Don't make me remind you again."

"I didn't start nothing! It was Matthew that was the trouble! Him and Naomi drawing their guns like that!"

"How so?" Liza asked.

"Mother! All they wanted was some coffee! They weren't gonna do nothing. But, oh no Matthew had to have on the big pants!"

"Big pants? That's an odd way of taking your brother's side. Protecting what is yours. Charlie showed more courage and he is no family."

The older man had proven on more than one occasion that he would be a devoted hand to the two wily women that had hired him. "I knew you'd find a way to make what happened my fault! You always do!"

"So, you believe that it's alright to allow someone to threaten your welfare on your own property? That's an odd conclusion." Liza stated in a disappointed tone.

"That's a fool's mixture for being dead, Mr. Jeffrey!" Lizzie snapped hotly.

Trying to put the nasty incident behind him he walked down the long stairway. "I'll show you a fool!" he mumbled.

"Breakfast!" Naomi hollered as she rang the huge metal triangle that sang like a strangled rooster across four states as she rattled it. When she turned to walk back inside the old log house, she ran smack dab into, Abe. Like a shining star she threw her arms around his full waist. "Morning, papa," she said in an adoring tone.

Abe held the young woman tight for several minutes. She reminded him more and more of her mother everyday. "Morin', sunshine," he answered warmly. "Our Little Feather."

Naomi loved it when her grandfather called her by her native name. The words seemed to roll like respected honey from his kind lips. "I love you too, papa," she said sweetly. Across the yard they could see the twins and Charlie heading in for breakfast. There was no missing the compassion in their cool blue eyes when they saw the engaging moment.

"Mornin, father," the twins said happily at the same time. Within minutes they all gathered at the long oak table.

"We'll be gone for several days," Liza said between bites.

"We'll be fine here," Abe insisted.

"We're taking Charlie, Naomi, Matthew, me, Liza, and Jeffrey. If he's up to it," Lizzie said matter-of-factly.

"He'll be up to it!" Liza countered. "Or, I'll tie his sorry butt to the saddle!"

"It's likely to be quite a rodeo up there," Abe said in a worried tone.

She looked into her father's concerned face. "We'll be fine," Liza added in a comforting tone.

"It's not you two I'm worried about," Abe stated. "Let's don't forget that you've got the kids with you."

"The kids!" Lizzie mocked. "Father, these so called kids can ride better than we can."

"It's a dangerous ridge to ride, Lizzie, you know that," he stated in a tone that said he was to be taken seriously.

"Father, Liza, and I will ride the highline. They'll snag them coming down. We're not that careless."

"I never said that you were careless," Abe argued half irritated at the insinuation.

"Father, this is a working ranch," Lizzie said just as irritated, "and I believe that the boy's and Naomi are more than up to the challenge. You've got to let them have a little fun, father."

"You call running down broken shallow shale at the speed of lightning or jumping ravines that could swallow a man whole fun!" he worried.

The identical women looked at each other, their cool blue eyes were full of excitement, "Yes, I do," they answered in unison. "And, we remember a time when you did too."

"Besides," Liza said softly, "let's not forget who taught us that in the first place."

A slow smile started to etch its way across his warm inviting lips as he spoke. "Yeah, let's not forget that! Well," he said with a twinkle in his tired eyes, "just make sure it's you two doing that and not my grandchildren."

The tiff was over and the conversation done when they heard a loud knock on the outer door. Abe assumed it was one of the hands as he hollered, "Come."

Within minutes a stocky built good looking younger man not more than a couple of years older than Naomi, filled the doorway. He held his dusty worn hat in his hands as his probing eyes met those of the twins then settled in on Abe. "Mr. Baxter, I didn't mean to intrude," Clinton said, "I, I just wanted to visit with you for a few minutes without my uncle if I might. Ma'am," he said to Liza, Lizzie, and Naomi. He even gave Dancing Bear a respectful nod.

"Coffee," Abe asked as he invited the young man in. There was something different about this boy. He didn't seem to fit in with the rest of the hoodlums that he was traveling with.

"Yes, sir," he answered in a delighted tone.

"Had breakfast?" Abe questioned.

"No sir, but I don't mean to impose," he said genuinely.

Without speaking the twins slid to either side and placed a chair between them. Abe had a look of regret on his face as soon as he saw the motion. Clinton didn't seem to be the least bit intimidated by the bold move as he slid into the chair and gave each woman a wide grin. "It's been a month of Sunday's since I've had a home cooked meal." Then as though he remembered his manners he hurriedly stood back up and introduced himself. "Please, forgive my manners," he said embarrassed. "Clinton, Clinton Small." Anxiously, he shook Liza then Lizzie's hand. "I believe that we have met," he said in a teasing tone. Then he reached across the table and shook Matthew's hand as he nodded at Naomi and smiled at Charlie. Then he sat back into the comfortable chair.

The twins were completely taken back at his genuine attitude as they smiled at each other. It was plain to see that he was completely at ease in his new environment as he politely filled his plate. "Man, this looks good!" he exclaimed as he looked from one person to the other. "Did I interrupt something?" he questioned.

"No," Liza said as she and Lizzie sat and watched the young man eat as the rest of the family did the same. "Father," Liza asked, "has Jeffrey been down yet?"

"Haven't seen him," her father answered just as the boy walked into the room.

It didn't take but a few seconds for Jeffrey to notice that they had company. When he recognized who it was he started for his gun.

Abe quickly botched the notion. "Not in this house!" he demanded as Liza and Lizzie came to their feet.

"But, papa, he's one of them! The one's that tried to rob us!" he yowled like a stepped on cat.

"Sit down, Jeffrey," Liza said in a tired tone.

"But, mother!"

"Sit!" Lizzie snapped in an annoyed tone.

Jeffrey did as he was told but he never took his distrusting eyes off of the stranger. "What do you think you're doing out here?" he hissed. "Where's your band of thieves!"

"I'm sure I don't know what you're talking about," Clinton said in self defense. "I'm a map maker, not a thief."

"Sure you are!" Jeffrey accused.

"Shut up, Jeffrey," Matthew injected. He'd grown tired of his twin brother's unruly outbursts. "Let the man talk."

"Well, little brother, he sure didn't seem to be doing much talking the other day!"

"No," Clinton said in a mocking tone, "I kind of like both of my feet. Wasn't a situation I wanted to get in to."

"How is the old goat anyway," Lizzie asked ignoring the outburst of her nephew.

"He'll be all right the dern'd fool. You missed any vital organs. Not that he didn't deserve it! Been that way as long as I've known him. Always aching for trouble."

"You're not buying that are you?" Jeffrey snapped in an angry tone. "He's probably here to spy on our operation."

"And what operation would that be?" Liza questioned, sorry that her son had even come down for breakfast.

"Why the ranch of course!" he looked at his mother as though she were insane. "What are you out here to sabotage us?"

Clinton gave the man across the table a queer look. It was obvious that there was trouble brewing within him that only a bullet was going to cure. "Like I said before, I'm a map maker. That's why I'm here. To draw up a map for a certain client, then I'll be on my way."

"You wouldn't be interested in drawing out one for me and this here ranch now would you?" Abe asked.

"Sir, I would be delighted. But are you sure that no one has done that yet? That's why I came back out here. Are you sure? Not on one small piece of paper somewhere's?"

"No, son, I don't recollect it." Then he rubbed his chin before he spoke, "Unless—no—no, I don't know why she would have."

"Sir, I have to be honest, if I do make you a map, the person I'm representing can contest it. You need to know that up front. I'm no backstabber." Clinton stated.

"I understand." He said in earnest.

Liza saw the heartache wash across Abe's wearing face. "Clinton," she said mostly to change the subject, "how do you feel about gathering a few horses? Give you a chance to see a big part of this ranch."

The handsome man looked Liza straight in the eyes as he spoke, "Honestly ma'am, it's been a while since I've done any of that kind of work."

"Probably, never," Jeffrey injected snidely.

Clinton ignored his remark as he continued, "But it would be a prime opportunity." He pondered the situation for a brief moment. "Yes, I'm in. Sounds great. I'm up for an adventure. But I'm not sure my horse will be. She's got a few years on her."

"We'll see that you're mounted," Lizzie said.

"Then I'm yours," he teased.

Matthew had taken an instant liking to the mapmaker across the table. "Listen," he said, "when we're done with breakfast I'll take you down to the corral and we can pick a couple of horses out. I mean if you'd like."

"I'd like that!. Just make sure they're gentle. I don't need my neck broke," Clinton chided.

"If you're worried about that, you can ride mine," Naomi offered, "he's very well behaved."

Lizzie couldn't help but grin when she saw the smitten look on Naomi's face. The young woman had no idea that the flour from the dough she'd used to bake the delicious biscuits, they were all enjoying, was dusted across the left side of her cheek and across the top of her forehead. All her wildflower circles could see was the handsome man sitting across the old oak table.

"What do you think, mother?" she asked Lizzie.

It was plain to see that some kind of attraction had developed between the young woman and the friendly mapmaker. "I have no say who rides your animal."

"What about me?" Jeffrey asked in a disrespectful tone. "You seem to have plenty to say about mine!" He glared at his mother and aunt. "I know one thing; I'm not riding that stinking mule on the highline!"

Liza let out an irritated sigh as she looked into Matthew's kind blue eyes. "You and Naomi go and find your brother a good solid mount. Take Clinton if you want. But the buckskin will be pulled behind the wagon and ridden by Charlie." Then, Lizzie gave Jeffrey a warning look. "I don't want to see any spurs on the heels of those boots young man. Charlie just got those open wounds healed up on the very animal that you seem to be so attached to. If I see another mark on one more horse on this ranch I swear I'll take those spurs and put them …"

"You're not the boss of me, Aunt Lizzie!" he snapped hotly. "You think you're all big and bad, bossing everyone around all the time! But you're not the boss of me!" he yelled.

"You don't talk to my mother that way!" Naomi threatened as she flew from her chair.

"Shut up you little half-breed!" he threatened right back.

At his last remark Abe came completely out of his chair and grabbed Jeffrey by the back of his collar. Like a mother dog hauling a yowling pup he yanked him by the back of the shirt and out of the door they went. "Don't you ever use that kind of vulgar language in this house again, young man!"

"Mother!" he whined as they descended the old log house in a huff.

Liza stared into Naomi's tear-filled eyes. "He doesn't know, he doesn't understand. I'm sorry Little Feather," she said sadly.

Naomi looked into the tired eyes of her loving aunt. She knew it wasn't her fault that Jeffrey was the way he was. So she did what her mother Lizzie had taught her from the beginning. "It doesn't matter, auntie, I love you no matter what." Then she turned and smiled at the boys, "Should we pick out a horse?" In low toned chatter the threesome left the house and headed toward the corral.

Nonchalantly, Charlie picked up his hat and started to walk out of the kitchen when Liza said in a concerned clear tone. "You watch yourself up there on the highline, Charlie, where my boy is concerned. He's got a bad ache in his heart. So you best be looking over both those shoulders." There was no denying the worry in her beautiful face.

"Yes, ma'am," he said as he left the serenity of the old log house.

"Lizzie," Liza said in a distraught tone, "what are we going to do about that boy?"

"I don't know, Liza. Tie him up behind the wagon and drag his sorry carcass to the Red Clay Ridge! Throw him into a deep ravine! I don't know." As she looked into her sister's tired face she added. "Don't fret so, Liza, we'll figure it out. He's young. We'll get there," she said in a hopeful tone. "But right now we need to get moving if we're gonna get where we're going before dark."

"See you in a few of days, father," the twins hollered in unison as they loped out of the pillared gate. Abe stood on the wooden porch as he waved to the small party. He gave the unwilling Jeffrey a warning look as the wagon followed along at a slower pace behind them.

CHAPTER 9

They'd gone several miles before Liza and Lizzie decided who would do what. "You take the north end of the ridge and we'll run them in that small canyon. What we can't get in we'll rope. How does that sound to you?" Lizzie questioned.

"I'm hoping they're not going to be that difficult."

Lizzie gave her sister a doubtful look, "Yeah. Would I want to go to a darn ole corral if I could run free?"

"Not hardly," they said in unison.

"So, who's going where?" Liza asked.

"I'll take Charlie and Matthew with me. You have Jeffrey and Naomi guard the gate. And Clinton can do whatever he wants. Most of the work will be ours anyway," Lizzie sighed.

"I know."

"Do you think it's safe to leave Jeffrey with Naomi? She might scalp him before the days over." Both women could hardly stay on their horses for laughing.

"Maybe!" Liza could hardly stay on her horse. "Who knows what that little heathen will do!"

"No, she'd shave him bald that's what the little imp would do," Lizzie giggled. "Remember how she used to boss me around? Little snot!" she laughed.

As they rounded the last ridge Liza and Lizzie sat on their horse's and waited for the wagon to catch up. The sight below them was awe-inspiring. The majestic beauty that sprawled out before them like a soft green carpet was breathtaking.

"Wow," Clinton said as he rode up next to Liza. "I don't think I've ever seen a place as beautiful as this."

"I know, I never get tired of looking at it," the twins sighed within the same breath.

"No, ma'am," he half whispered as he stared at the soft green rolling hills. There were miles of thick rich grasses that reminded him of a smooth rocking ocean. The gentle breeze from the warm wind looked like fingers as they lightly caressed the tops of the tall silky stems. It reminded him of a mother's gentle hand stroking her child's long glossy hair. There was every color of butterfly imaginable ducking in and out of the beautifully odd shaped blooming flowers. Their inviting ballet beckoned them closer and closer as they danced openly beneath the wispy breeze. At the bottom of the luscious meadow lay a blue winding creek the color of a young girl's ribbon that lazily etched its way across the beautiful meadow like a silver maze then disappeared into the shaley earth. But, the most magnificent sight was the powerful red rock cliffs that seemed to hang in the air with little effort as they disappeared one after the other into bottomless canyons. The crimson and golden colors entwined themselves within the heavy stone leaving the illusion of bloody veins just waiting to be exposed. He was completely mesmerized at the awe-inspiring picture in front of him.

As he turned his head to the west he could see a small herd of horses in the distance. Even from here the silky looking animals seemed majestic and solid like the very earth that supported their place of being. There were no words for the enchanting sight. A sense of calm enveloped his soul as something deep down in his gut told him that this was going to be an experience he wouldn't soon forget. Now, he was glad that he'd decided to ride along.

As Clinton gazed from one face to the other of the lovely women sitting to either side of him he couldn't get over how stunning they were! He just couldn't find a flaw on their faces anywhere. They were identical in every way. Their hand movements. The way they turned their heads. Their thought process. Right down to the way they dressed. It must have been amazing to be raised by such a rare breed of women. Clinton could only imagine what it must have been like when they were younger, why their beauty must have been staggering with their independent air and those cunning blue eyes that reminded you of moon drops on a lost forgotten lake. The only thing that he hadn't figured out was why Naomi, who affectionately called Lizzie mother, didn't resemble her in any fashion. She looked like the lady in the portrait above the fireplace.

"Hey!" Jeffrey hollered as he rode up next to the silent party like a cyclone. "What cha' all doing?" he sat a minute straining to see whatever it was that everyone was looking at. When he couldn't figure it out he continued, "I don't see nothing. Come on, we got work to do." And just like that he prodded his horse down the grassy slope ruining the lovely portrait that had been so graciously displayed in front of him.

But what Jeffrey hadn't planned on was the keg of dynamite that followed him down the grassy slope. "Mother," Naomi said in an overly sweet tone. "Aunt Liza." She gave them both a devilish grin as she came up behind her cousin's horse. What unfolded next was unthinkable.

"Oh, crap!" Lizzie whispered under her breath.

"She's not going to do what I think she is," Liza added in a knowing tone.

"Oh, yeah," they said in unison.

"Hello, cousin," Naomi said in a sweet manner.

"Now, Naomi," Jeffrey said in a jittery tone. "I didn't mean nothing this morning. I didn't."

"What makes you think that I'm mad about that?" she asked sweetly.

"Cause, you have that look on your face," he answered leerily.

"Well, maybe you should apologize. I mean if you're that worried about it."

"Apologize! For what, telling the truth?" he said exasperated at her arrogance.

They could hear Naomi's war cry from where they sat. One minute she was on the back of her horse and the next she was on Jeffrey's. The startled animal was on a full out lope across the open meadow as she clung to the back of her cousin. Liza looked at Lizzie and said, "Half way?"

"Middle of the pond."

"Yep, middle of the pond."

There was no mistaking the howling screams of terror from Naomi's startled cousin. "Get off of me you little heathen!" he threatened.

"Heathen am I," she struck back. "I'll show you a heathen!" Harder and harder Naomi slapped the horse's rump behind her.

"Stop," Jeff yelled completely terrified, "you're going to get us killed!"

"Scared?" Naomi seethed. "How about I'm sorry, cousin," she insisted seemingly unafraid.

"Go to the dickens you little spoiled rotten brat!" he hollered.

"I hope they don't break a leg on that horse," Liza stated calmly as she sat and watched her son. "I'd hate to have to shoot him."

"Which one, the boy or the horse?"

"The horse of course!" Liza stated in an exasperated tone.

"Me, too. It's going to be tough enough catching one gentle enough for him to ride home if that happens."

"Aren't you going to go down there and stop that?" Clinton wondered in a surprised tone. Shocked at how calm the two women were.

"No," Liza said. "I don't think she'll kill him."

"Do you sister?"

"Na, she might ruff him up a bit, but she won't kill him."

"She's half his size," Clinton stated in a flabbergasted tone.

"Yeah, but she's a lot meaner," the two of them said with pride in their voices.

"Oh yeah, she's an ornery one for sure." Matthew added.

Nonchalantly, the party headed the loaded wagon at a slow pace down the grassy knoll. There was no denying the half smile that circled the old cowpokes lips as Charlie clucked the team of horses grinning all the way.

"If you ever talk to my mother that way again," Naomi seethed through angry lips as the horse's hooves pounded the ground like thunder. "I will scalp you bald!"

"You'll try," he snapped back knowing that she would do just exactly that if she had a chance.

Then from out of nowhere the horse had no choice but to jump one of the small fingers of the creek. It looked as though Naomi had sprouted wings and was flying in mid air on the back of the startled animal. Everyone held their breath. When it landed she was still on behind. Then, as the horse skirted the small pond, Naomi gave her cousin an intended shove as he did a bellyflop across the water in front of her. She looked like a little heathen from where they watched as she stood holding the heaving horse's reins. Standing like a little barbarian in the middle of the saddle.

The twins knew that she could hold her own against her cousin. She wasn't a big girl but she was mean enough to be three times her size. Lizzie had instilled in her the importance of listening to her own being of self. "Listen to your gut!" she would say. "Know how important it is to trust your own instincts. Never second guess yourself." Lizzie made sure of that from an early age. A lesson in life that Naomi had never forgotten. Liza and Lizzie knew that no one would ever take advantage of Little Feather. She was too much like them. Head strong in her way of thinking, cunning in her actions and hard headed to a fault. Being proud of Little Feather came naturally just like her beauty.

Jeffrey on the other hand didn't have the disposition to carry out his own threats. He never worked hard enough to build any kind of muscles. Unless of course you considered a fifth of whiskey heavy. He always seemed to be able to pick one of those up. Still, he never seemed to know when to leave well enough alone. Drunk or sober. "You little heathen," he hollered again as Naomi brought the horse around and jumped right on top of her cousin.

With the fire of ten men she slammed his head under the chilly water. He fought her every move but she was quick like an otter in the water. Sputtering like a drowned duck he screamed. "Hold still you slippery snake!" But when he came up out of the water this time he had his pistol drawn. "Do it again!" he threatened through clenched teeth. "I dare you!"

Naomi stared at her cousin for several minutes before she spoke, "You don't get it do you?"

"I get that you are a spoiled little witch!" he seethed through angered frustration. That you can't do anything wrong!" Furiously, he pointed the shaking gun right at her.

"Shoot me, Jeffrey. Go ahead," she insisted. "And I can guarantee you that it will be the last thing you ever do." There was no way to miss the disappointment in her angry face as she turned and started to walk away.

"Don't turn your back on me!" he screamed completely out of control. "I'll do it!"

Naomi turned around and like a leaping frog she half walked half hopped back toward her cousin. When she was within inches of where he stood shaking like a leaf, she took the barrel of the gun and placed against her heaving chest. "If this is what you really want," she paused for a brief moment. "Then do it now or put that hog leg away."

Tears of frustration ran down her cousins wet reddened face just as the rest of the party rode up. But the boy was so mad that he didn't hear anything but his own breathing. As the two of them stood eye to eye, nose to nose, all he could see was a set of wildflower circles that had turned fearlessly black. She looked just like her! No, just like them! His eyes were cloudy and distant. In slow motion he reached his thumb to cock the hammer when Liza with one crack of her whip snapped the gun from his hand. Jeffrey let out a loud yowl as the pigging string stung his wet flesh.

"I think we'll leave Jeffrey down by the gate," Lizzie said matter-of-factly.

"Yup," Liza agreed as they headed to set up camp down by the mouth of the small canyon.

"Find that gun and clean it up," Liza instructed.

"Well, Charlie," Lizzie asked, "how do you feel about riding for the brand now?"

"Can't think of a better place to be," he half laughed. "Nope, don't rightly know one." Charlie had never met anyone like Liza and Lizzie. They were two women with one soul. All he could think of was if he was only a few years younger.

With little trouble they moved the loaded wagon to the bottom of the open meadow and into the front part of the rounded canyon that would work well as a corral. There was water and plenty of grass toward the back of the rounded out hollow. It would hold the horses for no longer than they would be up here and give them all the shelter that they would need in case a storm came blowin' northwest out of the mountains.

Like two well-trained generals, Liza and Lizzie prepared to set up the camp as they started unloading the wagon. "Jeffrey," Lizzie instructed take these coils of rope and pull it as tight as you can across that opening. Tie one to either side. I don't care which. Just make sure they can't get over or under it."

"Yes, ma'am," he answered, glad that he had something to do. Anything to get as far away from his wily aunt as possible.

"Matthew, unhitch the team and turn them out in the small canyon. Then get on your horse and go check out the lay of things inside. I don't want any surprises in the night."

"Yes, ma'am," he said without any hesitation.

"Naomi, take these small rolls of rope and get busy making me some makeshift halters. We'll need fifty. Can you do that?"

"Yes, ma'am," she said happily.

Then she turned and looked into the kind blue eyes of the mapmaker. "I have two things for you, Clinton."

"Yes, ma'am," he said enthusiastically, his facial features showed his excitement that he would be included.

"I need you to ride up on that ridge over there. Take a good look and see if there are any horses standing in the bottom of that big open meadow. It will give you a chance to get a different lay of the land. Take your time to look around."

"Yes, ma'am!"

Lizzie looked into Charlie's tired face as she spoke, "Charlie, I could sure use a fire and some hot coffee." She was extremely upset about his crippled hands. Especially since she knew that it wasn't arthritis that had made them that way.

"I can do more than that, Lizzie. You know I can," he said surprised at his easy task.

"I know exactly what you're capable of Charlie, but these young'uns have to learn that we can't do everything." She gave him a quick knowing smirk.

The old cowpoke knew exactly what she was saying. "I'll get right on it."

Liza and Lizzie busied themselves with the little chores that no one else wanted to do. After several hours of non-stop work they all gathered around the fire at once. "Nothing in the canyon, Aunt Lizzie," Matthew reported. "Clear as a bell."

"I have seven halters, mother," Naomi said.

"I need some help getting that rope tight enough. It's got a little swing in the middle," Jeffrey said.

"I can help with that, brother." Matthew volunteered.

"Thanks," he answered sincerely.

Then all eyes walked across the distance as they settled in on the mapmaker. He was busy drawing something with a lot of numbers on it with a small angled looking glass. "Clinton," Lizzie urged, "report please."

The young man looked up as though he were dazed at the question. "What? Oh, pardon; I get to drawing and...um, yes, there were about fifteen head at the bottom. Didn't seem like they were in a hurry to get anywhere." He gave Lizzie a wide smile.

"We'll start there in the morning," Lizzie stated. "The closer the better."

"What do you think, mother?" Jeffrey asked from out of the blue.

"About what?" Liza questioned in a puzzled tone.

"Well, Aunt Lizzie is giving all of the orders. What do you think? You're a part of this too," he gave his aunt a sour look.

Liza gazed into her son's trouble-making eyes. Like a lost kitten she let out a deep sigh. "Jeffrey, son, my sister, you're aunt knows exactly what she's doing. I would have done the same."

"Are you sure mother, or are you just saying that because she's sitting here?"

Liza smiled at her identical sibling from across the fire. "Whatever Lizzie and I have to say to each other has never been hidden by private talking. We say what we feel. There are no secrets between us." She gave her son an odd look. "You should know that by now."

"Why do you always take her side?" he asked plainly. "Are you afraid of her?"

"I didn't realize that you took sides against your own blood, Jeffrey. Is this where your trouble lies? You need to take sides?"

"No!" he snapped. "But you always do what she wants! All the time! You and papa! Like, you're afraid of her or something."

"And why would I need to be afraid of my sister? My own blood. She loves me, I love her, we are from the same center. Are you afraid of your brother?"

"Of course not!" he boasted.

"Then why do you ask me such a black spotted question?" she asked suspiciously.

"Because you never stand up for yourself! You never tell her, no! Don't you ever get tired of being her patsy mother?" he asked in a frustrated tone.

Liza said in a motherly fashion. "I don't understand this patsy person. But, I'm not sure I like her. And, I'm sorry you see me that way, son. But if you're sideways thinkin' says I don't trust my own no how's then you don't know me. My sister speaks from my heart, from my lips. The way I speak from hers. We are one and the same. Yes I trust my own say-so's."

"You are not her, mother! She is not, you! Why can't you see that?" It was very obvious that Jeffrey was furious with his mothers' mixed up defense.

Liza looked into her sister's trusting eyes. It was plain to see that they shared the feeling of regret that the boy had for both of them. Of course Liza was Lizzie and Lizzie was Liza. They didn't know anything different. They had been one since the day of their creation. "It makes my heart heavy with pain that you my son don't know the difference."

Frustrated, Jeffrey threw his coffee into the fire as he stood up. It made a defiant hissing sound much like the voice of the man who threw it. "You two aren't normal! You're not!"

Lizzie gave Liza a huge smile as she spoke, "That's the only thing that you've gotten right all day, Mr. Jeffrey."

Furious, the young man walked away from the fire, "I'm going to bed!" he said as he kicked the dirt in front of him.

Matthew gave his mother a loving look through angry eyes. It was obvious that he had plenty to say to his disrespecting twin but Liza shook her head no.

Before the dew had a chance to wipe its nose Charlie had coffee, biscuits, and gravy ready for the hungry crew when they were done saddling up. "Smells good, Charlie," Liza said. "Listen, I don't know what to tell you about my son, he's just, well, got some burr under his saddle about his aunt."

Charlie gave her an understanding look, "For the brand ma'am."

"Yep," she said quietly.

Lizzie hurried her sister as she finished the last bite of her breakfast with a quick slurp of coffee. "C'mon, Liza. We best get started." Then she gazed into the old cowboys rugged face. "You mind my sister's warning about that boy, Charlie."

"Yes, ma'am."

CHAPTER 10

By the end of the first day they had twenty seven horses gathered in the open canyon. Naomi came riding in like a bullet, Liza and Lizzie were hot on her heels with ten more. Clinton was amazed at the agility of the identical twins and the riding skills of the youngest Baxter.

"Wahoo! You look like a tick stuck on a mules butt! Ride em Naomi!" Matthew yelled as he watched the young daredevil whiz past him.

"Don't egg her on, Matthew," Lizzie injected in a bored tone, "she's bad enough!"

"She rides like the wind, Auntie!" Matthew stated in an excited tone.

There was no doubt about it; the young woman rode the way a single drop of rain clings to the back of a water-soaked horse. As though the animal brought her soul to life. Like the beating of her heart was as wild as the hairy beast beneath her. Fearless was an understatement.

Lizzie was both happy and sad that they were nearly done with the
gathering. It had been a momentous week of wonder and the twins dreaded the thought of going home to the stodgy work at the ranch. They knew tomorrow morning they'd break camp before the sun wiped the sleep from its eyes and everyone would get their allotment of horses to lead back to the ranch.

The gathering had gone better than they had expected but Lizzie wanted five more head just in case some didn't work out. Naomi told her mother she'd seen a small group down at the bottom end of the lush meadow.

"You're sure?" Lizzie questioned in a tone that said she didn't want to go on a wild goose chase.

"Yes, ma'am." Naomi answered plainly.

"Then, that's where we will start."

Morning came and the Baxter clan was on their final descent with the last five horses. It was especially warm this early morning and Naomi's horse was nearly spent. The so-called small group of horses had been a lot wilier than they had expected and had given them quite a run for their money. So, she stopped at the bottom of the small still meadow to give herself and the animal she rode a much deserved water break. As she stepped down from her heaving horse she could see Charlie resting on the top of the highline rubbing his old hands. And although he seemed close, she knew he was a good mile away. As she stretched and gazed the other direction she could see Liza and Lizzie on the top ridge watching over the whole outfit like two lionesses protecting their pride. Their presence always gave her a sense of security. She smiled to herself, from this distance even she couldn't tell who was who. It was no surprise that Jeffrey had refused to ride today, swearing his butt had enough blisters! Lizzie put him on gate duty. In fact he had contributed very little on this trip. Matthew was about a half mile on the north side of, Charlie. She didn't have a clue where Clinton was but the last time she'd seen him he'd been leading a beautiful black stallion and three other horses down the side of the sloping ridge.

The mapmaker had surprised everyone with his capable ability. Especially, Naomi. There was just something about him that made her gut fill with butterflies every time she looked at him. He was quiet and kind. He'd never once flaunted his skill. And he respected his instruction from the wily duo simply doing what he was told. She knew the twins had been glad that he'd pitched in as much as he had for the old cowpoke had slowed his pace considerably the last couple of days.

Purposely, Naomi knelt down and washed the dust from her heated face in the small cool stream. The water felt good against her warm skin. And, even better as it slid down her dry thirsty throat.

Naomi was lost in deep thought when an old familiar scent drifted past her sunburned nose. "Oh, no!" she whispered to herself. "Stupid! Stupid! Stupid!" Then, she swore she saw the tall grass move. Squatting down she strained her eyes as she stared into the brushy reeds for several minutes. She took in a deep sigh of relief when she didn't see anything.

Then, from out of nowhere she saw a clump of black fur. Regret filled her senses. She didn't have to see it! She knew! And, if she knew anything about anything where there was a cub bear, there was a momma looking for it. Then, just like that the small cub popped up out of the tall grass. Her heart pounded like thunder in her ears. She knew she was in deep trouble. Like her feet were made of feathers she crept backward through the tall reedy grass trying to make a quiet but hasty retreat. If she became invisible like the wind she just might get out of this alive. She hadn't gone far when the young cub discovered her whereabouts. Being curious about his newfound toy he started bawling and bouncing in her direction. Determined to capture his prey.

"No!" Naomi whispered in a panicked voice. "Get back!" But the small creature was completely intrigued with its new discovery. Hurriedly, Naomi tried to mount her skittish horse but he pulled away and ran toward the top of the barren hill when the momma of that little critter popped up out of a muddy bog where she'd been bathing. Naomi was left to fend for herself. "Mighty One help me!" she said as she started running as fast as her two feet would carry her.

It was plain to see that the huge mother grizzly wasn't happy that an intruder had spoiled her frolic in the mud and to make matter worse, the small curious cub was in hot pursuit tailing the fleeing creature. The mother sow let out a loud warning growl as she jumped up and down with her strong front paws, pounding them like a sludge hammer in the squishy mud, throwing her head side to side like a snarling two thousand pound ravenous beast! When the baby cub didn't stop the heavy sow started running after them both!

Charlie spotted the disastrous situation first. Completely stunned at what he was seeing. Like a madman he waved his old arms and shot his rifle high in the air. The booming sound echoed across the open valley as all heads jerked upward in his direction. Anxiously, he pointed to the bottom of the small meadow.

"Liza!" Lizzie screamed. "No!" But the twins were too far away to get to the fleeing young woman before the mother grizzly did. They both took careful aim but shooting was out of the question for fear that they would miss and hit Naomi. Both women sat stunned at the picture that was unfolding in front of them as they headed like two warriors to do battle to save their offspring.

Matthew saw Naomi running too but he was also too far away. All he could do was yell, "Run, Naomi, run!"

Clinton saw the older man waving his arms like a nest of bees was attacking him. As he glanced toward the bottom of the ravine his heart nearly stopped in his chest. Naomi's horse was spent from the chase of the morning and he knew that there was no way the gentle animal would hold up running down the rugged terrain and back again. Especially with two riders. With little thought to his own welfare he let go of the horses that followed him like a mother dog and jumped on the back of the sturdy black stallion. "You'd better fly you black beast!" Clinton said as he rode in the direction of the fleeing girl.

Clinton was ready for the attempt to get thrown from the back of the black at any moment. All he had for control was a rope slipped over the horse's nose and two pieces of rope to either side. This was going to be a wreck start to finish. Still the stocky man pounded the sides of the sure-footed animal as he bailed down the embankment of the rocky ravine. It was as though the animal beneath him knew the urgency of his flight. His large, muscled body flew through the air like the tail of a falling comet. Faster and faster the beast pounded the soft dirt. Digging his feet into the waiting soil then pushing off like the devil himself was hot on his heels. Closer and closer Clinton came to the rescue of the berry-headed girl that he had grown so fond of.

But the Grizzly was gaining ground fast. She was hell bent on catching the intruder that dared trump her territory and interrupt her afternoon mud bath. Angrily, she bellowed behind Naomi as she pushed harder and harder to claim her prey.

Clinton could hear Naomi's screams in his disbelieving ears. She was running for all she worth. Her fleeing legs looked like hummingbird wings as she ran through the thick grass. He knew beyond the shadow of a doubt that the grizzly would lay her skin open like a straight razor to a chin.

"No," he whispered. "Please, no!" With little thought to his own safety, he urged the fearless beast down the jagged ravine.

Naomi knew if she hadn't gotten a good head start on the overprotective momma she would already be dead. Faster and faster she ran! Tears of regret escaped her terrified eyes like rain. She should have waited to get a drink of water! She shouldn't have been so greedy! She knew better! Run! Run! She couldn't breathe! But slowing down wasn't an option; the mother grizzly was right on her heels. She could hear the loud pounding sound as its huge paws hit the mushy grass like thunder behind her! The grizzly's weight alone shook the ground beneath her feet as it echoed like death in her ears.

Out of the corner of her eye Naomi could see the black horse and rider flying at break neck speed down the dangerous ridge. Who was that? What were they thinking? There was no way to beat the crazed animal. "No!" she screamed just as she did a summersault landing in the waiting arms of the heavy black mud. The sudden impact stole every ounce of breath that was left from her aching lungs as she rolled, landing on her back. She could hear the crazed pounding paws from the huge mankiller behind her. She knew she was dead!

"Naomi!" Clinton yelled. "Naomi, get up! Run!"

Disorientated, Naomi tried to get to her feet just as the enraged animal did a complete summersault over the top of her downed body. The black matted fur pushed her backward as it smeared black rancid mud across her shocked face and across her heaving body. It was raining mud! The old sow must have tripped over the same thing she did! There was no mistaking the ferocious bellow as her massive bulk slammed into the edge of the stagnant marsh. Sputtering, and shaking Naomi started running in the opposite direction just as two bawling cubs ran past her like she was invisible.

The unbelievable distraction gave Clinton just enough time to grab Naomi by the back of the pants pulling her as close to the side of the black as he could. She looked like a dangling spider. Half running, half riding, half being drug in the direction of the rocky ridge.

"Hey, Liza," Lizzie stated in a surprised tone, "look! That ole sow has a set of twins, too!"

"I'll be jiggered! She sure does! No wonder she was so mad!"

The immense bear stood on her hind legs, bellowing like a stuck pig. She was two thousand pounds of angry flesh as she tossed her massive head side to side. Dirty black slobber flew from her enraged muzzle. You could hear her threatening roar echo across the canyon bottom. Furious that her intended prey had tricked her again. In a relentless state of fury the grizzly started running like a rabid dog in the direction of the fleeing duo.

Liza and Lizzie knew that the black horse would never make it half way up the ravine with both riders. It was an impossible feat to think the black could outrun the bear at the speed it was traveling. They also knew that Clinton was the type of person that would protect Naomi to the death. It would be a double massacre. So, the two of them took in a deep breath as they carefully aimed their rifles, placing a matched set of bullets right between the snarling animal's front feet. The bear was completely oblivious to another human being within miles of her. The echoing blast of the rifles and placement of the bullets caught her completely off guard as the muddy rock chips stung her snarling muzzle. She had no idea where they had come from. She let out a confused high-pitched yowl as one foot stumbled over the top of one of the cubs. The fall was inevitable as they heard a loud grunt. Within seconds she slid across the muddy marsh like a skipping stone. When she stopped sliding in the muddy slop the bear never moved.

"Your gun sighted in?" Lizzie asked shocked at the condition of the animal lying on the ground.

"Did we hit her, Lizzie?" Liza seemed so shocked.

"I didn't hit her, I was aiming in front of her," Lizzie stated matter-of-factly. "Unless she ran into it."

"So, are you saying that I hit her?" Liza questioned

"I never said that!" Then on second thought she added, "But she's not moving."

"Ah, that's gonna make me sick!" Liza scoffed.

"Are you sure your gun's sighted in?" Lizzie questioned again as they rode in the direction of the downed animal.

Then just like that the huge bear came to life shaking the hanging mud and grasses that clung to her matted fur like dripping honey. Like two small children that had been playing hide and seek, the naughty cubs shamefully got as close as they could to the grunting sow as she sounded out her crazed warning at the world.

Relieved that Naomi would live and the sow wasn't dead, Liza gave her sister a dirty look as she thought about what she had really been insinuating. "Did you call me a sow a few minutes ago? You know, the whole twin thing, did you?" And by the way, what did you mean was my gun sighted in? Are you saying that I missed?"

"Honestly Liza, I don't know where you come up with this cock-n-bull!" With a twinkle in her eye Lizzie hurried her horse to the side of the ravine.

"Lizzie," Liza hollered in a frustrated tone. "I'm talking to you! Lizzie!"

On the other side of the small knoll Naomi slid to the ground in a heap. The black gelding was heaving like an old steam engine and Clinton's face was as white as a sheet. "I thought she was going to get you for sure!" he said breathlessly as he grabbed her and pulled her to him. "Where are you hurt? Did she claw you?? My word!" he exclaimed as he turned her lose.

"Wow!" Naomi exclaimed. "Where did you learn to ride like that?" Completely oblivious to her near death experience as she stared into his scared eyes.

"What?" Clinton was completely baffled at her odd question. After all she'd nearly just been eaten by a two thousand pound grizzly.

"Where did you learn to ride like that?" She asked simply.

"Ride?" Clinton was shocked at her question.

"You risked your life for me! Why?" she asked in a calm tone.

Deep down he was wondering the same thing. Why had he risked his life like that? He certainly didn't owe her anything. Then, he stared into her intriguing face and he knew exactly why he had done what he'd done. This beautiful berry headed fireball was perfect for him.

"You're an odd man, Mr. Mapmaker." Naomi stated.

"More like a raging idiot!" he said once the reality of what he had just done started to sink in.

Naomi gave him a warm understanding look as they stared at each other. It was an odd feeling. One that was new to both of them. Naomi was getting ready to say something else when over the hill popped Liza and Lizzie.

"Good heavens, child are you all right?" Liza asked as she stepped down from her winded horse. "Why you nearly snatched me of ten years of my life, not to say what you did to your mother! Let me see," she demanded as she turned Naomi round and round. "No broken bones, Lizzie," she stated with a sigh. "Everything else is fixable."

"I'm fine," Naomi said honestly.

"So, Mr. Mapmaker," Lizzie said in an expressive tone, "that was some kinda riding you did there."

Clinton knew that the woman sitting like a judge on the tall red horse was a lot more concerned than she was putting on. So his answer never wavered one way or the other as he answered her with his heart. "Ma'am," he said honestly as he looked directly into those blue honest eyes, "it's been years since I've ridden an animal like that." His tone was so respectful as a slight mist covered the trusting circles that never left her face. "He didn't care where we were heading just being asked to perform the strength of ten horses was enough. He knew the ground and he knew what I was asking him to do, I could feel it in his giving spirit. This is his terrain, not mine. He could have unloaded me any time that he wanted to. So, don't give me credit I can't be accepting it. In a tender expression of respect he ran his trembling hand down the sleek sweaty neck of the beautiful black horse whose sides stood heaving for wind. "You did it buddy, you saved us both," he whispered. "You're a magnificent animal. Thank you."

Liza and Lizzie were quite taken aback at the emotion the young man displayed toward the frothy animal. The heaving beast stood sixteen hands if he was an inch. And not once did the affectionate man mention his skill of handling the large green-broke horse with nothing more than two pieces of frayed rope. It was plain to see that he didn't expect any recognition for his part in the dangerous rescue. He'd simply done what any red blooded American male would have done, he saved the life of a dying girl.

The two women looked into each other's eyes as they made the mental choice. "He's yours," they said in unison.

"What?" Clinton said in a shocked tone as his head popped up. "Mine? What's mine?"

"Take him," Liza said again in a voice that rang with authority.

"He'll never be rode like that again," Lizzie added.

"I could never pay for such an animal."

"From now on he's yours," they said together. "That's the end of it."

Clinton looked into the stern disciplined faces of the two women that sat like proud warriors in front of him. He knew that the horse was a gift and not to be taken lightly. He knew that these two self-made women didn't give things away at a whim. The respect that creased their brows was double fold. "Thank you," he said sincerely.

Just then like a whirlwind, Matthew flew over the hill dismounting his horse on the run. "Naomi!" he hollered in an excited tone. "Are you all right!" Anxiously, he picked her up and twirled her around in his huge protective arms. It looked like he was hugging an old rag doll. "I thought she had you! I did!" he exclaimed as he placed her back on the ground. "A few scratches, some mud. That's all fixable! She'll live, Aunt Lizzie!" he chided.

Naomi was overwhelmed at her cousin's compassionate display. "I'm fine," she giggled.

Then Matthew turned and looked into Clinton's serene face. "And you," he said in an exuberant tone as he grabbed the man's hand and shook it furiously, "you saved her life!"

As Matthew stood expressing his gratitude, shaking Clinton's hand there was no missing the indisputable exchange the mapmaker saw pass between Liza and Lizzie Baxter. Clinton stood in a daze and watched two single souls, one raging with fear and anger, one consoling and steadfast collide like two mighty warriors! He shook his foggy head in disbelief as he witnessed the raging storm explode within those blue circles that had turned black and dangerous turning day to night tangled within a protective mortal vine. He felt the worry, then the horror and grief explode like rotting flesh from the twins' aching chests within his own! Why? Then...complete calmness. The storm subsided. He witnessed the vines gripping snare release them both as they placed a protective barrier around the young woman's soul. Naomi was safe for now.

When the twins gazed into the mapmaker's wondering eyes they knew their calm demeanor sitting upon the perfectly matched red horses hadn't fooled him. He knew what the centers of those dark blue eyes were saying when the distance of time had melded between them as one. They knew there would be no fooling the young mapmaker. They knew his character wouldn't be on trial again as the three of them gave each other a knowing nod.

Just then Jeffrey flew over the top of the hill completely out of breath! "Naomi! You're in one piece!" he hollered in disbelief. "I was coming but my horse bucked me off! Are you all right? She was going to eat you alive!"

"Did you see that?" Naomi exclaimed.

"I did!" he answered in an exhausted tone. "C'mon, down by the gate and tell me all about it!" he demanded as the twosome started walking down the hillside toward the camp. "I thought it had you," they heard him say as they disappeared from sight. "I did."

Charlie led the four horses that Clinton let go of to save Naomi as he rode up to the small party. "That was something," he said in his normally quiet tone.

"I guess so." He said still somewhat confused.

"How'd you like that ride?" he asked Clinton with a twinkle in his eye.

"I'm not sure." He stated matter-of-factly. "It was fast."

"I had a horse just like that once."

"Really," Clinton said as he climbed aboard Naomi's gentle palomino and led the black toward camp, "around these parts?"

"Let me tell you about him," Charlie said with a laugh in his voice as the two disappeared down the grassy hill.

Liza looked into her sister's stony face.

Lizzie shook her head as she spoke. "My whole life flashed before my eyes in about a second. That was too close," she said in a barely audible tone as light tears filled her cool blue eyes.

"Yup, well, if'n your gun would'a been sighted in she'd of never gotten that close," Liza said with a controlled snip in her voice as she headed toward camp.

"What's that supposed to mean, Liza? I'm having an emotional grip here!"

"A what?" Liza injected before she could finish.

"Emotional grip! I'm losing my gription!"

Liza started laughing aloud. "You're losing something alright! Honestly, Lizzie I've never heard that word before! Gription! What in a mules butt is that? Pull it together sister!"

"Oh…shut…up! Here, I am pouring out my heart and soul and you make odds about a new word I learnd'ed and talk crazy bout my gun! What's that posed to mean?" she snapped as she hurriedly caught up with her identical sibling. "How's that posed to make me feel, sister? I'm talking to you, Liza! Liza! You're the ones whose gun wasn't sighted in not mine! Are you hearing me? Liza!"

CHAPTER 11

As Liza and Lizzie made their way into the small camp the cousins were busy talking about Naomi's near death experience. Laughing it off as though it had been nothing. Applauding Clinton's superior horsemanship.

But when the young maiden looked into the scolding eyes of her mother the talking stopped immediately. The air became silent as the conversation changed. Naomi knew that the risk had been irresponsible, a foolish mistake on her part. And from the scolding look on Lizzie's face she knew that it was only a matter of time before she would be reprimanded about her recklessness. As their eyes met Naomi walked to where her mother dismounted.

"Quite a deal huh?" Lizzie said in a stern tone.

"Yes, ma'am. I mean no, ma'am," she said quietly waiting for her punishment.

"How many times have you been told to always know your surroundings?" Lizzie asked in a tone that said she didn't want to hear any lame excuses.

"Forever," Naomi answered simply. Then she quickly added. "Since I was a child."

"What happened?" Lizzie asked in a voice that said she'd better have a good explanation for scaring her half to death.

"I was hot. My horse was hot." She stood like an old oak, never wavering, ready to take her punishment. "I didn't see her. I barely saw the cubs."

"Didn't you smell her?" Lizzie continued in a scolding tone. Her eyes were far more threatening that her voice.

"Yes, ma'am," she said. Her eyes never left her mother's gaze. Everyone knew that when Lizzie was making a point you looked her directly in the eyes or you wound up in the dirt.

Lizzie cocked one meticulously arched brow. "And?"

"I ignored the scent." It was the truth. She had ignored the salty smell and ignored the birds' warning. A mistake that had nearly gotten her killed.

"You didn't hear the warning of the birds or the whispers of the singing grass?" Her dark eyes probed into Naomi's accepting face.

"Yes, mother," she said honestly, "but I ignored them. I let my thirst override my senses."

Lizzie stared lovingly into her daughter's beautiful face, "Are you sure that was all that had your head distracted?"

"No, mother, there was other things." Naomi had learned a long time ago not to lie to Lizzie. Somehow, she knew the truth without asking and it was a waste of breath to come up with some lame excuse. "It was a foolish mistake. I didn't mean to scare you."

"I know how it feels to be distracted, Naomi. And I know how it feels to ignore what you know to be right, but," she took in a deep breath, "that doesn't excuse it. We get one life. One. What we do with that life determines who we are. I don't expect to see that life wiped-out in the gut of a mother grizzly."

"Yes, ma'am."

"So, next time you will do what?" she continued in a low authoritive tone.

"There won't be a next time," Naomi answered matter-of-factly.

"Exactly."

That was it. The reprimand was over. Naomi let out a sigh of relief as she walked away. That was the most amazing thing about, Lizzie. She never screamed her discipline or embarrassed her. She simply said it like it was and made a person use their own intelligence. She was truly a rare individual.

The rest of the day was uneventful as they gathered round the campfire. Lizzie doled out each rider the amount of makeshift halters they would need in the morning. She gave four to Charlie, two for each side of the wagon.

"Looks like we might be riding home in the rain!" Lizzie said as she glanced at the darkening sky.

"Yeah let's just hope we don't have a runaway tonight! You boys might want to pitch a tent tonight," Liza said, "it sure looks like rain. Get your slickers out to where they are handy just in case."

"And let's pray those stinkin' hairballs stay put tonight," Matthew stated. "I don't want to be running all over this canyon trying to catch their wet hides! I'm ready to go home. The lumber company is a piece of cake compared to this," he stated simply as he looked into the older cooks tired face.

Charlie busied himself with getting the fire up and going and started some good old fashioned rabbit stew. The longer the slow boiling concoction cooked the further the smell drifted through the open camp tempting the pallet of any hungry passerby. The hired wrangler had turned out to be quite a remarkable cook and Liza and Lizzie appreciated every bite of his delicious concoctions. If it did rain the warm stew would surely warm a belly and if it didn't well, the aroma alone would be worth the eating. The twins sat without talking just studying the older man in his field of expertise. They knew now without a doubt where Charlie would fit in with this outfit.

Clinton had decided to ride to the top of the tall ridge to finish what he had started a couple of days earlier. After all it might be several months before he would be able to come back out this direction to scale any of the chartered ground and the high lying plateau gave him quite an idea as to where Abe Baxter's land started and ended. At least in this section. There was no missing the laughter and conversation as Matthew decided to tag along. It was plain to see that these two were going to be the best of friends.

It was just nice to listen to the singing birds, and to feel the caress of the soft warm wind. It had been a long day and the twins were glad to have all of the horses that they needed. It would be a welcome sight to see the ranch late afternoon tomorrow. They'd been gone long enough. They couldn't help but smile as they sat and watched Jeffrey and Naomi as they played a blood-thirsty game of checkers. Each one trying to figure out a new way to cheat the other. But, being the cutthroat connivers that they were, neither one could get away with anything. It reminded them of someone else they knew.

It was nearly dark when everyone gathered round the fire with a bowl of freshly made stew and sweet biscuits. It was plain to see that the older man had outdone himself this time.

"This is great, Charlie!" Clinton said with an enthusiastic grin. "Man, I burn coffee!"

Liza and Lizzie gave him an affirming smile. They had come to like and appreciate the young man. He was witty, charming, and honest to the bone. Not once did they hear him complain about the jobs that they had given him, big or small and he never bragged about what he knew. He just pitched in with all he was worth to finish the chore at hand. It was a good combination on a job like this and he was a good hand. They would see that he was well rewarded for his part in this journey.

The sun was nearly gone and the darkening sky was still threatening rain as Liza said to Jeffrey, "I want you to take a horse and ride inside the corral there and check things out. The last thing we need is a fiasco in the morning. "Ah, mother," Jeff whined in a disappointed tone. "Do I have to? I was just getting ready to go to bed. I have blisters you know!"

"Did I say you?" she replied back, put out with his whining attitude.

"I'll go," Naomi, said not wanting to have to deal with her cousin's ugly disposition or the rude words that he would place on her loving aunt. "I'll do it. My horse is still saddled. I'll do it."

Liza let out a deep sigh, "One circle, that's it." Purposely, she gave Jeffrey a disappointed look.

"Mind if I go along?" Clinton asked.

"You might get wet," Naomi laughed lightly.

"Been wet before."

"Sure," she said completely taken aback at his whimsical disposition. "Jump on behind." Jeffrey opened the makeshift gate as twosome disappeared into the small canyon.

They rode in silence for a while before Clinton spoke, "You're sure lucky to have all of this. It will be yours someday you know."

"I know," she sighed. "It's funny, there's so many people my age that want to go back East, find a new life, school. I've never dreamed of leaving where I am. I love it here. I hope to raise a family on this very ranch someday."

"Yeah, I know what you mean," he said honestly. "I fully intended to do that too but after my family..." He stopped dead in his tracks.

"Your family?"

"It's not a pretty picture." He stated.

"Sometimes life isn't a pretty picture. What matters is who we share it with."

"One hot afternoon, when I was just a young pup I was out in the field, plowing. In the distance I could hear gunshots. Never once thinking that there was trouble. I just assumed my father was hunting. But, when I got home that evening someone slaughtered my whole family. My mother, father, both of my younger brothers and my baby sister. She was two. Not a day goes by that I don't try to forget what I walked up on that day. I found one man still breathing. I nearly blew his head off but he said he was my mother's Uncle who had come to help with the planting. Rode right in on the ugly shoot out. They opened fire before anyone knew what hit. Thus, my Uncle Ben. I nursed him back to health and long story short, here we are."

"That's a sad story," she said thoughtfully, "kind of like my own."

"Really?" he said, interested in what she had to say as they wandered through the mulling animals. "How so?"

"I've never told anyone about it. I'm not sure that I know the whole story. But, I, unlike you, never got to know my mother or my father." She let out a slight laugh. "I'm sure you've noticed that I don't look like my mother, Lizzie. Papa says I'm the spit-n-image of Sarah."

"Sarah?"

"My real mother. Aunt Liza and Lizzie's younger sister."

"Oh, so that's your mother hanging in the portrait above the fireplace?" he concluded. Completely shocked at the comparison.

"No, that's my grandmother, Becky."

"Really?" he exclaimed. "You could have fooled me."

She let out a deep sigh. "When my mother was young, she fell madly in love with a young Indian boy by the name of Flying Eagle. Together, unbeknown to her family or his for that matter, they had me. No one knew about me for months. Somehow, I'm not sure about all of the details, they've kept a lot from me, but my mother got kidnapped and then killed in the rescue. I guess my papa Abe nearly died when Sarah got killed. He blamed himself. Still does I think. Anyway, in the winter of that year Chief Flying Eagle, my father, and his whole tribe got sick with some awful disease. They all died except for Dancing Bear. And she only survived because of my Mother, Lizzie." She stopped for a moment, turned around in the saddle, and faced the saddened face of the man behind her. "I guess the Marshal that was supposed to save Sarah, fell in love with Aunt Liza. They got married and Jeffrey and Matthew showed up nine months later. They're the Marshal's son's. But for some unknown reason Aunt Lizzie hated him."

"I wouldn't want that kind of trouble," he said honestly.

"I know!" she agreed. "But on the day that Matthew and Jacob were born, something awful happened. Something that we've never been told the whole truth about. All I know is my mother Lizzie has a long jagged scar that runs from one side of her shoulder to the other. They won't tell you about it, believe me I've tried. She raised me and Liza raised the boys."

"So, you are the daughter of Chief Flying Eagle?" he asked quietly. "The one that there's so much controversy about? That Chief?"

"Yes," she answered proudly as she stared at him with those different colored eyes. "Some people would call me a half-breed. Some would call me dirt. I call myself a Native American. Don't let the color of my hair or the tone of my skin fool you. I am the granddaughter of the mighty war Chief, Mad Dog and daughter of his son Chief Flying Eagle, niece of Dancing Bear. I'm not ashamed of it. I'm proud of my heritage. I just wanted you to know."

"What a wonderful story!" he stated sincerely. "The way you said that, just now, it makes me proud of it, too."

"I get this feeling that you're not like the rest of the men you're with. You're kind and smart. And you need to know that what my mother and Aunt did today, giving you the black, that just doesn't happen. They guard their horseflesh like their secrets. I've only seen them do that one other time and that was Charlie." Naomi let out a slight giggle. "And I think that was just to humiliate, Jeffrey."

Clinton knew that the young woman sitting in front of him was genuine. "I am honored to even be the smallest part of this party, horse or not. Your mother is quite extraordinary."

"Yes, she is," she answered softly.

"Your secret is safe with me, Naomi," he said honestly. "I will take it to my grave."

"And, while we're being honest," she gazed into his understanding face, "I can't get this odd feeling out of my chest whenever I'm around you." She placed her hand over her heart as she searched his face for answers.

"Me, too."

For several minutes, the two of them just stared at each other with nothing but the warm wind caressing their faces. It was a wonderful feeling being a part of the same breath. Sharing the naked truth of their confessions with someone that you knew wasn't going to exploit it. Feeling the heat of their bodies without touching their skin. It was a wonderful feeling.

Gently, Clinton reached up and touched Naomi's soft cheek with his rough fingers as he pulled her to him. "May I kiss you, Naomi?'

"Yes," she whispered.

When their lips met it was like a magical sleigh ride. Cool and yet warmly inviting. She had heard many wonderful stories about falling in love but she never expected that it would happen to her, not out here in the middle of no where. A God-forsaken place where few wanted to be. And yet, here he was, touching her soul with his lips. The mapmaker. There was no doubt in either one of their minds that they were meant to be together. When their lips parted Clinton gave her a teasing smile. "I'm glad your mother didn't see that; I might have lost a foot."

In the distance Liza and Lizzie saw the flock of white birds that descended from the evening sky seemingly from out of no where. They gave each other a knowing smile as their eyes crossed the distance between them. "Young love," they whispered in unison.

Naomi let out a loud laugh as she turned back around in the saddle, placing Clinton's hands firmly around her thin waist. They felt good there. Like that's where they should have been all along. "You're quite a special man," she whispered as she leaned against his chest.

"And you, a woman," he concluded as they continued their journey.

When the twosome arrived back they were met with two sets of questioning blue eyes, "What say you?" they said at the same time.

"Nothing, mother," Naomi answered as she unsaddled her horse. For some reason she just couldn't shed those butterflies.

Lizzie looked into Clinton's kind blue eyes. "Nope," he reiterated, "quiet as a mouse."

"So you say," Lizzie said in a lighthearted tone.

"Hey, Matthew, you up to a game?" Clinton asked as though nothing had transpired between the two of them. But, he too couldn't get rid of those butterflies.

"Put your money where your mouth is," he said teasingly.

The small camp had been quiet for several hours when the first rumbling of thunder started. It had just begun to spit a little rain when they saw the lightning strike light up the night sky like a burning lantern. Liza and Lizzie were wide awake in the back of the wagon listening to the angry grumbling of the darkened sky. Neither one wanted to move, yet they both knew that it would be only a matter of time before the heavens gave them no choice.

"Great!" Lizzie said. "Now we're gonna get wet!"

"Balls!" Liza countered nearly within the same breath. "One more night was all we needed!"

"Mother!" Matthew hollered in a loud tone. "We got trouble!"

When Matthew yelled his warning, both women bolted upright like two wet willows. Both forgetting that they had stuck an odd, shaped log in an upright position in the middle of the wagon bed so the rain would roll off of the canvass. Both women hit the odd shaped piece of wood point blank at the same time. "Aww!" they yelled in surprised pain as they slid backward holding their head's as though they'd been kicked by a mule.

Lizzie looked at her sister in disbelief. "Are we daft, Liza!" she accused.

After they gathered their wits about them, they haphazardly exited the makeshift tent like two fighting cats! Each one being mad at the other for even putting the large piece of wood in the middle of the wagon. That is until they saw the matching marks on their foreheads. Lizzie laughed at her sister when she spoke, "I'm not taking all of the blame for that!" she insisted. "I told you we needed to put that more farther toward the back! Now look, look at your head!"

"My head! I wouldn't talk!" Disgusted, Liza reached her hand to her forehead; the goose egged bump had definitely started to form. "I never said to put that thing in the middle, why are you blaming me! Honestly, Lizzie, if we weren't in such an all fire hurry we'd be having this discussion in the mud!" she seethed as she rubbed her forehead.

"There you go blaming me!" Lizzie echoed in a put out tone like a scolded child. "don't let a little water stop you, sister! We can play in the mud! I'm ready!"

But before either woman could square off one with the other, Matthew hollered again, "Mother! Please!" Like two fleeing fireflies, Liza and Lizzie headed for the makeshift opening to the small canyon as one shoved the other. "Here," Matthew yelled between intervals of the pounding thunder, "pull this tight, we've got to make this thing hold or we'll lose them all!"

"Higher!" Clinton hollered. "We need to get higher!" Like a mountain goat he climbed up the side of the rocky opening. Several times he slipped but never stopped till he got where he was going. Like a well schooled marksman he threw the rope across the wide ravine, catching a rock on the other side. Quickly he pulled it tight and tied it off as he did it again and again. By the time he was on the top of the opening he couldn't believe his eyes. The night sky was rumbling its warning like a herd of running buffalo. Lightning was popping all around him as it lit up the sides of the canyon walls the way a lone candle lights up a dark room. He knew they were coming; it was inevitable.

Clinton felt the pounding of their panicked hooves long before he saw them. It felt like a deep quaking in the earth. He could see the hot steam rising from the backs of their wet hides as foggy matter escaped their blowing nostrils. Their dark terrified eyes looked like the reddened end of a branding iron when the lightning scattered its electrifying fingers across the blackened sky. They were coming all right, fifty head of terrified horses, traveling at the speed of light with one berry-headed young woman ridding smack dab in the middle.

At first Clinton thought his eyes were playing tricks on him. There was no way that anyone would risk their neck like that! But there she was, sitting on the back of one of the largest red horses in the herd. Pounding his hairy sides for all she was worth. Trying her best to get ahead of the stampeding herd. He could hear her chanting some kind of cry that he'd never heard before. A language that he didn't understand. In complete horror he hung there holding his breath watching as the courageous young woman clung to the back of the rain-soaked animal. Faster and faster she flew through the herd like a lit fuse on a stick of wet dynamite. Trying her best to turn the spooked horses before they made it to the end of the opening. Closer and closer she flew through the mist, her red hair flying like a kite behind her, chanting at the stampeding animals. She was about a quarter of a mile away when the lightning struck the ground in front of the lead horse with such an intense force it shot little sparks of lit stones in every direction. The big red horse let out a shrill scream as it jumped in the air like a terrified rabbit. There was no stopping the unescapable event as the steaming horse fell over backward. Naomi hit the ground running like the devil himself was hot on her heels. Fearlessly, she grabbed the mane of one of the other horses and swung herself with little effort onto its back. Like a tick she clung to the snot-blowing horses' puissance hide. She was so close to the rope gate that all Clinton could imagine seeing was a young woman's torn body tangled and bloodied within the rain-soaked hides of several crippled dying horses. He tried to worn her but nothing, not one syllable exited his shocked lips. He sat there completely helpless as he watched the fearless ride as he clung to the jagged rocks. He'd never seen such a sight. He'd never been exposed to such an irresponsibly dangerous stunt. He was both mesmerized at her skill and furious at her carelessness. There was no way she was going to make the turn! There were too many of them. She was going to be trampled to death!

  What was she thinking? Then, in complete control she spun the large yellow mare around on a dime in a full circle, chanting those unfamiliar words that made no sense to him. Within the passing of a breath the wild-eyed rain soaked beasts followed her like a litter of lost pups. Within an instant, she disappeared into the darkness of the rocked canyon. When he finally climbed back down to the ground he was livid.

  Clinton and Naomi arrived at the gate at exactly the same time. Like a raging bull he grabbed the wild little heathen by the shoulders, "Are you crazy!" he yelled frantically. "Are you! You could have gotten your fool neck broke pulling an asinine stunt like that!" He pulled her face close to his. "What's the matter with you? Do you think that you're indestructible? Do you! Are you bullet proof, Naomi!" he seethed completely out of control.

Liza and Lizzie didn't know the young mapmaker had it in him. But his face was white and it was plain to see that no one dared intervene in this conversation.

Jeffrey hadn't missed the ugly encounter and he didn't like the way the mapmaker was yelling at his cousin. Not that he hadn't said a lot worse. Intent on doing bodily harm he started running to where the hotheaded couple stood, eye to eye, face to face.

Out of the corner of her eye, Liza saw her son's hot pursuit. He went for his pistol just as she stuck her foot out. Jeffrey fell face first like a skipping stone in the mud. His gun went flying in the opposite direction, landing directly in front Lizzie's feet. Within seconds the chunk of steel disappeared into the darkness. The twin's shook their heads as they continued to watch the argument unfold.

"Do you have any idea what it was like to watch you risk your life for a bunch of horses that we could gather again in the morning?" His brilliant blue eyes were so angry that it looked like little daggers were shooting from the pricked centers. "That was a ridiculously selfish stunt!"

Naomi glared into Clinton's angry face and being the proud little princess that she was, she determinedly reached up and took his fingers from her shoulders and stepped backward. Her eyes were coal black as she confronted her accuser. "First of all, don't ever put your hands on me like that again!" Her tone was icy cold and anyone standing within ear shot knew that she meant what she was saying. "And second of all, I don't need to ask your permission to do anything! I did what needed to be done! Not only would we have lost horses, there'd be lots of dead ones, Mr. Mapmaker! Do you honestly think that twin of rope would have held them?" Then in a far more menacing tone she added, "And third of all don't ever question my judgment again!" With that, Naomi turned and looked into her mother's amused eyes. "I will stay with the herd the rest of the night." Instantly, Naomi jumped back on the horse she'd rode up on and disappeared into the darkness.

Clinton turned and stomped toward his tent mumbling the whole way. "Women!"

"C'mon, Liza, we'd better look after these lumps," Lizzie said as they walked away from the gate and back toward the wagon. "Maybe we should take that lump of wood out of the wagon."

"What for, the storm's not completely over, sides, we're the only ones that will have a dry tent in the morning. A little lump ain't gonna hurt us none. We've had a lot worse!" Liza stated.

The rest of the evening went on without a hitch as the striking lightning subsided and the misting storm headed toward the other end of the ranch. Liza and Lizzie made fun of each other's injuries as they resituated the standing log. Within minutes, both women were sound asleep.

As the sun crested the morning peaks and the camp came alive with activity, Naomi was still mad, that was plain to see by her snotty attitude as they gathered round the campfire for breakfast. She wouldn't acknowledge that Clinton was even sitting there. Clinton completely ignored her mood as he went along his way, kidding with Matthew and Charlie, pitching in where ever he was needed. That seemed to infuriate the berry-headed woman even more!

Liza and Lizzie had been up for hours gathering the horses that would make the journey home and turning out the ones that wouldn't. Leading in the ones that would travel behind the wagon and handing off the others. It was a wet soggy morning when the small party started back toward the ranch. Matthew, Naomi, and Jeffrey were long past ready by the time Charlie got the wagon loaded and ready to roll. With just the slightest twinkle in his dark blue circles, Clinton gave the twin's a quick wink as he headed out with the rest of the moving party.

"I like that, boy," Lizzie stated.

"Yeah, me, too." Liza agreed.

Abe saw the dust long before he saw the traveling party. "It's about time," he mumbled as he mounted his horse and rode out to meet them.

The twins recognized the lone rider as soon as they saw him coming. "Father," they said in unison in a cheerful tone.

"Have some trouble," he asked as he looked at the blue bump on Liza's head, then Lizzie's.

"Nope, pretty good going," Lizzie said as she followed her father's gaze. "Oh, that happened before we ever got out of the wagon," she giggled. "It was Liza's fault."

"It was not my fault and it's not funny, Lizzie," Liza disagreed.

"Well I got one too, you big sissy!" Lizzie countered.

Abe had heard this argument a hundred times! Nothing was ever their own fault! So he purposely headed his horse to the back of the group. He gave Charlie a quick nod. The man didn't look any worse for the wear. No bullet holes that were visible. "Charlie, good trip?"

"For the brand Mr. Baxter," he smiled through a crooked grin.

Abe knew exactly what he was thinking. It was always an adventure wherever the twins were. But, when he looked at the hired man's crippled hands as he held the moving pieces of leather to the walking team it made him furious. Someone would pay for that!

Abe gave Naomi a big smile. "So, how was it? You're still in one piece I see."

"It was all right, papa," she said quietly. "Mother and Aunt Liza did the hard riding."

"Clinton," he stated, "you see some territory young man?"

"Did I!" he exclaimed. "I wouldn't have missed this for nothing! I got lots of measurements and locations that I think you will like."

Then Abe rode back to where Jeffrey was struggling with his string of horses. He couldn't help but notice the line of blisters across his raw hand and the frustration on his red face. "Where's your gloves?"

"Back on the stinkin' prairie where they belong!" He was over this whole trip!

"Here," Abe offered. "Let me take them."

Jeffrey relinquished the line of horses with no resistance to his grandfather as he turned his horse and started toward town. "Tell mother I'll be home later, not to hold supper for me."

Liza was surprised to see her son riding in the opposite direction of the ranch. "Where do you think he's going in such a hurry?" Liza asked in a disgusted tone.

"I don't think we want to know," Lizzie answered.

CHAPTER 12

Lizzie couldn't help but notice that Charlie had been favoring his shoulders since the return of the gathering. They supposed that sleeping on the hard unforgiving ground probably hadn't helped matters any. There was no denying the fact that his crippled hands caused him a considerable amount of pain but he never once complained about the jobs that were assigned to him.

The older cowhand had a worried look on his face when the twins approached him. "Charlie," Lizzie said, "how bout we take a look see at those fingers."

"Awe, they're all right, Lizzie. Reckon the weather's gonna change," he said in self defense as he rubbed one through the other.

"Let us be the judge of that," Liza insisted as they led him into a small clean room toward the back of the barn.

"But Lizzie, Luke, and me we got several more head of horses to tend to," he said in protest, making sure that the two lady bosses knew he wasn't a slacker.

"Matthew and Jeffrey can help finish that up," Lizzie stated matter-of-factly.

Like two well-schooled physicians, the twins took their time looking over Charlie's crippled hands. First Lizzie would run her long slender fingers across his leather-like skin, then Liza would do exactly the same thing. Gently, Lizzie would pull on a certain bone then press another, always with her identical twin following the same motion. One finger was a dark gray as they both ran their work-worn fingers across the discoloration. Between them they mumbled several words that he couldn't comprehend. Their eyes never left the destination of their work. Then in unison and in a calm rotating motion they pulled the darkened finger with an intense snap. Charlie heard the noise but for some unknown reason the swift action didn't hurt. Puzzled, he stared into their trusting faces. Then once again they started jabbering in a language that he didn't understand before they asked, "You all right?"

"Yes," he nodded, then he noticed the fleshy color of his finger start to return.

The twins looked up when Naomi walked into the room. She too started talking in the strange language as she listened to her aunt's command. Within seconds the young woman walked back out of the hidden room and into another part of the barn. When Matthew made his presence known, they did the same with him. All Charlie could do was stare. Completely mesmerized at the two women's doctoring skills.

"Will these do," Naomi asked as she handed Lizzie a handful of finely sculptured pieces of wood.

"Perfect," Lizzie said as she cocked a wondering brow.

Naomi gave her mother an adoring smile, "I saw them up on the high ridge when we were gathering the horses. I liked the smell." Gently, Naomi laid her hand against the older mans broad shoulder. There was no missing the automatic whence. Naomi gave her aunt a strange look.

"How bout you take that shirt off, Charlie," Liza insisted.

"What fere? My hands a long way from my back." He protested.

"I just need a look see." Liza stated firmly.

"It ain't nothin'," he scoffed half embarrassed. "Just a scratch."

"The shirt," Lizzie commanded not taking no for an answer.

"Don't you's two woman's know what kinda word 'no' is?" Charlie begrudgingly unbuttoned the red checked flannel shirt and laid it neatly to the side. "My favorite," he said in an apologetic tone.

From the look on Naomi's face, Lizzie knew it was more than a scratch. Without even being asked the young woman hurried from the room.

Liza and Lizzie stared at the hideous looking laceration for several minutes. "That's a little more than a scratch, Charlie," Lizzie stated. "Wanna tell us about it?"

"Nope," he answered in a tone that told them it wasn't worth repeating.

"Why didn't you say something before we drug you half way across this ranch? I bet that was a bit uncomfortable the last week," Liza said in a compassionate voice.

"I don't know why," he said honestly, "I reckon it just felt good to be needed. I guess I didn't want you to think you'd hired some old cripple. I can hold my own."

"Charlie," Liza said in a caring tone, "no one would have said a thing. It's just now, they are infected. Both of them."

"What we are going to do today will cause you considerable pain." Lizzie stared into the kind older man's eyes. "Are you up to it?"

"Been in a lot worse fixes I reckon," he stated without much thought. "Pain ain't new to the likes o me."

From the scars on his broad back they were sure it was true. Liza smiled at the older man then at her sister. No one could say that he wasn't courageous. They spoke once again in a tongue that he didn't understand as Naomi reappeared with a large green leather bag.

Lizzie gave her a loving look as she placed several instruments on the wooden table. Like clockwork, Liza poured steaming water over the utensils as Naomi poured whisky over the top of that.

"Mind if I have a swig," he asked like a scared child.

Lizzie gave Naomi a nod as Charlie took a good long pull. "That ought to do it," Charlie said politely. "Thanks little lady."

"Have as much as you want," Liza offered, "you'll probably need it by the time we're done."

"Nope, I need my wits about me," he said soberly.

Lizzie squatted down in front of the worn out fellow. Caringly those blue crystal's exploded with worried feelings, "Charlie, what we are going to do today is going to cause you a lot of pain. If you need to drink the whole bottle..., well."

"Ma'am," he said honestly through steely eyes, "I ain't never been much of a drinking man. Has a way of turning my guts all around. So, if'n it's all right with you, I'll just hang on tight and ride out the pain." He looked directly into her crystal blue eyes, "Sides, I don't want to be giving out any of my secrets."

Liza spoke to Lizzie in the foreign tongue just as Jeffrey came waltzing in like a king on his throne.

"What the hell!" he squealed as his squeamish stomach full of liquor turned inside out. "He's been cooking our food with that on his back!"

"Jeffrey," Lizzie warned in a stern tone, "shut up! Go get Clinton and the two of you finish helping Luke." There was no need to say it twice: before the last syllable left her lips Jeffrey was gone holding his hand over his mouth.

Lizzie gave Liza a look that said to get ready as she started to straighten the old man's bent fingers. Everything was done mechanically, and in perfect time. Between the three of them their rhythm was automatic. Like a slow dreamy waltz. They were phenomenal teachers. Taking Naomi's hand, showing her every move. The young woman never said a word she just absorbed her mother and aunts instructions like rain on a piece of dry ground.

"Naomi," Lizzie said lovingly, "take that moss over there in the large white jar and wrap it in between each finger and then around his whole hand. Be very careful not to disturb the small sticks."

"Yes, mother." Her instructions were followed without question.

"How ya holdin up, Charlie?" Lizzie questioned.

"I'm all right," he answered in a tired tone. It was plain to tell that the painful process was wearing on him.

"We're done with your hands. You did good. Real good. Now, I want you to lay on your stomach so we can take a look see about that back."

Charlie was glad to have the chance to lie flat. He was starting to feel a little nauseous. "I'm so much trouble," he fussed.

"Nonsense," Liza said. "We haven't had a patient in some time. Makes us use our bean," she stated in a cheerful tone as she looked into her sister's worried face. "Naomi, would you be a dear and get our patient a cup of tea?"

Naomi's head jerked up as she stared into her aunts commanding face. "Of course, Auntie." Within seconds she hurried from the room. Before Charlie knew she was gone she was back. "Here Charlie," she whispered sweetly, "I think this will quench your thirst."

The worn out cowpoke gladly sipped the wet liquid as he started to feel calmer and calmer. Within seconds his lids were heavy as the steely circles softly closed.

The lacerations were perfectly matched. As though someone had deliberately put them there. Entwined within the dried bands of flesh were tiny pieces of metal shavings stuck within the dark festering scab. "Where did these metal fragments come from, Charlie, did you get caught up against something?" Liza asked.

"No, just a bad game of Russian roulette," he said in a drugged voice trying to make light of the subject.

"What? What is that, Russian roulette?" Lizzie asked.

"It's where you play a game with someone else's life," Charlie said half asleep. "I won."

"Well if this is winning, then what does the loser look like?" Liza asked completely taken aback at his flippant attitude. "I was the loser too!" It was plain to see that the man wasn't going to tell them anything.

"Why in the world, who would do something like that?" Lizzie questioned.

"I know," an angry male voice said as everyone's heads snapped around. "It was you? You were the one my uncle was bragging about?" It was plain to see that Clinton was furious. "That low-lying-scum!" he seethed. "I looked for you! I did! I couldn't find you anywhere! When they told me what they'd done, I couldn't find you!"

"It's nothin to be bragging about young man," Charlie said in a down-trodden tone through sleepy eyes. "No ones business but mine own."

It was as though Clinton had lost his breath, "Noth, nothing! What they did was despicable!" he ranted. "You don't treat an old man like that! You don't treat anyone like that!" Clinton walked to where the man laid on the damp table. Intentionally, he squatted down to eye level. "I'm sorry," he said genuinely. "I am. If I could trade places with you right now, I would. What you did was a very brave thing."

Charlie had grown quite an attachment to the younger man. "It wasn't your fault. You weren't even there."

"If I would have been, it would never have happened! If saving the life of a little girl is losing the game, then you're the best loser I've ever seen." There was such a genuine honesty that always appeared when Clinton showed up. Like he couldn't keep his emotions in check. "Now that I know, I want you to know, that I will deal with this. He's such a bold-faced liar!" he seethed. "Pardon, ma'am," he said in a frustrated tone as he tipped his hat and left the room.

All three women had blank looks on their faces. Whatever happened or didn't happen, they weren't about to be told. "You know, Liza, the more I'm around that boy the more I like him."

"Amen!"

Naomi gave the disappearing man an odd look. He never ceased to amaze her with his unique character. Maybe she had misjudged his outburst on the highline. From the way he acted in here, he was genuinely concerned. It wasn't about control at all. It was raw emotion for doing the right thing.

CHAPTER 13

Several weeks came and went and Charlie was healing up quite nicely. On more than one occasion he'd asked if could take the bandages from his hands and from his back. His complaint, they itched like crazy and felt like he had on a pair of boxing gloves. If they didn't come off soon he'd threatened to take them off himself. Lizzie told him that if he even thought of touching those bandages he would come up missing one of the protruding parts of his body. And, it would be the last thing he ever took off.

Today, the self proclaimed female doctors had listened to his whining long enough so they decided to lay him outright in the sun and let the golden rays and warm breeze finish drying up what was left of the clean healing lacerations. "One more week," Liza said. "They should have a nice crust in one more week." Satisfied with their diagnosis the two of them left Charlie lying in the sun like a baking potato. "We'll be back in about half an hour. Don't move!"

As the twins walked into the sweet smelling barn to retrieve a can of ointment that they had made the night before and grab a quick nip of their special concoction, they could hear muted voices. When they recognized who it was they slid into one of the small stalls like two thieves in the night. Each gave the other a devilish grin.

"I'm going back into town today," Clinton said. In a flawless motion he saddled the black horse that the twins had given to him. Lovingly, he gave the glistening beast a gentle pat. "I feel kind of guilty taking him."

"Why?" Naomi asked in a sober tone. "He was a gift."

"He'd better take him blast it," Lizzie whispered to her sister as they sat hidden in the straw like two nosy mice taking turns sipping the soothing whiskey.

"Shut up!" Liza whispered back. "We're gonna miss what they're saying!"

"I know," Clinton said, "but it was too generous. How will I ever be able to pay them back?"

"Take him, leave him, I certainly don't care," Naomi snapped in a snotty tone as she stared into the handsome map-makers face.

"Besides, I doubt they expect you to pay them back. It was a gift. You do understand what a gift is?"

"Why you snotty little imp!" Lizzie seethed. "That's just how she use to treat me!"

"Look at that! Why she's acting just like you!" Liza's response was quick.

"Shh!" Lizzie interrupted as she gave her sister a dirty look. "I can't hear!"

"How long are you going to be mad at me?" Clinton questioned in a determined tone as he looked directly into Naomi's odd looking eyes.

"She'd better straighten up!" Liza scolded as she stared into her sister's so-called innocent face. It was plain to see that she blamed her for the young woman's flippant attitude.

"I didn't teach her that!" Lizzie snapped as she took another short nip, appalled at her sister's reaction.

"You yelled at me in front of my family, Clinton!" Naomi concluded in a huffy tone. "Like I was some kind of child! What did you expect?"

"I might have taught her that," Lizzie confessed with a slight scowl to her forehead.

"I know I did," he conceded. "I apologize about that."

"No! No! Don't concede!" they said in unison as they both took a nip.

"You are?" Naomi was completely shocked that he would give in that quickly.

"Oh, he's doomed for sure now," Liza whispered.

"Yeah, but you nearly turned my hair white." Clinton turned and gazed into the lovely woman's surprised face: then he turned back around and faced the black horse.

"Don't stop now!" Lizzie hissed. "Don't let that little snip walk all over you!"

Then he turned back around. "You, your family, they're a special breed of people."

"Well, at least he got that part right," Lizzie whispered through a puffed up chest.

"He wasn't just talking about you!" Liza spit back at her sister completely miffed.

"I've never been anywhere like this. It's almost magical," Clinton exclaimed through twinkling blue eyes of sincerity. "Every day it's something new. Why would a person need to go anywhere else? It's amazing here!"

"Oh, I like this boy," Liza reiterated as she placed her hand over her heart and handed the bottle to her sister.

"And your mother, your aunt, why they are the most stubborn, life-threatening, strong willed women that I've ever had the pleasure to meet! And, and no one even appreciates what it is about them that make them so unique! They're powerful! They're so powerful! They scare the daylights outta me!"

"I know what they're like!" Naomi said in a huff. "They raised me or did you forget?"

"Snot!" the hiding duo said at the same time.

"How could I forget!" he said in a gentle tone, "Look what they raised. Why, you're the most beautiful woman, aside from your aunt's," he teased, "that I have ever seen."

"Oh, I know I like this boy," Lizzie swooned in a knowing tone as she placed her hand over her heart and handed her sister the bottle.

"You're lovely. I mean it! From the top of your berry-colored head to the tip of your toes. Enchanting, that's what you are. Why I can't imagine what my life was like before I came here!" There went that irresistible honesty.

"Are you thinking matrimony?" Liza questioned.

"This could be the one," Lizzie answered.

"For you or me?" Liza questioned.

Lizzie gave her sibling a dirty disbelieving look.

"What?" she snipped as she threw her hands up.

"And when I saw you take such a risk, why my heart nearly exploded right through my chest." His clear blue eyes told her that he was telling nothing but the truth. "So if I scared you or hurt your feelings, then I am truly sorry. That wasn't my intention."

"Ah, dogs!" Lizzie's voice dropped as she threw up her hands. "It's over now."

"Yep, too much ammo," Liza added.

"But if it makes you stop and think about what you're going to do next time, before you decide to break your fool neck, then I'm not sorry," Clinton added.

"Oh, he's building up some pressure," Lizzie whispered in an excited tone as she took a quick nip.

Liza looked at Lizzie. "He's good," she said.

Naomi stood and stared into the handsome mapmakers face for several minutes. It wasn't going to make any difference what she said, it wasn't going to come out right. So, instead she took one step closer and looked him squarely in the eyes as she spoke, "I'm sorry too, I am. For scaring you."

"He's got her now!" Lizzie said in a bold manner.

"But you can't expect me not to be who I am. I would never expect that from you." She stated wholeheartedly.

"She got that from me," Liza's face had a smug look as she took the bottle from Lizzie and had a quick nip.

"I am the daughter of Lizzie Baxter. She has taught me well." Naomi said.

"No denying that!" Lizzie stated proudly.

"You are going to have to except that fact if this feeling in my gut is going to go any father." There was no missing the hope in those flowered circles.

"Do you always have to have the last word," he sighed with a twinkle in his eye as he pulled her closer.

"Yes," she smiled back as he gently placed a soft kiss on her waiting lips.

"Ohh," Liza held her breath. "Young love."

"Young love! You know what young love leads to! He'd better watch where he puts those hands!" Lizzie snapped.

Liza gave her a dirty look as she snatched the bottle away and popped the cork back in.

"It' will be a couple of weeks before I get back out this way," Clinton said as he held her close. I will miss you." His finger lightly touched the tips of her delicate nose. "Tell your mother and your aunt bye for me."

"Good bye," the two of them whispered in love-struck awe as they peeked through the wooden planks, hidden in the dry yellow straw like two naughty mice.

"I'll see you at the Harvest Dance?" she said, sorry that she had wasted so much time being mad.

"Every dance will be yours," he said as he mounted the large black horse and headed back toward town.

Naomi stood for several minutes and watched as Clinton disappeared from sight. He was wonderful and there was no doubt in her mind that she was in love with the kind mapmaker. With a slight skip to her step she headed toward the back of the barn.

"We have to get out of here!" Liza insisted. "Charlie is gonna be baked to a crisp!"

"Blast it!" Lizzie's face was full of remorse, "I forgot all about, Charlie!"

Like two sneaking detectives they started out of the small straw-filled prison. But Naomi was headed back in their direction leading one of the horses that they had gathered. "Do you want to shoe this guy in here, Luke?" Naomi asked looking over her shoulder.

"No! No!" Liza whispered as she shoved Lizzie's face into the straw.

When Lizzie came up for air she was fighting mad. "Have you lost your mind?" she seethed as Liza pointed her head toward the duo.

"Not now!" Lizzie moaned.

"Or, outside?" Naomi continued.

"Outside, outside!" Liza insisted. "Please, outside!"

Luke was about to consider outside when he noticed the two human rats caged in the small stall. He had a devilish twinkle in his old checker-cheating eyes as he spoke, "I don't know, it's awful hot out. She might not swat at as many flies in here."

Lizzie knew that the wily old fool had seen them as they frantically waved him outside. When he ignored them Lizzie started to her feet shaking her fist as Liza grabbed her by the back of the pants and pulled her back down. Lizzie landed in the straw with a thud.

"What was that?" Naomi questioned as she turned around and glanced toward the small stall.

"Packrats!" Luke hollered in a high-pitched tone as Naomi jumped and spun back around. "Had two of them in here the other day, I reckon they're back," he said matter-of-factly. "Black hairy devils! Big butted old rats! One had a big wide wart right between his eyes! Ugly! What I sawed of em they'd probably scare the fur offn' their own mother's." He gave the hiding duo a cagey look.

"I swear when I get my hands on him, I'm gonna kill him!" Lizzie hissed furiously.

"You startled me!" Naomi was completely baffled at the horse wrangler's behavior.

"I did? I'm sorry," he apologized sincerely. "Here, help me throw some of this compost over there. Maybe we can... Nope, I've got it." Anxiously, Luke grabbed the pitchfork and threw several scoops of the soiled hay in the small stall. "Oops, that last one was a little wet," he laughed. "They'll leave, now. Nosy varmints!"

Naomi was completely baffled at the older man's goofy conduct. "I think maybe we'll shoe this one outside," she said with a wrinkled brow, not knowing what to expect next.

"Suit yourself," Luke agreed, "but we can stay here till supper if you want." He gave them a wicked smile as though he had some kind of dangerous critter treed. "Lots of things to do in this here barn."

Luke could see the two women cowering behind the wooden stall with the manure in their hair. Their cool blue eyes were black like a viper and he knew that they were furious. "Shame on you two, ya sneakin' eavesdroppers," he mumbled as threw another pitchfork full of fresh manure in the small stall when he walked past. Lizzie did everything she could to reach his foot and trip him. But Luke was too fast as he stepped on her fingers. Lizzie let out a yowl just as Liza covered her mouth.

"What?" Naomi questioned as she stared toward the large barn door.

"Do you need your bonnet," he said.

"Nah, I don't think so, besides the wind will feel good," Naomi said as they walked out into the open yard and disappeared toward the corral fence.

"I'm gonna kill him!" Lizzie seethed. "Look at me! I'm full of ...! Look at you!" she said through a fit of laughter as she stared at her identical sibling. "You look like you've got the scours, Liza. You're full of horse s...!" Lizzie couldn't finish her sentence as she laughed at her sister hysterically.

"That nasty old goat! He knew we were in there! He knew!" Liza was outraged. "He did that on purpose! The dirty old goat!"

"Well, he's gonna get his. Yes sir'ee, he's gonna get his! Calling us fat butted! I know he wasn't looking at me!" Lizzie concluded matter-of-factly as she stomped out of the grassy stall. Her trailing sister gave her a quizzical look.

Like two fleeing bandits, Liza and Lizzie exited the side of the barn only to run smack dab into their father. He gave them both a curious look then stepped aside and held his hand to his nose. They stunk! As he gave them a wide berth his humored features said that he didn't want to know what it was that they had no business getting into. So he simply let them pass.

The two escaping bandits gave him a sheepish grin and headed for the sanctuary of the well. Liza pumped the clean refreshing water for Lizzie and Lizzie for Liza. Once the nasty chore of getting all the manure out of their hair was done they headed back into the house at a high lope to retrieve their baking patient. Hoping that he didn't resemble an over-cooked loaf of bread.

"What in the world happened to you two?" Charlie asked in a grumpy tone. "I'm cooking out here!"

"Other business!," Lizzie answered matter-of-factly.

"C'mon, Charlie," Liza said as she looked at his sunburned back. "We have some special salve just for those cuts." They gave each other a quick wink: now they would be treating the man for sunburn.

CHAPTER 14

Several weeks of solitude came and went on the Baxter ranch. With no major life and death catastrophes it was a nice laid back time to be had by all. In the process of the lazy days, Liza and Lizzie had taken off Charlie's bandages from his back and his hands. There was no doubt that there would be a minimal amount of scaring on his shoulders but for the most part the lacerations on his back had healed quite nicely. The reddened marks would be neatly added to his collection of scares tucked neatly away on the rest of his body.

The twins were both shocked with the results of his hands when they cut away the puffy bandages. His old worn fingers were a little swollen but perfectly straight. His motion of movement with certain exercises had nearly all come back. It was an amazing sight that even he couldn't believe. But even more amazing than his healing hands and back was to see how fast his whole persona was changing and how strong he had become. He was like a wild woody flower that had resisted the constraints of Mother Nature's hardened wrath and budded right before their very own eyes. This was not the haggard, dirty looking old man with no place to lay a blanket. No, this man was well groomed, well mannered and in his cleaned up state looked to only be about twenty years older than the twins.

Most of Naomi's time over the past several weeks had been applied to cutting and tying the new blue dress that she was making for the harvest dance. Maria and Dancing Bear both helped her with the intricate stitching and when it was done improperly she had to do it again. She was so patient with the two older women when they would discuss her mistake.

Liza and Lizzie sat back like two well-groomed cats and watched as her patient fingers followed their master's instructions perfectly; it was refreshing to watch her learned skill. The twins certainly had never taught her how to sew. The only thing that they had ever sewn in their lives was flesh. Yet here was Naomi, busily getting the dress sewn, offering to do the same for both of them. As they sat and watched her put the cotton dress together her long slender fingers reminded them of Sarah. It was as though each stitch on the lovely fabric was like a stroke from her dead sister's brush.

Liza and Lizzie hadn't decided yet if they were even going to go to the dreaded 'Harvest Dance'. It seemed like a long way to go for a lot of fancy hee-hawing. Why all of those do-gooders had to show up out here and disturb the serenity of their isolated existence was beyond them. But then, they also knew that Naomi had her heart set on going and trusting Jeffrey to take her alone was out of the question. And expecting Matthew to be her continual escort was asking too much from her cousin. Not that he wouldn't have done it if they asked but Matthew was a young man himself it didn't seem right; he needed to have some fun, too. Besides, there was nothing physically wrong with either one them. So, against their better judgment they both sullenly conceded to go. They acted like they'd been invited to a hanging. Grudgingly they climbed the narrow steps up into the attic after conceding to the tear-filled pleading.

They had forgotten about a lot of the stuff that lay hidden up there full of dust and cobwebs. Nonchalantly, they looked through a couple of the dusty trunks and dug out two yellow dresses with short puffy sleeves. The twins looked at each other in a completely dismayed fashion. They hadn't worn these garments in years. For all they knew the cotton fabric could be rotten by now. Maybe the dresses wouldn't even fit. The two of them decided if that was the case going to the dance was out of the question.

As they stumbled around the large open room their eyes settled on a small trunk sitting alone in the corner like a scolded child. There was one lone Indian blanket spread across the top protecting the cherished piece of wood from any harm. The twin's both had saddened looks on their faces as they gazed at the small chest that had belonged to Sarah.

"I'm so thankful we have, Naomi," Lizzie whispered as she ran her work worn fingers across the embossed looking wood. As long as the two of them lived they would always carry a part of the blame for not saving their younger sister's life.

"Amen," Liza answered as she delicately opened the forsaken box that had sat barren in the far corner of the large room for years.

At first they felt guilty when they opened the sweet smelling lid. Like they had disturbed the sanctity of the dead woman's privacy. But then, they both knew that they had ignored the contents that laid dormant there for years. It was time to let out all of the bad memories so that the good ones could be remembered.

Drudgingly, they took one deep sigh and continued their search. There was no missing the familiar odor that escaped the small chest. Sunflower's and sweet pea's. Her favorite. It left them with a lump in their throat's. Wishing now that they had left the wooden box alone.

There were all kinds of little trinkets that were neatly confined within the small wooden prison. Several delicately folded dresses of every color, a pair of soft brown moccasins that they'd seen on her tiny feet more times than they could count. Doilies outlined with flying eagles and colorfully matched feathers. An old worn out piano book that had a feather bookmark in it from the last song that she had played on the abandoned piano that sat in the parlor. And, of course her sketch pad.

The twins sat cross-legged on the wooden floor, shoulder to shoulder, hip to hip as they untied the leather string and opened the large book laying it across both of their laps. Together they took a breath as they recognized the familiar face of the handsome Indian Chief. As they stared starry-eyed at the identically drawn image on the heavy thick paper, they held their breath and tried to justify how time had a way of taking a structured memory, placing it against the years, both past and present and then forgetting the physical image all together. They'd forgotten him, the handsome man. But, inside this amazing leather-bound book the memory of Chief Flying Eagle was alive and well. They sat and stared in complete awe at the way she had captured his amazing image within the lines of his forbidden portrait. He stood proud and straight with his long black braids, wide determined jaw line and those warm black eyes.

They couldn't help but gasp as their misty blue circles followed the delicately written passage at the bottom of his picture.

Here, in the wisdom of his eyes lies my
death
the essence of my soul
breath

LOVE OF THE BLOOD

*heart
our innocence
love
one forbidden one undeniable
cheek to cheek the two of us stand together
bound within the united yearnings of our love
two hearts daring to encircle our culture's
one within the arms of the other
both forever denied
when our fleshed shells have been depleted of all human
existence
turned to dust
this legacy will live on
life has a way of finding death
just like death has a way of finding life
this innocent seed which grows silently within the womb of my flesh
is,
His
Ours
and, from the fire of our forbidden love the strongest flower will be
born
this figure will become the miracle of our
Secret Love, Lie's, Heritage, Death
and, within the miracle of that love a baby will come forth,
an arrow of salvation for
His family and **Mine**
our everlasting love will be known as
Little Feather
our Little Feather will seal the love
of the sisters' blood
with the tribe of Chief Mad Dog
the roots of existence will seep like blood
deep into this dark rich soil we call home
beneath the shaded protection of
Willow Walks
the spiritual guardian the of the Big Horn Mountains.
forever & always
Sarah Baxter Flying Eagle*

Liza and Lizzie stared at each other through mystified tears in complete disbelief. The mere mention of Naomi's native name before her birth was haunting. They'd never read this passage before. Why? Neither woman said a word as they continued to turn the tattle-telling pages.

There were pictures of the ranch from every angle. A perfect layout of the main house, the barn, the corrals, the high ridge, the low ridge, the Old Willow Pasture, and every other piece of ground connected to the Lazy AB Ranch. Even the lumber company. Her accuracy was perfected only by the dimensions of her drawings. It described the lay of the land perfectly.

The bewildered twins looked at each other their eyes asking the same question, *When did she do all of this? How did they miss it?* Both women grinned as they read each other's minds. They would put this in a private place that only the two of them knew about for safe keeping. Let the mapmaker draw his deeds. They'd see what kind of sand he was made of soon enough. For now they knew they had the original score right here. And, when the time was right they would show their father what they had discovered. A sense of security washed over them as they continued their journey into a world long forgotten.

There were pictures of Abe standing within the tall pines from the lumber camp. He was much younger than he was now. Handsome. Pride showed in his dirty face. There was Maria making her famous tortillas. In the corner of the white pad she was shushing the twins out the kitchen door. There was a picture of Luke laughing aloud at the breakfast table. The comically drawn pictures were funny and made the two women giggle uncontrollably. The drawings were so real! It was as though they could have jumped right off of the pages. But, when they turned the fading paper to the last page their fingers froze like flesh to ice as they stared at the final drawing. It was unbelievable how her fingers had sketched the look of little black and white featherlets across the top and bottom of the fancy writing.

Both sisters took in a deep breath as they stared at the frozen image in front of them.

SISTERS

 In the center of the page stood Liza and Lizzie's dominant silhouettes. Shoulder to shoulder, back to back, standing naked to their waists within in the rippled water of a crystal blue pond. A thousand sparkling stars lingered like jagged lace against a blackened sky above their quixotic heads. The large oval moon cast a sinister shadow over the glistening water as though it was hiding a secret about the two of them no human needed to know. A slip of their long black hair tossed by the unruly wind laid protectively over their shoulders shielding the silhouette of their firm naked breasts as the coal black strands floated on top of the waiting water. At first glance it looked as though one twin was standing directly within the form of the other. Yet amazingly, their bodies were separate. Their tanned skin stood out like the dust on a rolling prairie against the matt of the white paper. Their deceptive blue eyes looked like moon-drops on a lost forgotten lake seductively warm and enchanting, inviting you into the bosom of their desired domain as they looked directly at you, but not. They both caught their breath when the book tipped slightly and their calm demure turned dark and threatening. The perception being no one knew the truth of their real nature. But, the expression Sarah had captured within the lines of life on their sculptured faces made them both sit back in complete awe. The stroke of her pencil brought to life the ruthless battles they'd claimed in their position as women of West. It said they surrendered to no one. That they stood united against the elements of this hostile land both animal and human. No backing down. That the fearless spirit placed in their heart of hearts believed in truth and justice, wielded by the hand of the Mighty One. Sarah had grasped the true portrayed beauty of the devoted twin sister's to the tee. They seemed so real they swore they could feel the warmth of their own breath on the tips of their fingers! This part of the penciled painting told the real truth of Liza and Lizzie Baxter. It was the most amazing illusion they'd ever seen.

 Together they sat back and stared at the disturbing image for some time before they closed the sweet smelling book. As they slid the trunk lid shut both sisters stared into each others faces. The price that had been paid for the life of their younger sibling had been too much. They would never tolerate a travesty like that happening again on Baxter soil. Not without someone paying the price of that mistake with their life.

    Without talking they quietly closed the lid of the wooden trunk and carefully placed the Indian blanket across the top. Grudgingly, they placed the yellow dresses across their arms, climbed back down the hidden ladder and closed the trap door behind them. Sealing the disturbing image within the barren trunk. Dreading the moment that they would have to put the starched fabric on. Sorry that it would be their feet dancing across the wooden floor at the harvest ball instead of dear sweet Sarah's.

CHAPTER 15

"Mother," Naomi hollered from the bottom of the stairs. "Aunt Liza, come on, we're going to be late!"

"Yes, yes," Lizzie said as she and her sister descended the long staircase arm in arm smiling and laughing with each step.

Naomi stood at the bottom of the landing with her mouth gaped open when she saw them coming. She and everyone else that was waiting at the foot of those stairs were speechless. The two of them were stunning. That was the only way to describe them. Like two freshly made pearls in one shining shell. Identical in every way. The soft yellow dresses moved like a wispy summer wind that was hiding within the starched fabric as it swayed with every step they took. The puffy laced sleeves clung to their muscled arms leaving just enough room for movement. The intricately designed dresses had tapered square necks that slightly exposed the curves of their full tanned chests. They each had a yellow ribbon entwined with tiny feathers that were delicately braided within one strand of their long dark hair that hung like black satin to their thin waists. Each woman had a soft brown leather strand of newly made beads that hung loosely like a whisper around their thin tanned necks. Their long black lashes were thick and alluring beneath those cool blue eyes that looked like moon drops on a lost forgotten lake.

"Mother," Naomi breathed with tears in her eyes as the two sisters's escorted each other down the wooden stairwell. She was sure by the nonchalant look on their faces that they had no idea how lovely they looked.

"Mother," Matthew breathed in awe as he held Naomi's arm. Both children were star struck.

"Diamonds," Charlie breathed under his breath. "If I was only fifteen years younger."

There was no missing the shocked look in everyone's eyes as they watched the beautiful pair descending the stairway like two crowned princesses. "Beautiful as ever," Abe stated in a fatherly tone as he met them at the bottom. "I always said I had the most beautiful daughters in the whole valley." Purposely, he took one daughters arm in his and then the other. "Come, our chariot waits," he giggled cheerfully.

"Thank you, father," they said in unison as a soft blush caressed their tanned cheeks making them even more lovely than they already were. They adored their father's praise and not once had it ever gone unnoticed.

The ride to town seemed to come and go quickly. One minute they were leaving the safety of the open yard and the next they were pulling the team up to the hitching post by the large barn-like building. There were lots of people gathered here tonight to take in the festivities and the Baxter family knew nearly every one.

Clinton spotted them right away as he came running. When he saw Liza and Lizzie he stopped dead in his tracks. He couldn't tell one from the other. Not dressed the way that they were. That is until Lizzie opened her mouth.

"Oh, stop your gawking," she said in a scolding tone, "we feel awkward enough."

"It's better than a shot in the foot ma'am," he grinned teasingly. "Come on, Naomi," Clinton said as he helped her down from the wagon. "I believe this is our dance." Then he whispered in her ear. "You look beautiful. I'll be the envy of every man here," he chuckled as they disappeared inside.

Abe proudly took each one of his twin daughter's arms as they walked into the large building. There was no missing the fact that every eye was on them as they walked toward the laughing crowd. It had been years since anyone had seen the twins dressed so lady-like. It was quite a jaw dropping ordeal. In some people's opinions they might have been too old to be considered matrimonial material but they were still the epitome of breathtaking.

The music was light and lively and a welcome addition to their ears. They all grinned as they watched Clinton swoop Naomi across the floor like she had wings on her tiny feet. They made such a nice looking couple. The tables were heavily garbed with freshly baked food as the twins added several of Maria's brown sugar cakes and two cherry pies to the feast. Their stomachs growled just looking at all of the different dishes. It was going to be a wonderful affair.

The twins stood quietly and watched the festivities for quite a while when Lizzie noticed Charlie watching her from across the room. She gave him a friendly grin as she started to walk in his direction. She'd long ago lost sight of Liza and her father was dancing with Mrs. Paul's, a wide hipped woman who'd been quite smitten with him since her husband's death. He looked as though he was enjoying himself as well. But just as Lizzie was ready to encounter the cowhand, the owner of the small mercantile magically stepped in front of her. "Lizzie," he said shyly, "would you dance with me?"

The thin storekeeper was a good foot shorter than she and half her size. A bit of a frail looking man. But he had such a sincere look on his pale face that she didn't have the heart to turn him down. She gave the man a friendly smile as she spoke, "I'd love to, Mr. Dott."

Like the man had been practicing his approach for weeks it was plain to see that he was thrilled when she accepted. Like a runaway team of horse's he practically drug Lizzie out onto the floor. "I'm not a very good dancer, Lizzie but I couldn't help asking the most beautiful woman in the room."

Completely taken aback at his sincere compliment she laughed quietly. "I think you need to change your glasses, John." When the song ended he thanked Lizzie profusely as she half walked half hobbled in the direction Charlie stood against the frame of the open door with a smirk on his rugged looking face. But, once again before she made her intended destination, she got blind-sided and drug back out onto the dance floor. After that dance and several others that followed, she declined any more until she'd had a moment to catch her breath and have a drink of something cool. When she finally did get to where Charlie was standing, he and the small petite dressmaker were completely enthralled in conversation.

She turned when Lizzie walked up. "Hello, Miss Baxter," she said in a friendly tone. "You look absolutely radiant. You and your sister I mean."

"Thank you, Nelly," Lizzie said surprised at the young woman's rattled condition.

"I'd love to have the opportunity to make you a dress one of these days. Not that anything is wrong with the one you have on mind you. I just have so many beautiful bolts of cloth and you and your sister would look so, I mean with your skin and …" she stared into Lizzie's amused eyes. "I'm sorry," she apologized, "I don't even know what I'm saying, I get nervous when…"

"Aunt Lizzie," Matthew interrupted out of breath from the last dance, "I'd like to introduce you to someone." His sweet face was so full of apprehension.

"Of course," she answered grateful to be saved from the gibberish of the annoyingly jittery woman.

"This is Emmy, my," he looked at the young girls beaming face for permission, "date for the evening."

Lizzie was surprised at Matthews's selection. The young lady on his arm was nothing like Lizzie had expected. There were several young petite looking women far lovelier than the one that held his hand. And there was no missing the eyes of envy that followed her around the room. She was every bit as tall as he was and out weighted him by at least fifty pounds. To say the least, she was a big boned girl. But she wasn't fat. She carried her weight well. She had thick blonde curly hair that hung in a loose ponytail to her waist. She had the biggest brown eyes and a wide happy smile to match. "Nice to meet you, Emmy." Lizzie said sincerely as she took the young woman's hand in hers. There was no missing the calluses in her palm. Lizzie knew that this girl knew her way around a ranch.

"Me, too!" she said in an admiring tone. "I've heard so much about you. I've wanted to meet you forever." Her voice had a way of letting you know that she meant exactly what she was saying. There were no tricks of the trade wrapped up like a stick of candy in this girl. Between the two of them they simply glowed. As they strolled away to the other side of the room Lizzie couldn't help but say. "I'll be dogged." As she gathered her whit's about her she turned to finally speak with Charlie. Surprisingly, he wasn't there. He was out on the floor dancing with Nelly, smiling like a cat licking cream.

It had been weeks since Lizzie had actually taken a good look at Charlie but there was no missing the fact that something had definitely changed about him. As she watched him dance across the floor like one of the younger men she noticed that his peppered grey hair was freshly shampooed and neatly cut as it lay at the nap of his neck. His typically scruffy face didn't appear to be as hard and barren looking. He was clean shaven and was very neatly dressed in his polished boots and leather vest. His hands, even though they were still a little sore, had healed up wonderfully and when he stood, he no longer slumped over. It was an amazing transformation. Like a sickly butterfly that had emerged from a darkened cocoon. It was as though Lizzie was looking at a completely different individual. It was quite unnerving.

Liza walked to where her sister stood as she followed her gawking gaze. "Doesn't look like the same man does he?" she sighed.

"No," Lizzie said simply as she stared in confusion at the cowhand. Somewhere in the middle of all the commotion on the ranch the real Charlie had become present.

"Well, it looks to me like you're not the only one that has discovered that little secret. I'd say that the dressmaker is spinning more than just yarn," Liza said as she rolled her eyes backward in complete distaste, dismissing the dancing couple as though they had some type of disease. "I have to tell ya, my feet are killing me! I don't think I've danced this much in years. Next time I'm wearing a gunny sack!"

Lizzie looked into her sister's distressed face and laughed out loud. "Well, get ready cause here comes Mr. Johnson." But Lizzie noticed that her identical sibling had a different kind of look on her face as the stately looking man approached.

"Miss Liza," he said in the most respectful tone, "would you do me the honor of another dance?"

"I would." she gave her sister a quick wink.

Lizzie stood in shock as she watched her sister glide across the floor like a floating feather. It was an odd match to say the least. He was several inches shorter than she with thick rimmed glasses and just a hint of a mustache. He had large, muscled arms that went from his wrists to his broad shoulders. He had just a hint of gray at his temples and a wide friendly smile with a confident air that said you wouldn't want to tangle with him without good reason. But there was no denying the look of admiration on his face. He thought Liza was enchanting. And from the smitten look he was proud to hold the beautiful woman in his waiting arms.

It was good to see the engaging smile on Liza's face and the blush on her cheeks as they twirled around the wooden floor. It seemed her identical sibling was quite smitten as well. It'd been years since anyone had seen that transformation run across her sister's enamored features. Lizzie let out a deep sigh as she turned to walk to the punch table. Much to her regret, Mr. Dott was standing right behind her. There was no place to run.

"One more time," he said hopefully, delighted that he had caged his prey as he drug Lizzie like a plow horse going to water out on the dance floor once again.

After several minutes of stepping on Lizzie's feet she saw a man's hand tap her partners shoulder. "You'd better let me have part of this dance," a commanding male voice said out loud. When she turned around there stood, Clinton with a huge smile on his delighted face. "You looked like you needed rescuing. How are the feet?" mused.

"Bruised," she whispered as the song ended. "You saved my life!" she sighed gratefully.

Together they started to walk off the dance floor when Lizzie felt a soft touch on her elbow. She was afraid to turn around for fear it would be Mr. Dott again. There just didn't seem to be any escaping the annoying man. She didn't want to hurt the storekeeper's feelings but she wasn't sure her feet couldn't take any more bruising. As she turned around she looked directly into Charlie's humored steely eyes. "Might I have this dance Miss Baxter?" he smiled like a teasing school boy.

An odd feeling washed across Lizzie like a cool cup of creek water as she answered lightly. "Of course, Charlie."

There was no missing the shocked whispers from the single ladies and the jealous glares from the wanting men as they stared at the miss-matched duo walk toward the emptying dance floor. She, the scorned enchantress, and he the hard core, ruggedly handsome cowhand. As though she were a delicate prairie flower, he placed his wide work-worn hand securely in the middle of her thin muscled back. Lizzie was surprised at the strength in his once broken fingers as he pulled her close. It felt as though those fleshy stems had nested there on her brown quivering skin her whole life.

Charlie stood only inches away from the stunningly beautiful woman in his arms. His intense gaze never left hers. His steely eyes probed the very depths of Lizzie's being as she willingly allowed him to search her soul. When the sweet melody of the music started their feet glided like two perfectly mated swans as they waltzed across the crowded dance floor. The rhythm of the alluring melody was in perfect harmony with their footsteps. Lizzie's gaze never once strayed from the cowhand's handsome face. In fact the vision in her mind said the floor was completely void of any other human beings. All she could hear was the rhythmic sound of their quiet breathing as she studied Charlie's rugged features. One, two, three, back, back. The motion of the dance was like a mating call as they gracefully moved in and out of the vine of people on the crowed floor.

Closer and closer they danced as the floor became fuller and fuller. When Lizzie touched her cheek to Charlie's softly shaven skin it was like a shot of lightning etched its way right through her. Jolting the vessel that had lain dormant in her chest for years. She could feel the beating chamber that had been exiled in darkness slam back to life. He smelled so good! Like the leaves of a spring aspen.

Closer and closer they melded together as their bodies relaxed within each other's arms. She could feel the swell of her breasts as they brushed against his chest then stayed pressed there against him. Her heart was pounding in her ears like rolling thunder. As she gazed into those fascinating eyes she couldn't help but wonder if he could feel the beating of that tainted vessel that had betrayed her so many years ago.

Closer and closer they danced until the shadow of their silhouettes became one solid persona. Pressed together like a lone slender reed, one rhythmic beat entwined within the other as they glided across the open floor like a gentle babbling creek. Neither one took their eyes off of their elusive partner. It was a magical display of unfettered chemistry for anyone that was watching the enamored pair. And whether they knew it or not their silhouetted movements had captured the attention of everyone in the room and everyone let out a disappointed sigh when the song ended.

"Thank you, Lizzie," Charlie said in a warm gentlemanly tone as he released her like a child releases a bird with a healed wing.

"Thank you, Charlie," she whispered back surprised at the faintness of her voice. Breathless from her flight.

On the other side of the room Abe stood like a silent old oak as he watched his daughter glide across the wooden floor with the determination and grit of a woman, yet she carried herself with the grace and elegance of a young girl. Lizzie had always been a handful for him. Questioning every breath of air that she ever drew in, judging every breath of air he expelled. It had been years since he'd seen the look of contentment that covered her enamored face. It had a way of making his heart smile, but more than that, it gave him the slightest ray of hope that maybe, just maybe, she had found a way to forgive herself for the enigmatic decisions she had shouldered that had been beyond her control. He knew the man holding this priceless paragon was a good twenty years her senior. Maybe more. And yet he seemed to fit her like a well-worn glove. He knew instinctively how to counter, then compliment her every movement. As though he was gently breaking a wild mare that had been carelessly turned out on the lonesome prairie, then forgotten she existed.

Caught up in the paragon he watched as the kind cowboy gave her all the room that she needed to breathe and yet held just enough of the mystical rein to elude her intended escape. Their movements were fashioned together like the very ribbon that bound her dark hair as it floated through the air within the circle of their heated wind.

There was no need to express his delight or worries standing there watching them. Abe knew after all of the years of emptiness his rebellious daughter had finally lifted one of the rusty chains that blocked the protected entrance to her broken heart. That she had allowed the tiniest speck of light back inside her soul. He knew that this would be the man that would courageously seal the deep crack that had bound Lizzie's daunted being for so many years. That he didn't see the dated bruises or the branded scares that she carried on her strong shoulders. All this noble-minded cowboy could see was a beautiful wildflower that he and he alone held within his guarded arms.

It was a mixture of happy and sad emotions knowing that this beautiful twin had finally been pulled in by nothing more than the timeless wind. Like a whisper he whisked across her unforgiving heart like tumbleweed. They were a good match. A pair of gypsy's with limitless boundaries. Abe just hoped that Charlie knew what he had captured.

Several dances passed as the folks on the floor swirled in a total rhythmic pattern. Charlie and Abe were across the room talking to several of the other men. Liza and Lizzie were enjoying the whole scenario, watching the laughter roll from the lips of their children when from out of nowhere Ben and his band of thugs walked through the door. From their appearance it seemed like they had already indulged themselves in the dark smooth liquid that gave a man all the courage he needed to make a fool of himself.

Clinton spotted his Uncle first. "Stay here!" he commanded Naomi. Like a bullet he headed across the dance floor. But every time that he tried to gain access through the crowd, he got cut off. By the time he had made his determined destination, it was too late. It seemed that his uncle had zeroed in on the older cowhand as he started to walk to where the twins stood.

"For a dirty old cowpoke," Ben boasted through a red puffy face, "you clean up pretty good. What, the Baxter way of life proving to have more hidden benefits than most?" he let out a hideous laugh. When he got no response he continued, "Pot of gold at the end of someone's rainbow!" Then Ben poked his face within inches of Charlie's. "You best steer clear of me cowpoke, or I'll break your feet next time!" he threatened like the bully that he was.

Charlie merely looked him straight in the face. There was no doubt that he disliked the puffed up man. He wasn't afraid of him in the least, he'd dealt with men just like Ben his whole life but he'd just gotten his hands put back together. This man wasn't worth breaking them for again.

"What, cat got your tongue?" Ben challenged in a loud arrogant tone just as Lizzie walked up behind him like a whisper.

"I believe that this dance is ours, Ben," she said in a sweet loud voice as she pushed the small sharp knife into his side beneath his vest.

Ben jumped a foot at her sudden appearance. It was obvious that he didn't know what to do. "Why, yes, Miss Baxter," he said in an overly polite tone, knowing that she would put that knife plumb through him given the right opportunity. Like a lumbering elephant he hobbled to the floor. Trying to protect the very foot that she'd so uncaringly put a bullet in during their last encounter.

Like a sleek otter gliding on water Lizzie steered the man in and out of the staring crowd. Like a magician she slipped the honed blade from his side to the top of his neck. Barely pricking the skin. "You're scum," she hissed like a venomous snake through sparkling white teeth. "It's all I can do to put my hands on your filthy body!" Like a well conditioned actress she smiled at the curious onlookers. "I should cut this vein in your neck and let you bleed out like the dirty pig that you are," she threatened through darkening eyes.

"You wouldn't!" he exclaimed in a skeptical tone as he tried to escape her threatening grasp just as Lizzie felt a tap on her left shoulder.

"My turn," Liza stated lightheartedly.

"Certainly, sister," Lizzie smiled, "he's quite a good dancer." The man let out a loud moan as Lizzie purposely stepped on his foot.

"Oops!"

There was no missing the jealous glares from several of the irritated cowboys in the crowd that had been waiting to dance with the lovely duo all night.

Ben took in a deep sigh of relief until he felt the metal blade against the other side of his neck. "Witch!" he seethed. Why one was just as bad as the other!

"Now, is that any way to talk to a lady?" Liza smiled as she led the burly man across the floor just as she lightly broke the skin with the tip of the hidden knife blade.

"I'm sorry," he pleaded.

"You got that part right." She hissed.

"I didn't mean it!"

"Of course you did, silly." She gave him a scandalous look. "Hello, Myra. Beautiful apron."

"Why thank you, Liza," she gushed.

"Please! Let me go. I, I'm sorry."

"Oh, you're sorry all right," she hissed through dark accusing eyes. "You know, I've dealt with your kind all my life. It's always the same. Nothing is ever your fault. And everyone owes you." Liza knew the song would end soon so she gave her sister the nod encase it did. "So, let me tell you something. I don't like you. You're nothing but trouble. Eager to lead any young'un down the wrong road. So, it's only fair that you know if anyone in my family gets hurt I will personally take great pleasure in finishing what I started here tonight. You my friend will have more missing parts than a wind storm up a turkeys butt. You'll come up missing. Like I said there's lots of deep canyons on our ranch." Liza stared into the man's terrified face. "Tell me you understand," she threatened through tight lips as she tipped the knife into his skin a little deeper.

"Yes! Yes, I understand," he whined desperately.

"Good," she hissed. Then, like a well-schooled actress she stated loud enough for everyone to hear, "Oh, dear," she said in a regrettable fashion, "the songs over!" She gave him a menacing smile. "Maybe you would join my sister and I for a cup of cider." It was plain to see that the invitation wasn't optional. Like guiding a child she led him to where Lizzie stood waiting like a black widow spider patiently spinning her sticky web. One look was all her sister needed to know exactly what was going on.

Charlie started to walk across the floor to the women's rescue when Abe touched his shoulder. "Just watch," he chuckled with hidden admiration, "and learn."

"What?" Charlie questioned. "They could get hurt!"

"Yeah," Abe smirked, "like a snake with a rat." He saw the worry in the cowhands face. "It's all right. Watch Lizzie's right hand then Liza's. One if not both have a knife. They carry them in the oddest places. I'm guessing his ribs, the other near his neck. It's hard to tell which has which. But rest assured they both have one and they won't hesitate to use them."

Ben was standing stiff as a board directly in front of Lizzie when Clinton approached the small group. He gave the younger man a stiff smile but his eyes begged for his help.

Clinton pretended not to understand. "Uncle," he said cheerfully, "I didn't realize you were coming. And look at this! You sporting the most beautiful women in the building. I think I'd watch myself." he winked. "Lots of admirers!"

Lizzie's eyes twinkled like a cat with a rat bound securely within the confines of her steel jaws. "How does it feel?" Lizzie hissed in his ear as she smiled at the curious people. "Sally," Lizzie said sweetly when the friendly lady walked by, "great dance."

"Thank you, Lizzie," the woman beamed as she gave Lizzie's hostage a huffy look.

"Love your pie," Liza added.

Like the debutant that she was, Lizzie pressed the end of the small knife into Ben's fleshy side. "Are you scared yet?" she asked in a sweet threatening tone.

"No!" he snapped in a braver fashion than he felt.

"You should be you pompous little ant! You and I, we can walk right out of this door, no one would be any the wiser. I've already committed the most ghastly sin a woman can commit in the eyes of all of these fine upstanding folks. Tell me, do you think that you hitching your wagon up with me would change their opinion?"

"I don't think so, sister," Liza added before the cagey man could answer. "I believe that your reputation has already been soiled quite nicely."

"Now this is the point where they completely distract their prey." Abe whispered proudly to the starring cowhand. "I know, they've done it since they were babies!"

"Thanks, Liza!" Lizzie snapped as she gave her identical sibling an angry look. "What was that nasty remark supposed to mean?"

"Nothing," she said simply.

Ben stood in shock as he stared at the two battling women. "Now, now," he injected nervously, hoping not to be involved in a scene.

"Nothing! Then what in blazes did you say it for?" Lizzie snapped back as the twosome slightly loosened their grip giving the heavy-set man the false notion that he could make a clean getaway, which is exactly what he tried to do.

But, their dark threatening eyes settled in on him and it was like dealing with two black-eyed vipers. "Going somewhere?"

Ben was afraid to move. "Of course not!"

"Liar," Lizzie whispered.

"Move again and we'll gut you like a fish," they said in unison. Purposely, they pressed the ends of their knives even harder into his mushy flesh.

"Try it!" he challenged shakily.

"Take a good look around you worthless cowpie! Your own men don't even know you're in trouble. Look at them all jealous that you are over here being fondled by two beautiful women."

"Smile," Liza said, "they're watching."

Ben gave them a weak nod praying one of them would walk over to where he was. These two women were beyond normal!

"Let me tell you a little secret, not one person in this building will even notice that you're gone," Lizzie stated matter-of-factly.

"They don't want to know you're here do you think they'll miss you?"

"Not likely," Liza answered coldly.

"So, let me give you some good sound advice, Ben Parks," Lizzie said in an icy threatening tone meant only for him. "If that really is your name, which I doubt, if you want to keep that other foot dangling from your ankle then you best stay away from anyone that's connected with the Baxter ranch."

"That means all of the hands," Liza hissed as she pressed her knife on his other side. Smiling all the while. "Betty, love your dress."

"Or what!" he challenged.

"Or we-will-find that nice deep ravine with your name on it," they said at the same time as they snapped their knives closed like they'd never been opened. Within seconds they had them hidden inside the leather of their shoes. "Nice to talk with you," Lizzie said through cold lips as she stepped directly on his swollen foot. Then they dismissed the man without so much as a thought. Like the fleeing rodent that he was, the Ben quickly hobbled away holding his side and rubbing the back of his neck.

Liza and Lizzie's gaze crossed the distance to where their father stood proud as an old peacock. The understanding that passed between them was unconditional. They knew it, and he knew it. His expectations were realized through their determined commitment. As those chocolate circles held the icy blue crystals safely within the rein of his command, a familiar twitch etched its way across his sturdy jawline. The well-known gesture told them they were well within their boundaries.

"See, I told you," Abe grinned as Charlie stood completely baffled as he stared with pride at the two hellcats across the room. "You don't be worrying about Liza and Lizzie, they know how to take care of themselves," he said proudly. "I made sure of that the day they were born."

Clinton stared in awe at one lovely woman then the other. He shook his head in disbelief at what he had just seen. "I just love those two!" he boasted. Then he instantly disappeared into the crowd. When he found Naomi she was surrounded by the very men that Ben had brought in. She looked like a cornered coyote. Ready to take any one of them on. "Naomi," Clinton said, "there you are!"

Protectively, he grabbed her hand and led her toward the dance floor. She was so angry that she was shaking like a leaf.

"Troublemakers!" he mumbled. "They are always looking for a way to get into something!" When the dance was over he insisted that she stand by her mother until he had a chance to settle this matter with his uncle.

Liza and Lizzie studied the small group of thugs and were both surprised that Jeffrey had attached himself like a leach to the troublesome group. Liza gave her sister a knowing look. One thing about Jeffrey, he was easily led astray. They couldn't see him being stupid enough to hook up with the like of these men yet, here he was right in the thick of it. Maybe they should have told him the truth about the day that his father was killed.

Both women took in a deep sigh as they walked to where the restless hoodlum stood like a cocky rooster, crowing his snide remarks and insults. The other men departed instantly when they saw the dark-eyed duo walking their direction. Ben immediately stumbled like a three legged dog to the other side of the room. He didn't need another encounter with the two dark-eyed she-devils. He was sure that they might cut more than just his neck next time.

Jeffrey seemed unaffected by their dominating presence and never offered to move. "Hello, mother," he said with little emotion in his voice. "Aunt Lizzie," he said in an icy arrogant tone. Jeffrey had never seen his mother or aunt in a dress that he could remember. They were stunning. There was no covering up the surprise in those cocky sea green eyes that he was taken aback at their appearance. But more than that, he couldn't tell which one was which.

From across the room, Abe noticed his grandson's reaction. They were lovely his twin daughter's. Two peas in a pod.

Liza said in a motherly tone. "I wondered where you were."

"Like you care," he snapped. Pretending to be offended at her warm motherly remark.

"What?" Liza was surprised at the hostility in his voice.

"You've got your precious Matthew, what are you worried about me for?" he questioned openly.

For once in her life, Liza didn't know what to say. All she could do was stare at her son in disbelief. The alcohol on his breath was prominent.

But Lizzie knew and she didn't waste any time. "What is this nonsense, talking to your mother in such a way? Comparison is the devils tool, Jeffrey. Be careful how you use it."

He gave Lizzie a dirty look. She always knew how to get his goat. Like his soul was a mirror and she could see inside of it. "As if what I think is any of your business."

Lizzie took a step closer as she stood to the side of the snotty boy when she spoke, "Please don't tell me that there will be a lesson in manners here tonight in front of all of these nice people."

"You wouldn't," he spit back in her face.

Lizzie cocked one delicately arched brow. "Wouldn't I?"

Jeffrey knew all too well that his aunt would do exactly what she said. He wasn't about to cause a scene. He'd been humiliated enough at her hands lately. So, instead he turned and looked at his mother's beautiful face. "Would you like to dance, Mother?" Like an astute gentleman, he took Liza by the arm and led her out to the dance floor.

Within seconds Matthew swooped up his Aunt Lizzie and off they went, too. He hadn't even realized that his brother was there. When he did it was very obvious. "Jeffrey!" he hollered, delighted to see his sibling. "When did you get here?"

Jeffrey tried to ignore his brother with little results.

"Mother," Matthew said proudly as he twirled Lizzie past in a circle, "you look radiant." Then out of nowhere he traded partners. "Mother," Matthew whispered, "may I?" as his huge smile engulfed her.

Hesitantly, Jeffrey took Lizzie's hand. "You're not going to kill me or anything are you?" he asked as her dark eyes cloaked his face.

"That depends," she said in an off-handed tone.

"On what?"

"On whether you can dance or not?" she said teasingly. Jeffrey was glad when the dance was over and he walked back to join the group of men he'd arrived with.

CHAPTER 16

After several hours of dancing had come and gone, it was time for the musicians to take a break as the pooped out dancers started gathering around the long table of food. Everything looked delicious. Yams, taters, ham, beef, rolls, sliced bread, salad after salad, cakes, and pies galore. It was quite a feast.

Liza and Lizzie had just filled their plates when they noticed from across the room how red Matthew's face was. He, his brother and two of the thugs that Jeffrey was with were in a heated conversation. Liza gave Abe a nudge as they silently watched. Within minutes Abe politely excused himself and quietly approached the arguing party. He was somewhat glad that he'd only gotten in on the end of the conversation.

"Shut your mouth!" Matthew seethed in a threatening tone. "Just shut your filthy mouth! You don't know anything about her!"

"I know she has the ass the size of Charlie's old mule," Jeffrey laughed, trying to impress his newly found friends. "I'll bet the rides a lot smoother though," he chided. "Holy jeebers, Matthew, how would you ever carry that across the threshold! With a team of horses?" Jeffrey and the two men that he was with whooped it up like the school-yard bullies that they were. In the corner Abe could see the teary-eyed face of Emmy as her mother Hattie held tightly to her trembling hand. He was furious at the arrogance of the rude young Baxter.

"If you say one more word, so help me I'll..." Matthew threatened.

"What? Go running to mommy? She'll protect you, you're her favorite. The good son! Or better yet, go tell Aunt Lizzie, she hates me anyway!"

Within the breath of the last remark Abe quietly reached across Matthew's shoulder as he grabbed Jeffrey by the back of his shirt and pulled him backward to where he stood. The action took Jeffrey by complete surprise as Matthew silently stepped aside. There was no missing the hurt that etched its way across his grandson's angry face.

At first Jeffrey tried to resist the restraints of the intruder. That is until he discovered it was his grandfather. "Papa," he said in a defensive tone. "I didn't see you."

"I'm sure you didn't," Abe said in a stern voice. "Gentlemen, if you'll excuse us."

Like a pack of wolves in an enclosed fence, they instantly backed out of the way. They weren't sure that they wanted any more dealings with this Baxter family. They were a ruthless group, nothing like they had encountered before. Their retreat was immediate.

There was no missing the angry intent on the older Baxter's face. Like a cat being drug to water Jeffrey tried to resist Abe's intended destination. It did him little good to resist. His grandfather was strong, embarrassed, and furious. When they arrived in front of Emmy and her mother Hattie, the younger Baxter was beyond humiliated. Abe gave them each an apologetic nod.

There was no missing the hurt in Hattie's worried face. She was a lovely woman, maybe five years younger than Abe. She had her brilliant blonde hair pulled up in an attractive French roll on the back of her head with tiny tendrils of the massive curls dangling like earrings from either side. She had warm kind eyes and her smile always made you feel welcome. She was a woman who'd definitely had her share of sorrows but you rarely heard her complain about any of it.

She and her husband Ed had come out West for a better life just like everyone else. They'd settled their small family on the outskirts of the Lazy A B ranch, tending to one hundred acres of land that they farmed with all sorts of different vegetables and fruits. They'd had four well-schooled, intelligently groomed children. Three girls and one young boy. But one summer her husband caught a bad cough from plowing out in the rain that turned into phenomena. He died three weeks later. That same year her oldest daughter was tending to the large acreage of seeded vegetables when her horse spooked from a sunbathing rattler as she fell from the startled animal and broke her neck. And if that wasn't enough to push any normal human being over the edge of insanity her only son at the young age of four drowned in the small pond behind their barn playing with the ducks. It had been a devastating time for the woman to struggle through alone. Now, all she had left was, Emmy. She had literally been the young woman's shadow for sixteen years and she was very overprotective of her only surviving child.

"Apologize," Abe insisted firmly trying not to cause a scene. When he got no response his grasp became more aggressive and his tone more menacing. "What you have said and done here tonight is not the behavior becoming a gentleman or a Baxter. Apologize," he said roughly.

"That's because I'm not a Baxter!" Jeffrey snapped back at his grandpa through thin white lips with a venomous tone. "I'm a Jones! Jeffrey Baxter Jones!"

"Don't make me repeat myself, Jeffrey," Abe said in a voice that sounded just like Lizzie's, "or you'll be sorrier than a dead skunk! I don't care if you're a Baxter, a Jones, or a dog!" It was plain to see that Abe was furious with the young man's disrespectful mannerism. "I will not tolerate this kind of rude behavior!"

"I'm sorry," he said in an untruthful tone. Terrified of his grandfather.

Abe tightened his grasp even further. "Say it like you mean it boy or the consequences will be far worse."

"I'm sorry, Emmy, I am. We were just having a little fun, that's all. I didn't mean nothing by it," Jeffrey said in a half-hearted reply knowing that his grandpa meant exactly what he said and by now his firm grip had completely cut off the circulation in his arm.

Emmy stared into Jeffrey's wild green eyes with no resentment as she spoke, "Thank you."

Her unconditional surrender caught Jeff completely off guard as he stared in disbelief at her forgiving face. "You're welcome," he said with honesty. "Darn it," he mumbled under his breath, "Matthew always get the good ones!"

"Ladies," Abe said in a controlled voice as he led the lad outside, directly to the horse trough. It was plain to see that Abe Baxter was livid with the young man that had disrespected his brother and the Baxter name. After several good solid dunking's he handed Jeff the reins to his horse. "Go home, young man, you're an embarrassment to our family name! We'll be discussing this further in the morning!"

Humiliated, Jeffrey mounted his horse and rode out at a fast pace. It wasn't long before Abe saw the other hoodlums following close behind him. They were going to be trouble. Plain and simple. As he strolled back into the noisy room he looked for his two lovely daughters, then continued to the finish the supper meal that he had started earlier. When the band resumed its musical poetry he politely walked over and asked Hattie to dance. "It's the least I can do for the disrespect of my grandson," he said teasingly, fully expecting to be turned down. But once again the dignified woman did completely the opposite.

Hattie gave him a wide un-offended grin. "Thank you," she said sincerely, "for everything." With a twinkle in her eye they danced across the floor while Abe told her how much he'd enjoyed her food.

At the stroke of midnight, everything came to an end. One last slow dance the fiddler said as everyone paired up. It was a magical moment watching Matthew and Emmy as they swayed across the floor like two young colts whose pairing seemed only natural. Abe with his charming smile as he escorted Hattie to the waiting floor. The adoring face of Clinton as he gazed into the odd colored eyes of their precious Naomi. And Albert Johnson with his newfound love, Liza. It was a breathtaking moment as Lizzie stood watching and waiting for Nelly and Charlie to stroll by since that was who he'd been dancing with most of the evening. When she felt a light tap on her elbow, Lizzie was surprised at her suitor.

"Shall we?" Charlie asked with an admiring gleam in his steely eyes.

The inviting expression on Lizzie's contented face said nothing and everything. There was something truly amazing going on here tonight. A feeling that hadn't been allowed to escape her chained heart since the lying deception of Jeremiah. Like someone had opened a floodgate of emotions that she could no longer control. As his steely grey eyes invaded the hungry pools of blue, Lizzie whispered, "For the brand, Charlie." Like two young lovers they floated across the dance floor. They could see their reflection in the lantern light as they swayed cheek to cheek in a wind of undenied bliss.

But standing just outside that very window of the lively building, stared an objective set of angry sea green eyes shaded by the glow of the glass as he watched the oblivious dancers. He stood lurking like a peeping-tom just waiting until one of the Baxter women danced by. He saw the satisfied look on Liza's contented face as she slowly glided at the hands of the stone-faced livery owner. "Stinking harlot," the shadow said with venom in his voice.

Then he watched as Matthew danced by with Emmy in his arms. He was sure no one had missed the interlude between grandfather and grandson about harassing the big, butted woman Matthew seemed to be so proud of. The older man had made such a fool of him. He reminded the hidden shadow of a love sick bull! With all of the lovely young ladies scattered throughout the room this is the one he'd chosen? The thought of it made him furious. She would have never been his choice! But, as he stood alone hidden within the darkened shadows he knew that Matthew was a Baxter through and through. His mannerisms, the way he carried himself with a dignified air screamed that he had the inner bred values of his grandfather. But more than that, standing here in the dark, he realized how much Matthew looked like Liza and Lizzie. And Liza and Lizzie looked just like, Abe Baxter.

Then his breath caught in his throat as Naomi and Clinton slowly etched past the window, totally smitten with each other. From this distance it was shocking to see how much she looked like her mother. He'd studied the silhouette of her flawless face from a distance and not until now did he see how much the reality of their beautiful features were identical. He watched in awe at the way she carried herself with a self-righteous attitude and determined body structure. There was no doubt that she was Lizzie's daughter. "Your day is coming too you snotty little heathen!"

As the shaded personage took a step to the side he could see Abe Baxter smiling and dancing with the mother of Matthew's so-called, date. She was comely enough but she would never make it to the alter. She wasn't dignified enough; she just didn't know it. "Stupid woman!" he mumbled.

Then out of the corner of his eye, the silent snoop saw Lizzie and Charlie slowly glide by as though they were in a world all their own. He had to admit she was mesmerizing! It seemed unbelievable as he watched the amazing transformation as the two of them gazed into each other's eyes. It was like they had been affectionately connected all their lives. Strolling across the wooden floor like they were on a pond of ice as his hand lazily lay across the small of her tanned back. The intruder didn't like the way those blues eyes that looked like moon drops on a lost forgotten lake lightly touched the steely circles of the old cowpunchers. Her actions were humiliating! What a trashy witch! Why, she was allowing her full lips to lay innocently against his scruffy cheek, whispering something in his ear! Disgraceful! Hadn't they embarrassed their family enough? One was just as bad as the other! The cowboy didn't want Lizzie! Just like the blacksmith didn't want Liza! No! All he wanted was the Lazy AB Ranch! Something he'd planned on laying claim to for himself! "You stinking two-faced rounder's!" he hissed to himself. "Both of you unfaithful pirate's!" Angrily the hidden image wrung one hand inside the other. All he could think about was choking the man in Lizzies arms to death and putting a gun to the head of the livery man. Couldn't they see how humiliating their display really was? What a fool she was making of herself? What fools they were all making of themselves? Then just like that, grumbling obscenities to himself, the shadow disappeared back into the safety of the night.

The last dance ended as the steaming dancers said their goodnights. The Baxter party loaded into the wagon and headed back toward the ranch together. The atmosphere of the small group was light and lively. It was as though no one wanted to go home.

They teased Liza unmercifully about her new beau, Albert, which she admittedly denied. He was nothing more than a good dance partner and she threatened to shoot the next person that said otherwise. But Lizzie saw the moon-struck look on her sisters blushing face and knew that she was quite smitten.

Naomi rattled on about every dance that she and Clinton engaged in. About how he had stuck up for her and told his uncle just what he could do with his so-called band of thugs. "Mother," Naomi said in an excited voice, "wasn't that wonderful of him!"

"He'd better protect your reputation young lady or I'll put a bullet in him!" the twins said in unison.

"Mother!" Naomi scolded. "Auntie!"

The two women gave each other a knowing nod as Abe laughed out loud.

"Can we go again? The next time? Can we, mother? Please? I never dreamed dancing could be so, so wonderful!" she sighed.

Lizzie rolled her eyes to back of her head just as Abe started in on Hattie's cooking. Why the woman had made several masterpieces as far as he was concerned and was going to ask her if she would bring one of her cakes out to the ranch some Sunday afternoon. "Are you sure that's what you really want her to bring?" Lizzie teased.

Matthew could hardly contain his enthusiasm when Abe suggested that Emmy's mother come out to the ranch. "Could they, papa? Maybe we could go on a picnic!" But when he gazed into his mother's suspicious eyes he added. "With permission of course."

"Of course," Liza added.

Matthew was so smitten with the lovely blonde that he kept saying over and over what a wonderful girl she was and how much he loved her personality. She was so warm and kind, nothing like the other stuffy women.

Lizzie'd nearly had it with all the hoop-a-la and made sure that everyone knew about the bruises that would swell her feet for the next six months. How she and she alone had saved the Baxter reputation by dancing every song. That she had gone far and above the call of duty. That she'd probably never get her boots on in the morning and that tomorrow she would be walking like a crippled duck. And next time, if there was a next time, she would wear two wooden buckets on her feet and a pair of coverall's full of cow manure! "That'll teach em!" she mumbled to herself. But, no one was was listening. They were all telling their own tales. One interrupting the other.

"Well, I for one," Abe stated, "had quite a nice time."

Not once did they mention the ugly incident that happened between Matthew and Jeffrey. Or the dunking in the water trough or the quick exit that he made. But it was lying there just beneath the surface like a festering boil waiting to erupt.

"Highline to the left," Lizzie whispered to her sister.

"I see them," she answered softly as their father pulled the walking team to a stop. Then, as though they were a band of well trained soldiers, Liza and Lizzie stood up in the back of the wagon, rifles drawn. The three outriders, Matthew and Charlie followed suit. No one moved.

From the top of the ravine the sight was frightening. The small band of men that had been following the wagon like a pack of jackals hadn't planned on this kind of resistance. The worst part was, they knew that the set of dark-eyed twins standing on the back of that wagon wouldn't miss. Like a litter of beaten pups, the band of men hurriedly rode in the opposite direction, down the ravine and out of sight.

"I can follow them, mother, find out who it was," Matthew stated bravely.

"Not tonight," Lizzie said firmly. She knew who the small band of riders were. "Sister and I will take care of it tomorrow."

CHAPTER 17

Hattie and Emmy bounced along the rutted road as they laughed and recounted the evening's festivities. Emmy told her mother she didn't understand why Jeffrey disliked her so much when he didn't even know her. "Jeffrey," Hattie stated, "he's trouble that one. You stay clear of him."

"I will mother," she said as they continued on their jolly way. "Did you see the way Matthew stuck up for me?"

"I did."

"He's such a gentleman, mamma." She swooned.

"I can see that," she smiled as she patted Emmy's thigh.

The presence of the small group of men both startled and surprised the bouncing duo. They seemed to appear from out of nowhere as they rode up alongside of their moving wagon. As though they had been waiting just inside the shadowed trees like a band of raiding thieves. Hattie had her shotgun loaded and fully intended to use it.

"Ladies," a masked voice that they didn't recognize said. It was plain to see that the man was drunk. "Beautiful night don't you think?"

Hattie gave them a distrusting stare. "What ya want?" she said in an angry confronting tone. Afraid for the safety of her daughter.

"Why nothing, ma'am," he slurred.

"Then what ya got those covers over your face's for?" she accused.

"No reason," he lied.

"Only cowards cover their faces," Hattie stated as she pulled back the hammer on the waiting shotgun.

"It's awful late to be riding out here alone, don't you think?" the masked man continued.

"I'm not alone," she said stiffly, "but even if I was, it ain't none of yourn business!"

"Well, I can see how you would think that," the masked marauder said as his eyes undressed the younger woman sitting next to her mother on the wagon seat.

Hattie didn't miss the intended exchange. "You come one step closer you filthy bandit and I'll put this buckshot right through your saggy gut!" she said with no fear in her voice.

"Now hold on!" from the look on Hattie's fearless face he knew the hearty woman would do exactly what she threatened. "We don't mean you no harm. Just want to sit a spell and talk."

"Ain't no talking going on here," she said matter-of-factly, "only shootin'." But in the midst of the conversation Hattie hadn't heard the man who'd been sneaking up behind the standing wagon like a slithering rat. As she felt the connection of the cold hard steel to the back of her head the loaded shotgun echoed across the distance. Hattie fell to the ground with a thud, her motionless body lay face down in the dirt.

"Mother!" Emmy screamed at the top of her lungs as she jumped from the safety of the wagon to where her mother lay unconscious.

"Well, Missy," the outlaw said in a slurred tongue as blood dripped down his sleeve, "seems we're gonna have us a party after all."

"No," Emmy whispered in disbelief as one of the men shoved her to the ground. But Emmy was a big girl and knew how to fight. Her days of physical labor helping her mother to survive on the small acreage that they called home had proven to be a good alli for the young woman. She scrambled to her feet like a leaping cat. She would fight till her death before they took her. And that is exactly what she did.

Emmy fought like a wounded bear. A kick in the stomach here. A blow to the jaw there. She clawed and scratched like a mountain lion cornered in a box canyon. Her fists bleeding from the impact of her defense. But there were too many of them. Like a sinking stone they ambushed her fatigued body and with one quick blow, she too lay motionless on the hard unforgiving ground.

But that didn't stop the band of marauding thugs. No, they had other plans for their trapped trophy. Roughly they drug her limp body to the back of the still wagon as they tied her bloodied hands to either side of the wooden wheels. Like a band of white teethed sharks they circled round and round her. Laughing as they dipped and dived in and out of her face, touching her virginal skin with their filthy drunken hands.

When she finally came to Emmy let out a loud shrill scream. Frantically, she spit at the lust-filled faces of the hideous bandits and kicked her feet for all she was worth. "Cowards!" she screamed, sobbing uncontrollably. "You're nothing but filthy cowards!"

Her accusations only enticed the marauding thugs to the next level of frenzied lust as they ripped her beautiful cotton dress completely away from her maiden body. Horrified, she screamed even louder, pulling like a rabid dog on the strand of ropes that held her captive. Hoping someone, somewhere would hear her desperate cries. Like a roped calf they roughly gagged her desperate screams with a sweaty neck scarf as tiny droplets of blood slid down either corner of her typically soft warm mouth. Emmy hadn't given up the fight as she kicked one then the other in the face. "Filthy, pigs!" she sobbed. "Let me go!" the filthy scoundrel's didn't hear her desperate cries; all they did was laugh. Then from out of nowhere a hand roughly threw the bleeding bandit into the dirt.

"She's mine!" the masked marauder demanded. Emmy fought him with all the strength that she had left. With the force of a mule her left leg kicked him hard across his chest as he flew backward into the dirt. Furiously he came to his feet as he leaned over her wiping the blood from the side of his cracked lip.

As she stared through a river of heated tears a spark of recognition ran across his determined features. This man knew her! How? When the horrible event was over he slapped her hard against her ghostly cheek as he defiantly stared into her cow-like eyes and said, "The mule would have been better!"

Emmy's disbelieving expression was full of hatred as she glared into those sea green eyes as he laughed like a madman. But the man had underestimated Emmy. All the fight wasn't out of her as she caught his boot inside of hers. The man started to fall backward as she kicked him as hard as she could in the back. If she was gonna die, then she'd die fighting! Shocked at the magnitude of the blow he kicked Emmy several times in her ribs and legs. Furiously he knelt down within inches of her face. "I should kill you for that! But, you don't win! I win! And, if you tell anyone about what happened here tonight, we'll come back when you're fast asleep and kill you both!"

"You'll try!" she threatened as she spit in his startled face. Tears of desperation ran like a raging river that had jumped outside of its muddy banks down Emmy's bruised cheeks. "You might have taken this body you filthy pig! But you'll never take my soul that belongs to Matthew Baxter!"

The masked man seemed shocked. Then he hissed, "You're not good enough to be a, Baxter!"

"Just like you!" she spit back.

"There's not much time," the outlaw stated angrily. "She's yours!" he said to his men as he strutted away. Emmy did her best to fight them off but the inevitable happened anyway. Emmy sunk into a hole of darkness. "Mother," she wept before the black cloak surrounded her broken body and overtook her for the last time.

It was nearly dawn when Hattie woke up. Her head spun like a whirlwind as her blurry eyes searched for Emmy. She let out a shrill cry as she crawled like a crippled pup to where she laid. Sobbing, Hattie gently cut the filthy bandana that stretched the crusted skin on her bloody lips. Then she cut the frayed rope that bound her bleeding wrists like a gutted deer to either wagon wheel. Emmy fell forward into her mother's hysterical arms like a fragile doll. It was an un-fathomable sight. A sight that no human being should have to go through or see. Desperately, Hattie climbed to her wobbly feet as she struggled to pull Emmy up into the back of the wagon. She knew the filthy jackals had been waiting for them. Hiding like cowardess curs just inside the blackened shadows. "Don't die, Emmy," Hattie sobbed. With one good slap of the reins the two patiently waiting horses jumped from the sting of the leather as they headed at break-neck speed for the safety of their little homestead.

CHAPTER 18

When the Baxter family rode into the ranch it was perfectly quiet. As they unhitched the horses and led them to the barn, Abe noticed that Jeffrey's horse wasn't in the corral or one of the stalls. Liza and Lizzie noticed it, too. Abe was disgusted immediately as he thought to himself, that boy was gunning to get shot. But no one said a word as they all said their goodnights and tucked their dreams away for the evening.

The next morning as they all gathered at the breakfast table going over last evenings festivities, low and behold there sat Jeffrey like a stuffed pumpkin. He seemed to be in good spirits for once and ready to join in with the rest of the family.

Liza gave him a distrusting stare. "Morning," she said lightly. "When did you get home?"

"Not too long after you did mother," he said in a know-it-all tone. "I didn't want to wake everyone so I slept in the barn. I knew Maria was up when I smelled her coffee drifting plumb across the yard. Why, your watch dogs out late?"

Lizzie gave him a look of complete disgust at the way that he disrespected his mother. "I see that you've made some new friends," she stated coolly wanting to walk to the other side of the table and slap that cocky mouth plumb to the other side of the ranch.

"Yeah, they're all right," he said as he tried to act like it was no big deal. "Wanted to know if I'd ask you and mother if you needed any hands," he said sincerely. "I said that we can always use good hands."

"Not out of that bunch," Abe said in a stern tone before either daughter had a chance to reply. "Besides, you and I have business today young man, didn't I tell you to go straight home?"

"Yes, sir." There was no hiding the disappointment in his wily face. He'd hoped that his grandfather had forgotten about the threat of punishment for today. "I'm sorry about all of that last night, papa. I am. I don't know what I was thinking."

"So you say," Abe countered in a tone that said he didn't believe him just as Matthew walked into the large old kitchen. There was no missing the tension between the two brothers.

Jeffrey took up the conversation immediately. "I'm sorry, brother, I am. I acted like a jack-ass last night. And the next time I see Emmy, I'll tell her the same thing."

Matthew was so taken aback at his brother's seemingly genuine confession that he didn't know what to say. "Well, don't do it again! That really hurt her feelings. Not to say what her mother thought."

"I know, I won't," he said sincerely. "I swear."

Lizzie knew that the young man was lying through his pearly white teeth. She could feel it in her bones and smell the foul play on his sour hungover breath. She wasn't sure why he was lying, but he was just the same. He was a scallion that boy. Trouble from the day of his birth. Nothing good was going to come from Jeffrey. And Matthew, God-bless his soul was just too forgiving. "So, where did you go last night?" Lizzie asked in a simple inquiring tone. "I mean after the dunking," she added intentionally trying to get him riled up so he'd get mad and tell the truth.

"Ah, me and the boys, we went and drank a little more whiskey then I headed home. I wasn't that far behind you." He knew what his Aunt was up to so he decided not to take the bait. He had bigger issues to worry about today.

"So then you heard the gunshot," Lizzie said as everyone looked at her inquisitively.

Jeffrey's head jerked up as he stared at his Aunt's probing face. "I heard something, but I don't know that it was a gunshot. "So to change the subject he asked, "What do you want me to do today, mother?"

"You'll ride with me today," Lizzie said before her sister even had a chance to answer. "We're gathering up by the Old Willow Pasture. A place that I'm sure you're familiar with."

"I don't believe that I asked you," Jeffrey snapped in an intense haughty tone as he directed his stare at his Aunt, "unless you have somehow miraculously become my mother!"

Lizzie knew how to get under the young boy's skin as she added in a cool tone, "I'm worse than any mother you'll ever have

Jeffrey, I'm your conscious." Her dark eyes probed his, "Besides, if you were my son, I'd of drowned you at birth."

"Lizzie," Liza said in an authoritive tone.

"Don't worry, sister, I'm looking forward to working with Mr. Big Mouth today. See what he's really made of."

There was no missing the fear in his lying sea green eyes as tiny droplets of sweat started to appear on his forehead. There was no telling what this mad woman would do to him alone out on the prairie with no witnesses. Probably castrate him! He had to find a way to get away from her. "Do you mind if I take a nap first, Auntie? I could sure use one, you know late night," he said sarcastically to provoke the probing woman.

"Far be it from me to say whether you can waste your drunken life away sleeping. I can wait right here." She gave the younger man a looming smile.

"Don't waste your time," he said back in a snide tone.

"You know, Jeffrey, someday, if you don't change your lying scandalous ways, you'll be napping permanently." Her cold dark eyes told him that she meant exactly what she was saying. "In the dirt!"

"You don't own me!" Jeffrey hollered back, terrified that she knew something she didn't need to. "You're nothing more than a dried up old crone!"

"A dried up crone am I? Let me tell you something you loud-mouthed piece of cow dung, all of these ugly little stories that you seem to think you're so good at telling." Her eyes were dark and intensely focused only on him. "They're' going to come back tenfold and bite you right on that hunk of flesh your sitting on. And me, personally, I could care less! Good riddance!"

"Mother!" Naomi stated in shock. "Jeffrey!"

"Lizzie!" Liza was even more shocked at her sister's off-handed remark than Naomi. "Jeffrey, that is quite enough!"

"Naomi," Lizzie said in a protective tone, her eyes not leaving the destination of her squirming prey, "you'll go with me today."

"Yes, mother," she said simply, completely baffled at her mother's change in disposition.

"Morning," Clinton was his typically cheerful self as he sat in his designated place. "What'd I miss?" Purposely, he followed Lizzie's intense gaze as it drifted to the other side of the table. "Hey,

Jeffrey, nice to see you. Gee's man, you missed out on all of the fun," he said as he gave Naomi a quick wink.

"I wouldn't say all of the fun," Jeffrey replied with a cocky look on his face as he tried unsuccessfully to stare down his brazen Aunt. "I did get to dance with, mother." he said warmly as those sea green eyes swallowed her whole.

Liza gave him a loving smile.

Lizzie gave him a look that said she could see right through his cowardess eyes and he'd better be watching his back as far as she was concerned.

"Father," Liza did her best to change the subject and to get away from her son. "When is Hattie coming over to help with the cooking. I do hope that's what you two were talking about last night. Maria's not feeling much better and it's a lot to expect from Dancing Bear."

"What about, Charlie?" Jeffrey asked from out of nowhere. "He cooked some pretty good grub up on the mountain."

"No, that won't work I need Charlie to help Luke." Liza stated.

"I'll send word with one of the hands," Abe answered lightly. "See if they can come for a week or two. Give them a couple of days to get ready."

Lizzie never took her inquisitive eyes off of her shady nephew. "That all right with you, Jeffrey?"

"Yeah, sure. Why wouldn't it be?" he snapped back. "I said I was sorry!"

"You know, I see your lips moving, Jeffrey," Lizzie's glare was so intense. "I just don't know what you're sorry for yet. But, remember this, if I hear one bad word come out of that pie-hole you call a mouth, I'll put my foot right in it!"

"I hate you!" he seethed as he jumped to his feet.

"I'm sure you do," Lizzie said unfazed by his obnoxious outburst.

"Why can't you just leave me alone?" he yelled. "I didn't do nothing!"

"No one said that you did," Lizzie continued in a cool collected tone.

"Then why are you so miserable mean to me!" he accused his aunt like a two year old.

"Because, if someone doesn't ride herd on you, Jeffrey, and I mean ride hard, you'll get us all killed!" She said matter of factly.

"Shut up you overbearing dried up old crow!" he screamed hatefully. "No wonder no man ever wanted to marry your…"

But before Jeffrey could get one more syllable out of his hateful lying lips, Clinton flew over the top of the table like a bullet. No one saw it coming and the younger Baxter never knew what hit him. Within seconds Clinton had both arms pulled to the middle of Jeffrey's back. The younger man was screaming like a child from the pain. "Don't you ever talk to a lady like that!" he seethed.

"I hate her!" Jeffrey countered completely out of control. "She's nothing more than an old dried up witch!"

"Shut up! Shut your filthy mouth or so help me I'll pull both arms plum out of their sockets!" Clinton might have been the smaller man but he was like a fighting bull as he pushed the howling man's face to the floor.

"Papa!" Jeffrey hollered through muffled lips as his face lay smashed against the wooded floor.

"Clinton." Lizzie spoke in a calm, soothing tone, "it's all right, you can let him up now. Clinton," she said again as she gently touched his shoulder.

When the mapmaker looked into Lizzie's cool blue eyes his were filled with angry tears. There was no denying the fact that he was fighting mad! An anger that she had never dreamed lived within the chambers of the young man's gentle soul. She knew from the fearless look that he gave her that he would have surely de-limbed the younger Baxter with little or no regret. Their eyes stayed entwined within each other for several seconds as Clinton recklessly let go of Jeffrey's arms. He stood staring at the downed man for several seconds. "I didn't mean no disrespect, Ma'am." Then he politely picked up his hat and walked out the large oak door. Closing it quietly behind him.

"Naomi, get saddled up, we have a long day ahead," Lizzie instructed as she placed several pieces of bacon and hotcakes into a clean cloth.

"Yes, ma'am," she answered softly as she stared at her Aunt's Liza's ashen face.

CHAPTER 19

Several days came and went since the fiasco in the kitchen as the rest of the family waited for Hattie and Emmy's arrival. It was early morning when the sweaty team finally pulled into the Baxter yard. There was no denying the huge smile of relief that covered the older woman's lovely face as she witnessed the waiting family. It gave her a sense of pride knowing that her services were so outwardly needed and a hidden sense of protection.

Liza and Lizzie both saw the mixed expression on the older woman's gaunt face as they gave each other a questioning look. And if that wasn't enough to make them suspicious, they both noticed that Emmy wasn't her typical self either. Her movements were slow. Not giddy like they had expected. She had on long sleeves which for a day like this seemed odd. The twins couldn't help but notice the bruises that ran down the inside of her writs as several of them lay like a snake on the top of her marked hands. Their suspicions were the same. Her normal, lighthearted, outgoing personality was noticeably quiet and subdued. Her eyes didn't have that lighted twinkle. No. They seemed almost ashamed as she stared into Matthew's inviting face.

"Emmy," Matthew said in a gentlemanly tone, "it's good to see you." There was no missing the look of adoration on his handsome face.

"Me, too," she said meekly as she looked adoringly into his kind trusting eyes, then immediately at the ground.

Liza and Lizzie didn't miss the hesitated exchange. Something wasn't right. Nonchalantly, they turned and walked the other direction. "Hattie," Lizzie smiled as she held out her hands, "I hope you plan on cooking; father hasn't stopped talking about your meat pie since we got home from the Harvest dance."

"I'll show you," she said cheerfully.

"Not me," Lizzie laughed. "I can't boil water!"

"I can vouch for that," Abe agreed as his burly frame joined them on the wooded porch. "Hattie, you're a welcome sight, please, come in," he offered in a jolly mood. He was always such a gracious host.

"My, that's quite a bump on your head," Lizzie said as she ran her hand across the fading bruise. Instantly, she cocked one delicately arched brow.

"This? It ain't nothing," the older woman half laughed. "Next time I'll duck before I chase that old fox out my henhouse."

"Ouch! Stinking four legged scoundrels! I hope you got him," Liza said in a happy tone showing her enthusiasm for the older woman's appearance. Knowing that she wasn't telling the truth. "Hattie, Emmy, we're so glad you made it! We've been expecting you for some time."

As they all entered the large old house, Dancing Bear was standing just inside the kitchen. "You good come," she said sweetly.

At first Hattie was taken aback at the sight of the lovely Indian Princess. Shocked at her natural beauty. Then she simply smiled and threw her arms around the petite Indian. "I've heard a lot about you. Why, you're just as lovely as I imagined."

Dancing Bears face blushed red. "Come, you show pie," she said in broken English as she and the hippy cook disappeared into the large kitchen. "Maria, well not."

"I'm sorry to hear that," they heard Hattie say in a disturbed voice as they disappeared.

"I suppose you two had best get going on your little picnic," Liza teased. "Just try and be back by dark."

At first Emmy seemed to hesitate at the invitation as she gazed into the young Baxter's anxious face. "Of course," she whispered as she quietly took Matthew's hand.

"Are you not well, Emmy?" Matthew asked in a concerned tone as they passed through the gates. "Cause, we can do this another time."

"I'm all right," she said in a quiet voice. "I've been looking forward to seeing you all month."

Matthew didn't know what to think as they rode to the steaming pond with little or no conversation. When Emmy saw the young man's intention her mind ran wild as she immediately started to cry. "What? What did I do? I just thought it would be fun to swim for a while." He looked deeply into her ashen face. "Please tell me what I did."

Emmy stepped down slowly from the wagon as she wiped her tear-stained face. It had been a long healing month and she was still a little sore from her horrible ordeal. When she was a safe distance away from Matthew's interrogating eyes she spoke softly. "It's nothing that you did," she stated matter-of-factly, "but I'm afraid if I tell you what has happened to me," she paused for a brief moment, "you won't want to ever see me again. And yet if I don't tell someone, I think I might just die."

The ashen look on her face scared Matthew half to death as he walked her sobbing body around the wagon and under the shade of the Aspen. "Oh Emmy, I love you there's nothing you could tell me that would ever change that," he said with a truthful compassion in his voice.

"You are a kind, good man Matthew Baxter. But, the words that will pass from my lips to yours will change everything." Her eyes continued to fill with water.

"Then don't tell me," he said simply. "We'll just enjoy the day. All month long I've thought of nothing but you. We don't need to hurry our day with bad news. Naomi has fixed us the best picnic basket in the world, let's just enjoy that and when you're up to it, then we'll talk." Matthew was surprised at the transformation that crossed her pale features. That was the look he'd been expecting.

"Yes, "she said with conviction. "You're right. Thank you."

The two of them lay on the soft Indian blanket for hours talking about their lives. Emmy told him how different her life had been before they came out West. How much she missed her father even though he had been a hard man to be around. Constantly demanding so much from her mother. Expecting even more. And how disappointed he had been in the unforgiving soil every time he would place a sharpened blade to it. "I remember how hard mother cried when he passed." With conviction she gazed into the handsome man's questioning face. "But I didn't. It was more like a since of peace for me. He seemed so unhappy. I think he's in a better place now."

Matthew watched the changing expressions on her freckled face so intently that he got lost in the rhythm of her words. Her soft voice was like a lullaby to his ears. He adored her smile and the honesty in her warm looking eyes. But more than that he loved the kindness that expelled from her heart like a warm ray from the afternoon sun. He could tell by her actions that she was intelligent.

But more than that she wasn't snotty or filled with untrue intentions. She was solid as a rock. A rare find in this savage land.

"Are you listening?" she giggled.

"To every word." He mused.

She told him how sad her mother had been at the loss of her sister's and little brother. That burying them nearly killed her. How hard it had been to get everything done alone on the small homestead in the time of her mother's grieving. "I sold as much of the livestock as we could afford to live without. I kept the milk cow and chickens." She let out a deep sigh. "They didn't bring much but at least it paid what we owed." It felt good to get so many miseries off of her chest so she told him how they struggled to plant the full hundred acres. "I didn't seem right putting the blade to the ground. I could feel its resistance. So, mother and I after she got better made do with what was tilled." She told him what a great cook her mother was and that she had taught her as well. How much she missed the old piano that laid in pieces on the prairie when it fell out of the wagon. She let out a light giggle, "Now, I did cry over that!"

"You're quite amazing," Matthew said sincerely.

"You don't know me well enough to give me that much credit," she laughed through embarrassed eyes.

"I think I know enough." As he looked into her wholesome face he knew that this lovely jewel fit him like an old worn glove. It didn't matter that she was a full figured woman. He enjoyed being able to look her directly in the face without bending over like a stooping willow just to talk. He'd enjoyed holding an ample body next to his at the Harvest dance. Not some petite scrawny stick that would break at his touch. Honestly, there wasn't anything about Emmy that he didn't love. And someday if she'd have him she'd be his wife. He could feel it.

"And you?" Emmy questioned.

"Me?" Matthew had been lost in her presence.

"I've sat here and done all of the talking. What about you, Matthew Baxter? Where do your dreams lie?"

"Well, as you know," he grinned at her lovely face. "I don't have just one mother. You should be grateful for that by the way. I have two. I learned from a very young age that their word is the law. Don't rebel against it. Believe me it doesn't work! I've a—had my breeches warmed up a time or two for that!" They both laughed uncontrollably. "But, their hearts are always in the right place. I wouldn't want to be the one that went against them. Stood on the other side of their values. I've seen what they can do and I don't want no part of that." Matthew stared intently into her engrossed brown eyes. "I saw my mother walk through a coiled nest of rattlers, pick up two or three of the scaly varmints, milk the venom from their fangs, then placed them gently back on the ground. I'll tell you one thing; I wasn't getting out of that wagon!"

"Why would they do such a thing?" Emmy asked breathlessly.

"It's for some serum that they and they alone know how to make. Chief Mad Dog taught it to them when they were really young. In fact, if you listen to papa he has all kinds of tales about Liza and Lizzie with Chief Mad Dog. The two of them were like little heathens. No one could control them but papa. And on more than one occasion he'd have to go to the Chiefs camp and bring them home. But," he gently brushed back her hair, "while they held him captive."

"They held him captive?" she giggled.

"That's what papa said. Who really knows? I guess it was the old Chief that taught them 'Magic Medicine'." He gave her a slight smile. "They live by it." He stated truthfully. "And, it has saved many a life."

"They sound so amazing!" she was so sincere.

"Those two," he laughed, "are as wild as the wind and just as unpredictable. Don't let them fool you. Cross them, you'll pay the price."

As the day progressed they ate their delicious picnic that Naomi had made just for them. "Do you swim?"

"Is the water deep?" her voice hesitated.

"Not for you and I," he said in a respectful tone.

"Mother hasn't let me go near the water since my baby brother drowned."

"There's no reason to be afraid of the water, Emmy. You and I, we're tall people. You won't drown, I won't let you," he said sweetly. "And not only that, it's perfectly warm." He gave her a reassuring smile. "I love it here. Mother says it's the pond of healing. Magic. I guess when Naomi was a little girl Aunt Lizzie brought her out here. Actually, they brought all three of us out here. Something happened in our family the day that we were born that no one will talk about and I doubt we'll ever know the real truth. Anyway, Aunt Lizzie swears that it's healing water." He gave her a confident smile.

Emmy looked into Matthew's warm trusting eyes. Maybe the water would do her bruises some good. Maybe it would be magical enough to wash away her wounds. Maybe it would have a way of erasing all of the ugly dirtiness that she felt inside. "I need some magical healing, Matthew," she said as she stepped into the warm water.

"Why?" he asked simply.

"There is something that I have to tell you. I don't want to," she said as she took a stand of conviction. "I've been trying to ignore it all day. But you don't understand my behavior and it's only fair that you do."

"You do seem different." Matthew confirmed in a worried tone. "I thought you'd be happy to see me. But, if there's someone els..."

Emmy stopped him point blank. "Matthew," she said as her eyes filled with water, "when mother and I were on our way home from the harvest dance," she paused for a brief moment. "Some men stopped us in the middle of the road."

Matthew's heart started pounding in his chest. "Men? What kind of men?"

Emmy looked directly into his face. "They were waiting for us just inside the shadows about a half mile from the ranch. The knot on my mother's forehead or the cut on the back of her head, they're not from the henhouse, Matthew. It's from falling out of the wagon when one of the dirty skunks hit her over the head with the butt of their gun."

"What?" He couldn't believe what he was hearing. "Who hit her over the head?"

"I don't know they had masks on."

"What?" he was so shocked at her confession. "Mask's! What kind of cowards hide behind masks?"

Tears of anger slid down her flushed cheeks as she slid the soft cotton dress from her body and stood in her shortened petticoat. Matthew let out a loud gasp as he stared at the paling bruises on her skin. "There were five of them," her voice was barely audible as she looked into his disbelieving face, "I think. I'm not sure. They all …," her voice caught in her throat. She hung her head and stared at the steaming water in shame. Then she faced him again. "They tied me to the wagon wheels. I couldn't reach mother. Believe me I tried! I thought she was dead! I thought they had killed her! I wish they would have killed me." She broke down. I don't remember all of it. Just bits and pieces till I passed out. It was dawn when mother finally came to and found me lying there. I never saw her cry that hard even when we buried father, Sissy, Toby, or little Sam. She was so dizzy she could barely untie me. But, somehow I managed to crawl in the wagon as she covered me up and took me straight home." Her long scabbed fingers skimmed the top of the steaming water. "I haven't told anyone," she stared into his reddened face, "but you. And you were the last person I wanted to tell." Her voice was barely audible.

Matthew's reaction was nothing like she'd expected. "Let me see!" he demanded fervently. "Pull up your slip! Let me see!"

"Why!" Emmy demanded, "So you can mock what has happened!"

"Pull up your slip!" he demanded in a more controlled tone.

"Fine!" Emmy said. "I've nothing to hide now!" Quietly she did as she was told.

"No!" he screamed as he saw the horrible blue and yellow colors that ran down her inner thighs. "Turn around!" he demanded. There was no mistaking his loud howl when he saw the festered blisters from the small stones and cactus that lay hidden in a puss-like mass on her fleshy skin. "Curs!" he yelled over and over. "I'll kill every mother's sons of em! I will!"

Emmy stood with her hands over her ears. Trying desperately to block out the aching pain in Matthew's voice. "I'm sorry," she wept shamefaced. "I am. I tried, Matthew, to fight them off! I tried! But, there were too many! I'm so ashamed! They said if I told that they would come back and kill us both in our sleep! I, I can't close my eyes without seeing them! They're everywhere I look! I haven't slept in weeks! I didn't know what to do!" she sobbed. "I'm so sorry!" She pounded her fists in the warm water. "I ruined it for both of us!"

In the next second Matthew stopped his uncontrollable ranting. Instantly, he put his large caring hands on her shaking shoulders. With his trembling finger he lifted her chin to meet his watered gaze. The kind compassion that lay there took her breath away. Those crystal blue eyes told her that he didn't blame her at all.

"I'm so sorry," she wept through sobbing lips as he pulled her to him and held her tight as they both slipped beneath the water in the warm steaming pond.

"I have to tell my mother," Matthew said matter-of-factly as he stroked her long curly hair as they lay against the side of the bank like two reeds of grass.

"She will hate me," Emmy wept. "She will think that I am weak. That my body is cursed."

"She will love your courage. She will hate whoever did this to you. They will help you."

"And you?" she asked through anxiety ridden eyes. "How can you love something that is spoiled?"

"Spoiled? What an odd word. You could never be spoiled to me, Emmy. I love you."

With that being said, Emmy threw her arms around his full muscled neck as they cried together. It seemed like an eternity when the warm afternoon sun started to play hide-n-seek with the late evening clouds. Neither one of them wanted to leave. It was so peaceful here in the arms of the healing pool. And as the daylight started to fade Matthew tipped Emmy's sweet face to meet his gaze as he spoke in a soft loving tone. "Emmy," tenderly he gently touched her long curly hair. "Will you marry me someday? Not tomorrow or anything like that, but someday when you're ready? Would you?" he asked lovingly. "I can't imagine my life without you now. Here in my arms, it's where you belong. I don't want to live without you. I don't want you to live without me. Will you?"

"Matthew Baxter," she wept. "You never cease to amaze me! I would be proud to be your wife," she said with a sigh. "Till death do us part?"

"Till death do us part. May I?"

"I've been waiting since the moment I laid eyes on you." She swooned. "Yes." Gently, as though she were a precious flower he placed a kiss on her waiting lips. "You'll always be my Emmy."

It was nearly dusk when the wagon pulled into the Baxter ranch. Liza, Lizzie, and Hattie were all waiting on the large landing anticipating the bouncing duo's arrival. Seeing them ride through the arched gate, knowing they were safely home they all let out a sigh of relief. It was very evident from the happy looks on both of their faces that something wonderful had happened.

Still there was no missing the concerned look on Hattie's worried face. She knew they would be returning home tonight in the dark, beneath the stars. She hadn't forgotten the last time they did that.

Emmy and Matthew were hand in hand as they approached the waiting women. "Mother, Auntie, Hattie, were you worried?" he asked sincerely.

"It's late," Hattie said in a concerned tone.

"Yes, Ma'am it is, that," he said without hesitation. "That's why I thought maybe you could spend the night and go home in the morning, when it's daylight. You two can have my room. I'll bunk with Jeffrey. If he even bothers to come home tonight."

"Mother, may I talk with you and Aunt Lizzie in private please?" His tone was so determined.

"Surely, we'll help put the horses away," Liza said in a motherly fashion. "Dancing Bear would you show our guests to Matthew's room?"

"See you in a while," Matthew said caringly to Emmy as he gave her a knowing wink.

As the threesome walked toward the barn Jeffrey rode in. Lizzie never gave him the time of day but Matthew acknowledged him immediately. "Hey, brother, listen we have company so try behaving would you?" he stated.

"That means you," Lizzie said in a hard tone just wanting him to say something crude.

"I despise you!" he yelled as he wiped his horse around and rode out.

"Good riddance," she mumbled under her breath as the threesome disappeared into the barn.

Once they were out of sight of the others Matthew turned with an ashen face and said, "Mother!" His voice was high pitched and hysterical both Liza and Lizzie jumped from the intensity of it. "They raped her! The dirty curs took turns and they raped her! She's got bruises everywhere! Everywhere! I, I tried to be brave so she would feel better but..." he sobbed. "She was mine and they hurt her!" Like a broken child he fell to his knees on the floor of the wide open barn. Lizzie immediately pulled his face to hers, startled at his abnormal behavior.

"Who hurt her?" she demanded.

"I don't know!" he countered.

"Aunt Lizzie," he wept openly as though his heart was dying, struggling for a breath of air beneath his trembling knees, "mother. She's so badly bruised. She is. Can you look at her? Can you fix her for me? Like when I was a boy? You always know how to make everything better. Please," he begged as he held his sobbing head in his hands. "They hurt her mother, so badly!"

Liza squatted next to her ailing son. "Who has done this terrible thing?"

Matthew's tearful face engulfed his mothers. "She doesn't know. They had masks over their faces. I, I said that you could help her. You and Aunt Lizzie. She's so ashamed!" he hollered completely out of control. "They hurt her and she's ashamed! What makes that right! What!" he hollered as his emotions ran rapid. "If I find them I'll kill em all! Every one of their filthy hides! I've never killed anyone, but I'll kill every mother's sons' of em!" he sobbed. "I will," he cried as his voice faded.

"How long," Lizzie asked in the most compassionate tone that Matthew had ever heard her speak as she held his chin in her work worn hands. Her cool blue eyes were sorry and he lost himself in the comfort of them.

"The night of the harvest dance. They were waiting for them. Hattie got bad hurt, too. Not like Emmy, but the knot on her head, that's not from some old chicken coupe, it's from falling out of the wagon. I bet if you looked she has one on the back of her head to match it. She's too old to fall from a wagon mother," he said compassionately. "They could have killed her!" He looked desperately into his mother's weeping eyes. "I should have escorted them home!"

Liza held her son for several minutes as his hysteria started to subside. Only he would find the worry to fear for the safety of an old woman. "You tell her that we will come when everyone is asleep. It will be just between us." Her cool blue eyes shared her son's heartache. "Now, wipe the worry from your face, and dry your eyes. This matter will be between Lizzie, me, and the Mighty One."

Matthew did as he was told. "Thank you, mother."

CHAPTER 20

There was no missing the terror in Emmy's scared brown eyes when Liza and Lizzie walked into Matthew's room with a small green leather bag. Immediately, she stared at the floor. Hattie folded her work-worn hands as she sat in the old rocker and said nothing. Her daughter had told her all she needed to know. The compassionate faces of the twin mother's told her the rest.

Lizzie walked to where the shamed girl sat on the edge of the bed and smiled down at her lovely face. Matthew was right, she was very pretty. Her size certainly didn't take away from that. And standing here, they could both see what a good match they really were. But more than that, there was no missing the heartache in the features of that lovely face. There was no denying the fact that some disgusting maggot had carelessly stolen the flower of her innocence. Ripped it from her young body the way you would tear a beautiful flower from the earth. Leaving nothing behind but a shallow hole of emptiness. She and Liza would see if they couldn't at least put a part of the bloom back. "Emmy," Lizzie whispered, "don't ever look down; it's not up to you to carry their guilt."

Tears fell like rain from her fevered eyes as she looked into the kind circles that she had respected for such a long time. "I fought as hard as I could!" she held out her large hands. She had the scabbed knuckles to prove it. "I knew what was going to happen," she stated matter-of-factly. "I wanted to run but I couldn't. I didn't know if they'd killed my mother or not when she hit the ground." Sympathetically, she looked into Lizzie's heartfelt face, "It was an awful sound. She hit so hard! I screamed for her but no one was there to hear me." Lovingly, she stared into her mother's tear-stained face, "I'm so sorry, mother." Then, she straightened her back, "I stood my ground! I kicked them, bit them did everything but kill them! But there were too many." She shut her eyes as if to block out the whole scene. "I screamed and screamed." Then she gave them a discarded look. "Only the weeping wind heard me."

"Of course there were too many," comforted Liza as she placed her hand on the young woman's forehead. She had a fever.

Then Emmy's eyes became stormy and frightened, "They said if I told anyone that they would come back and kill us while we slept!" Her eyes pleaded for their understanding, "I haven't been able to sleep for weeks. All I can see when I close my eyes are their ugly masked faces and smell their sour breath." Then, Emmy looked from one twin to the other, "I was going to kill myself. I wanted to, until today."

"And what happened today?" Liza asked sincerely. Glad that the woman hadn't taken her own life.

"I told…Matthew." She gazed into their questioning eyes. "I told him everything. At least what I could remember. I passed out." Then she gazed into Liza's concerned face. "You must be an amazing woman. Mother." she said through trembling lips. "Because not once did he blame me. He called them, cowards and said," her voice cracked, "how could one lone girl and her broken mother fight off so many. It was like he knew." She stared lovingly into Liza's angry face, "You must be an amazing woman to have raised such a good son."

"My son makes his own decisions. He is the master of his rights or wrongs. The Mighty One tells us not to interfere. But, in this matter our hearts say someone will pay for their hostile actions. They will feel his wrath."

"Thank you," she whispered.

Liza looked into her reddened face. "You set the worries of their voice behind you. We will set their eyes into darkness. No one will come into this house to hurt you. There are no bad worries here. Only peace."

"Coming threw me or sister will be the only way in, there'd be no way out. You're safe here," Lizzie stated in an understanding tone, "tonight, we will see to it that when you close your eyes, instead of dark looming shadows, sleep will bid you goodnight." Then, she continued in a disgusted tone, angry that someone would even use such a deceitful trick. "Now, let us see what can be done here."

"I'm really sore," she confessed like a small child. Thankful that she didn't have to keep the horrible secret anymore.

"Of course you are. Has your womanly time come since the attack," Lizzie asked in a soothing tone.

"No," she said meekly. "That's what scares me the most. What if…?"

"You need to take your nightgown off and lay on the bed now and let us take a look see," Liza instructed.

She was a sweet girl with a gentle loving spirit. That was plain to see. No wonder Matthew was so smitten with her. Even after all that she had been through she had a forgiveness about her that was overwhelming.

She followed the twins' instructions with no hesitation as Lizzie inspected her back and buttock. Matthew had been right. There was a lot of dirt under her skin and it was infected. That would be easy to cure with a bit of their special salve. As she lay on her back Liza let out a gasp. The sight of the front of her body was hideous. Lizzie shuddered at the thought of the pain that must have been inflicted to her young delicate skin.

It was plain to see that she was lucky she'd survived the attack at all. As they lifted her legs and inspected her inner thighs, they both were angry instantly. Their chatter was in Naomi's native tongue. Emmy didn't understand a word but she knew that the two sisters were furious.

Gently, Liza rubbed a salve along the inside of her delicately bruised skin as she explained the comforting effect that it would have. The throbbing sting started to disappear within seconds of its application as the young woman began to relax. As Lizzie felt up inside Emmy's torn body it was plain to see that she was in fact pregnant. A sad expression washed across her face as she looked into her sister's heated eyes.

"Emmy," Liza said as she sat by her side, "you are with child."

Emmy started sobbing, "No! I can't be!"

Gently, Liza held her in her arms. "There's so much damage." She held her breath. "I doubt that you will be that way for long."

"I agree," Lizzie said in a regretful tone. "There's just too much injury to the baby chamber." Together they stepped away from the young weeping woman. "Later will risk her life."

"We've seen it before." Liza voice was so quiet. "She'll bleed to death."

"It is not a decision we can make sister." Lizzie stated as her eyes filled with angry tears. "The Mighty One will chose."

"Mother," Emmy whimpered. "What do I do?"

Hattie gave her daughter a weak smile, "I cannot make that choice, Emmy."

"I don't want to die. I've barely gotten to live," she sniffed. "But, I ca." Emmy's words were cut short as her face turned white. Instantly, she grabbed her stomach. "Ahh!" she screamed in pain. "Mother! It hurts so bad!"

Immediately, the twins ran to where Emmy lay. "Today, the choice was made for you. The Mighty One says, you have suffered enough." They wrapped the bloody mass within the stained sheet placed it into a small basket. Then they started talking in the foreign language that she didn't understand. Their eyes carried the same relieved look.

As if their fingers were made of feathers they carefully cleansed the bruised area between her bloodied legs. Then they gently sewed several torn patches of skin. "Now Emmy," they said in unison, "this may sting for just a second. It will pass in the blink of an eye." Then, they gently placed their special poultice within the spoiled flesh and laid a thick heavy cloth between her legs. There would be no reason to carry the guilt of this unthinkable situation around anymore.

From the expression on Emmy's face it was plain to see that she was grateful that the two women had taken the time to help her at all. Her body had been badly beaten by a troop of barbarians but they hadn't stolen her soul. No, she'd fought for that. And they didn't steal the love in her heart, for she'd given her heart to someone kind and warm before this hideous deed ever happened. The two women could plainly see that it wouldn't be hard to fall in love with Emmy Paul.

"Matthew was right," she sighed, "you didn't blame me."

"There's no blame when the fault of the hurt is at the hands of another," Lizzie whispered in a compassionate tone. "Now, I want you to drink this tea. Close your eyes. And let the whisper of my voice take away the hurt. Can you do that for us?"

"Of course," she smiled as the warm liquid slid down her throat.

"We want you to lie still for as long as you can. Remember, you're safe here." Then, Liza looked into Hattie's tearstained face, "You're next."

"Is mother staying in here with me?" Emmy whispered. There was no missing the fear in her voice.

"Of course. This is a mother's place." Liza stated matter-of-factly. "Close your eyes, Emmy and sleep." Liza's voice was full of compassion.

Hattie knew that there would be no sense in arguing with the two self proclaimed doctors. She patiently sat in the old rocker as they inspected the mark on her forehead and the cut on the back of her skull. "Did this bleed very long?" Liza asked.

"A couple of days," Hattie answered regrettably.

"Sister, I need the scissors," Liza instructed. "I'm going cut some of the hair away, Hattie. Not much, just enough to tend the wound."

Lizzie sat and watched as Liza's skilled fingers cleaned out the wound, then placed some of their special salve on the bruised skin. "That will heal up nicely, Hattie. Just try not to hit it with your comb or brush. I didn't take off too much hair," she kidded. "We will be checking on both of you in the morning. I think maybe you'll be staying a couple of extra days." Gently, she patted Emmy's thigh as she stood up. "Good. She's asleep already. Now, you go to sleep too, Hattie. We'll see to it that no one enters the confines of these walls. Sister," Liza said. Like two well oiled machines they left the room and headed directly for the barn. When they walked within the confines of the open room they ran smack dab into Jeffrey.

"A little late isn't it," Lizzie asked, still furious from their last encounter.

"Maybe for you," he snapped back.

"You know, Jeffrey," Lizzie said as she backed the arrogant young man up against the wooden stall, "one of these days you're going to open that big yap of yours and someone is going to put a bullet in it."

"Is that a threat?" he countered.

"Nope, a fact," she seethed. Lizzie had come to dislike the smart mouthed boy even more since he'd been hanging around his hooligan gang of thugs. He reminded her so much of Jacob. Then she looked him straight in the face, hanging inches away from his nose. "Where did you say you went after the harvest dance?"

He was immediately on the defensive. "I drank some whiskey and came home. Why? Did you lose your pet rattlesnake?"

"If I did," she threatened, "you'd of found it in your bed. And by the way, you sleep in the barn tonight, we have guests." With her last remark she turned and walked away toward one of the other stalls.

"Why do you rile her so?" Liza asked in a tired tone. "You know she's going to win in the end."

"Someday she won't," he stated hotly.

"Well, if she ever comes up missing I'll know who to blame," Liza sighed

"Don't you ever get tired of hanging on to her shirt-tail mother?" Jeffrey was completely frustrated with his mother's constant defense of his meddling aunt.

"And what shirttail would that be?" she inquired patiently.

"Mother! You act like you can't think for yourself! She always tells you what to do, when to do it! Man!" he threw his hands up in the air, frustrated as his sea green eyes probed her unwavering face.

"I love Lizzie," Liza said simply with conviction, "she's my sister."

"I'm your son! Do you love me the same way, mother?" he countered putting her on the spot. "Do you?"

"You make it hard for anyone to love you, Jeffrey." Instantly, she turned to follow her sister.

"Mother," he said in a smart tone as he kicked the dirt with his foot, "Who's our so-called company that Matthew is so excited about?"

"Hattie and Emmy have come to help Dancing Bear out for a couple of days till Maria is feeling better."

Jeffrey's heart started pounding in his chest like a hundred drums. For a brief moment he lost his breath completely. How was he going face her? "It just keeps getting better! Who's the next stray dog you'll be bringing home, mother?"

"Did you hear me?" Liza asked as she stood inches away from her son.

Jeffrey jumped a foot. "Yes, yes I did mother," he said in a quiet voice.

"So, behave yourself!" Lizzie's voice echoed across the barn in a commanding tone as she headed back toward the old log house.

"What I do is none of your stinking business!" he snapped back at the fading shadow. "You're not my mother!"

As Jeff put his horse in the stall Liza couldn't help but notice a large bruise on the back of his neck just below his collar. "Goodness," Liza said as she got a better look. "Where did you get a mark like that?"

"Horsing around, you know guy stuff," he stated as he blew off her remark.

"Take off the shirt, let me see," she demanded in an untrusting tone.

Reluctantly, Jeffrey did as he was told. He had a bruise all right. Like a mule had kicked him in the middle of his left shoulder. It looked very painful and Liza was sure that it was. "Hold on a minute," she instructed as she rubbed some of her magic salve on dark skin as she spoke, "some horsing around."

"Mother, please don't tell anyone. Aunt Lizzie already thinks that I'm a sissy. Please don't give her any more ammunition. Please," he begged.

Liza let out a deep sigh, "I don't know where you get these notions. All right but you best be careful. You could have fractured your shoulder blade."

"Ah, I'm all right," he mumbled.

Liza gazed into her son's disconnected face. "I don't understand this new man that stands in front of me."

"What new man?" He seemed surprised.

"You my son. I fear for your life if you continue to walk down this path." She paused, "I see many lies hiding behind your fathers eyes. Lies I'm sure I would not understand. I've lost enough from this life, I pray I won't lose you, too."

Jeffrey stood there, shocked at his mother's confession, "Ah, I ain't going no where's momma." Then he abruptly turned around and walked to the back of the barn. Minutes later she heard the wooden door slam behind him.

CHAPTER 21

Several weeks came and went with little activity at the Baxter ranch. Emmy seemed to get stronger with each passing day. Liza and Lizzie made sure of it. Constantly checking her progress every morning. On the last day before their departure back to their small homestead Liza sat at the end of the bed and looked sadly into Emmy's soft brown eyes. "Emmy," she said gently, "there is something that needs to be said. Something that you need to know."

There was no missing the concern on the two women's faces. "All right," she answered bravely. "But, I am feeling much better."

"I see you are and it makes me very happy. But, I must tell you there was a lot of damage to the chamber which holds the fruit that you are so willing to bear. It was badly torn and now it is weak. The delicate chamber won't hold your delicate petals, Emmy. There will be no babies. We, sister, and I couldn't fix that."

"No, babies?" she whispered in a barely audible tone. "Are you sure?"

"Yes." They said in unison.

"Matthew wants babies. I want babies." Like a lost soul she placed her weeping face in her hands. "No one will want me now," she cried brokenheartedly. "I've ruined everything! I should have fought harder!" Her eyes begged for the older lady to understand. "I don't want me, why would, Matthew?"

A burning hatred started to grow in Liza's chest. She was so angry! So, furious with whomever had done this travesty to this lovely young girl. Then, her soul quieted as she touched her shoulder, "Then, you don't know my son."

"What?" Emmy said through sobbing lips.

"Matthew is a good man. He knows what horrible deed has been done here. And when I see the way he looks at you, I know that no baby will change that. So, you dry those eyes and stiffen that back young lady because you have paid a price that many will never pay."

Emmy threw her arms around Liza's neck as she held her tight. "Thank you, Liza, thank you for not blaming me."

"There's no blame for the innocent," she stated matter-of-factly. "Now, I'll give you a minute to get ready, then we'll see you down stairs." Gently, she touched Emmy's trembling chin as she gave her a knowing nod. Together the two women left the room.

When they closed the door behind them Lizzie stared into her sister's forlorn face, "If I find out that Jeffrey had anything to do with this, I will kill him."

As Liza stared into her sister's angry face she proclaimed, "If I find out that Jeffrey did this, you won't have to worry, I will kill him myself!" Like two warriors they headed down the long stairway.

Hattie had totally enjoyed teaching her student Dancing Bear the art of cooking. She was so willing to learn. And in doing so, Hattie had learned a few short cuts herself. The woman was beyond generous with her skills and her language. Between the two of them, they made the perfect pair.

Clinton made several sporadic unannounced appearances, coming and going, always jotting something down on his checkered tablet mumbling to himself. If he had any questions he would find Liza or Lizzie and ask them about some rock or tree in a ravine or ridge out in the middle of nowhere. "Are you sure?" he would say, then walk off with a smile on his face as though a firefly had lit a dark chamber in his brain.

Jeffrey spent hardly any time at the ranch since Hattie and Emmy had showed up. He said he'd been seeking refuge in the hills. Neither twin believed him. He'd given his mother the impression that he hadn't been welcome at the ranch lately and he was better off out on the prairie.

Abe and Matthew had been in the office all week working on some huge lumber deal that couldn't seem to wait. The men from the Eastern Building Co. in a faraway territory past the ridges of the Bighorn Mountains. They wanted a signed contract which was nearly impossible to fill on such a short notice. Abe said yes, Matthew said, no. No, was the final answer.

Matthew stood at the side of the wagon wishing that Emmy didn't have to leave but the time had come to go home. It was evident in those striking blue eyes that he wanted her to stay here forever. "We'll be checking on you from time to time," Matthew said caringly. "I'll miss you."

"Me, too," Emmy gushed through misty eyes as she gave him a huge hug and placed a sweet kiss on his lips. "Till next time." Then she turned and faced the two identical women that stood on the wooded porch. Purposely, she walked to where they were. Her eyes had an undisclosed amount of respect. They had saved what little dignity she'd had left and found a way for her soul to become blameless, blooming all over again like the wildflowers that caressed the prairie. There were no words to express how she felt about these two iron-handed women. As though it were as natural as breathing, she gave each one a heartfelt hug. For a brief moment they seemed embarrassed. No one hugged Liza and Lizzie Baxter! No one! "Thank you," she whispered, "for everything."

As the twosome rode out of the Baxter ranch, Jeffrey rode in. There was no denying the look of hatred that escaped his probing eyes as the wagon with the two women in it passed the hooligan. "Ladies," he said in a cocky tone.

Hattie stared directly into his inebriated face as she clucked the horses. "Git!"

Neither woman acknowledged Jeffrey's gesture which irritated him to the next level. How dare they snub me! Who did they think they are? Like a thundercloud he rode to the barn and dismounted. Seething to himself he decided that something would have to be done about Emmy and the old hag that she called a mother. They both needed to learn a little respect! Besides, there was no way that fat hog was going to marry his brother! They were Baxter's after all and only a proper woman would influx this family. He thought he'd taken care of that the night of the harvest dance. Obviously, his verbal insults hadn't worked. He was going to have to come up with something a lot better than what he did to sabotage this so-called love affair.

As he roughly yanked his horse's bridle out of his mouth, Jeffrey ran smack dab into Charlie. There was no missing the disgust on the older man's face for the way that he treated the sweating animal. "What are you looking at old man?" he challenged.

But, Jeffrey didn't see Luke as he walked up to the side of him. Furious with his mistreatment of the small bay he pushed Jeffrey aside like a raging bull. "What in the devil's gate is the matter with you? You'll break his bloomin' teeth off doing that!" Patiently, he scanned the mouth of the waiting horse. Satisfied that the animal's condition was all right he continued, "If I ever see you do that again you harebrained prairie digger, I'll put a bit in your mouth and do the same thing to you!" he threatened angrily. "You're lucky Lizzie didn't see that! She'd be riding your sorry carcass around this compound with a snaffle bit in your mouth!"

Embarrassed, Jeffrey turned his anger toward Charlie who stood there smirking at the fact that the boy had been caught red handed with his hateful conduct. "What are you laughing at old man?" he sneered.

Charlie chose to ignore the remark and walked toward the back of the barn, but underneath he sorely wanted to put a bullet right between those hateful green eyes.

"I'm talking to you!" Jeffrey hollered in an engaging tone.

"Shut up you durned fool!" Luke hollered. "One turn on that pistol and he'd put a hole in you the size of this ranch!" The horseman was so angry that he hollered, "Now, get outta my barn if'n you can't be more respectful than that you dern'd troublemaker!"

Furious and embarrassed Jeffrey half walked, half ran toward the old log house and slammed the door to his room. No one heard from him for the rest of the night.

CHAPTER 22

Later that evening Lizzie felt a demanding rap on her door. When she opened it, Dancing Bear's tear stained face was waiting. "She better, not. Need come."

Immediately, Lizzie grabbed her green leather bag and followed her to Maria's room. When she arrived she knew that the wonderful old cook wouldn't make it through the night. "Go get Liza and Naomi," she said in a stern tone to the shaken Indian woman. "So," Lizzie said through tear-filled eyes to the old worn out Mexican lady as she softly sat down on the bed, "you didn't think I needed any sleep tonight or what?"

The older woman lovingly placed her hand in Lizzie's palm. "I never tell you bout, mother. She no goot. Bad blood inside," she whispered as she coughed until her ashen face turned red.

"Your mother or mine?" Lizzie questioned in a puzzled tone just as Liza and Naomi walked into the room. The look that Lizzie gave them told the story of her impending demise.

Immediately, Naomi's wildflower eyes filled with unshed tears. "Hi, Maria," she whispered through trembling lips. "You need not fret so, we're all here."

The old woman patted the top of Naomi's soft young hand. "You goot girl just like mother, Lizzie. Her heart kind like butterfly, full honor. You honor," she whispered through fevered lips as she took her last breath. As Lizzie's trembling fingers closed her frozen eyes, all three women wept like lost children.

"I'll go tell father," Lizzie said in a forlorn tone. "He's going to be awful upset."

Upset was an understatement when Lizzie told her father the bad news. She thought he was going to collapse. "I, I knew she was sick, but not that sick!" he worried. "I would have done something, anything!"

"We did all we could father. It was her time to fly."

"But, I could have…"

"No, father, you couldn't."

"I should have…"

"No father, there was no time."

"We'll bury her tomorrow," he said sadly as he closed the old oak door to his den.

After they put sweet Maria's cold body to rest in the small cemetery everyone gathered round the kitchen table.

"Father," Liza said, "there is too much for Dancing Bear to do here alone. We need to hire someone to come in and help. Naomi can't do the extra work; I need her and the boy's with me right now."

"Would you consider hiring Hattie for a few months? I'm sure she could use the extra money," Lizzie asked.

"What about her livestock? What about her place? That's an awful lot to ask of someone, don't you think?" Abe countered.

"Father," Matthew said as he joined in on the conversation, "we can bring what they have over here. It can't be much. We have more than enough room to accommodate a couple of goats, chickens, and a milk cow for heaven's sake. Besides, Hattie has sold off just about all of the livestock they have to get by."

"You can ask her, but don't make it sound like charity. That woman has a lot of pride."

"Yes, sir," there was no missing the twinkle in Matthew's eyes. "I'll see if Jeffrey would like to ride over with me."

"That would be a nice gesture, maybe they would feel more comfortable if they knew that he was glad to have them here." Abe stated.

"Maybe." Cheerfully, he walked to Jeffrey's room and lightly knocked on the door, the smell of liquor reeked into the hallway. Matthew knew that he wouldn't be taking his brother anywhere.

CHAPTER 23

It had been at least a month since Maria's death. Hattie and Emmy had made themselves at home in the large old log house gladly excepting Abe's gracious offer. It couldn't have come at a better time as the town clerk had told them they would be losing the small acreage that they called home if their note of two hundred dollars couldn't be paid by the end of the week. It was a tremendous amount of money for a widow and her daughter to have to come up with before their harvest.

When Liza and Lizzie heard the distressing ultimatum that had been given to the kind older woman as she sat in Abe's office negotiating her salary they were both upset. "Who told you that?" Lizzie asked hotly.

"Dan Brans down at the clerk's office," Hattie said meekly. "He sent a man last week with papers. Twice. I have them in my bag." Then she looked into Abe's stern face. "I'm grateful that we, Emmy, and I have been given this opportunity. But, you don't worry. I will hold my own and Emmy will too. Charity never did sit well with me."

"I don't offer charity, Hattie. This is a working ranch." Abe stated matter-of-factly.

"Of course." The respect showed in her face. Glad this wasn't about charity.

Liza sat and watched the woman's calm and collected demeanor as she stared at the floor. "Hattie!" Liza snapped in a loud angry tone as the woman's head popped upward like a prairie dog from a hole. "Why are you looking at the floor? You're tougher than that! I know you are! Letting some jackal take your property without a fight! You're a hard working woman, don't you dare let anyone belittle you for that!"

"Honestly, Liza, I'm just about all out of fight. I am," she said through weary eyes "My losses here have been too much. I've nearly lost my whole family because of that piece of land. There's nights I don't sleep, don't eat. I worry all the time about how we will make ends meet." Hattie's older eyes were tired and worn out looking. "Maybe it's time to let go. Say, good riddance to it."

For a brief moment Liza was sorry that she had been so harsh with the woman. She had been through a lot. There was no denying that. So instead she offered, "Sell your land to me and Lizzie then."

"What?" The older woman was startled at her generous offer.

"Sell the land to us. I know just what we will do with it." Her blue probing eyes were intensely demanding.

"Are you sure?" Hattie asked through shaky lips. "That's an awful lot of money."

Liza's face was full of compassion as she stared into the wondering face of her identical sibling. There was no resistance there what-so-ever. Lizzie gave her a slight nod. "Yes."

"Father?" Liza and Lizzie said in unison as those crystal blue eyes drank in every ounce of his soul.

"By all means," he answered. Any other response would have been fruitless anyway.

"Well, that's settled then. Lizzie," Liza said in a business-like tone, "we'll be riding to town by the end of the week."

"Yep."

As the two hellcats walked from the confines of the large study Liza placed her hand on Hattie's shoulder as she smiled widely at her father with the slightest twinkle in her eye, "I expect we'll be flushing out a fox here shortly."

"It's about time we had a little fun, I was starting to get bored," Lizzie added.

Hattie gave Abe an odd look. "What?"

"Don't even ask. Just feel sorry for the fox."

Later that evening after everyone had gone to sleep the twins slipped within the confines of the barn. Together they saddled two of the green-broke horses to a special place within the shelter of their timbered escape. Today was the day of redemption and instead of going their typically well-trodden route, they went through the back deep within the thick timber so that no one would see them. A one horse trail that they had scouted out as young girls that never appealed to them. They were sure no one else on the ranch knew about. It had been years since they'd felt the necessity to use it. They'd never scouted it to the end.

Deep down in their souls, they knew that someone on the Baxter ranch was spinning yarns. Doing little deeds of deception that they didn't approve of. Putting people that they loved in harm's way. Hopefully today they would root out that demon and send them packing on their way to join the devil.

It was a beautiful ride and the two women enjoyed it immensely. Just sitting on the back of their horse's silently listening to the sweet melody of the chirping birds as they encouraged their journey. Feeling the beating hearts of the rustling leaves as they ducked their charming heads and waved them past. Hearing the sound of the cascading water from the cool clear creek as its feathered waves washed across the slick mossy rocks. Watching from afar as the blue open sky disappeared beneath the sheltering timber then reappeared from out of nowhere. It was truly an enchanting place.

The twins didn't want anyone to know where they were on this beautiful morning. They'd left their regular mounts at home on purpose so no one would suspect that they weren't around the ranch someplace doing chores. Purposely, they had hidden the animals in Albert's barn before they slipped within the confines of the small clerk's office. They had been there for quite a while hidden like two black widow spiders within the darkness of the small rooms.

Mr. Brans had no idea they were within fifty feet of him. They'd watched his demeanor go from glum to happy the closer it got to closing. They sat in silence as they watched him sift through the pile of papers on his desk. "Yes, yes!" Sweet surrender," he sighed as the clerk whistled a little tune. Nonchalantly, he walked to the safe but when he turned around he yiped like a dog getting clawed by a cat as he stared into the wily faces of Liza and Lizzie Baxter. They seemed to appear from out of nowhere.

"Liza, Lizzie," Dan Brans said in a nervous tone. "What brings you into town?" Anxiously, he looked around the room, there was no one else there but him. "I didn't hear you come in."

"It's Liza and Lizzie Baxter to you." Liza snapped.

"Of course." He said politely thinking how did they get in here?"

"We have some business that we need to take care of for a friend of ours," Liza continued in a stern manner.

"Really? And who might that be?" he questioned nervously as he gazed at the clock, then at his desk..

"Are you expecting someone?" The two women asked pretending to get up.

"No!" he snapped in a much quicker fashion than he had meant to. "There's no one," he continued in a softer tone as he glanced at the ticking clock. "Please." Neither woman missed the fact that the man had Hattie's file close at hand as he tucked it neatly beneath a stack of other papers. "And who might we be talking about?"

"Hattie Paul," Lizzie stated with a stone-like face.

"She sold us her property this afternoon," Liza continued.

"We've come to settle up on the deed." Lizzie was sure the pompous ass already knew that.

"Good, good," he said in an over exaggerated tone. "Believe me, I didn't want to have to do this. I've held off on foreclosing as long as I could. It's real nice of you to help Hattie out."

"We're not helping Hattie out of anything." Liza gave the man an unnerving look as though she could see right through him.

"We're buying a piece of ground that belongs to her," Lizzie injected.

"If we were helping her out, we'd of loaned her the money," Liza countered.

"Which we offered," Lizzie said.

"Which would have paid off the note," Liza said.

"And she declined," Lizzie continued.

"So, instead, we bought it." They said exactly at the same time in the same determined tone.

"I see, yes." He busied himself shuffling papers.

"It's a nice piece of property I'm surprised you don't have people standing in line to buy it." Lizzie studied his dishonest face.

"I have folks who are interested," he said in a defiant tone, trying to let the wily twosome know that he wasn't stupid. "It's a lot of money to come up with at such short notice. Especially since there are back taxes that have to be paid as well." He had an arrogant tone to his voice as he fiddled with his small spectacles making his tiny eyes look like a rat hiding in a hole.

"I didn't realize there were any back taxes. Hattie hadn't mentioned that. "Lizzie stated.

"You know how widows are, always looking for a handout." He was so smug!

"I don't know about handouts but I do have a piece of paper here that states she doesn't have any back taxes. Is that your signature?"

Anxiously, he grabbed the paper and pretended to squint to see it. "Yes, that could be my signature."

"Could or is?" Lizzies voice was demanding. "Look a little closer!"

"Yes! That is my signature!" his upper lip was starting to sweat.

So, in reality, the land shouldn't be in foreclosure. She has several months left to pay on it." Liza's probing eyes never left his. "So where is the back tax assessed at? I don't see it."

In self-defense he snapped, "Agnes must not have filed these papers properly!" Aghast he continued, "I've told her about that time and time again!"

"I'm sure you have," Lizzie said in disbelieving drawl. "What is the original amount of the payoff then?"

"I have a job to do too you know! I have my own responsibilities. If you let one person slide then they all want to!"

"Oh, I agree," Liza said. "I think it's only right that you yank a person's home out from over their head's. Throw them out into the prairie I say! Let the buzzards eat their bones raw!"

"Oh, I totally agree!" Lizzie stated. "Post diggin' squatters! Taking up land that ain't rightfully theirs!"

"Baxter land to boot!" Liza agreed with a warning look on her face.

Dan gave Lizzie a wide smile of recognition, totally agreeing with both women. That is until he saw their crystal blue eyes turn dark like a matched set of slithering vipers. The man sat back in his chair; he knew that they had been mocking him all along. His bottom lip quivered. "Well, we best get on with this. Five o'clock will be here before we know it. And I, unlike you, have an engagement to attend. "

"A hanging?" Lizzie questioned.

Dan gave her an exasperated look. "Yes, I see that the foreclosure amount is two hundred dollars." He was afraid to look directly into either woman's face for fear he'd turn to stone. "Yes, that's correct," he stuttered, "two hundred dollars."

"I'm wondering Dan, why there was such a rush on this particular piece of property. Did someone else want to assume ownership?"

"I've had several inquiries, yes," he countered trying to defend himself as he stared at the wily duo. He still hadn't figured out how they got into his office. "But then, I might ask you the same question. How did you come about purchasing this particular parcel. Don't you have enough land?"

"The land doesn't belong to us, Dan. We're merely its guardian." Liza's voice was calm and controlled. "We protect it from people like you that want to rip its veins from its beating heart."

"I can see wanting to sell it, but why would you stick your neck out on what appears to be an illegal foreclosure," Lizzie inquired. "Unless whoever this person is has the cash and you were hoping to make a quick buck."

"Are you accusing me of something Lizzie?" he snapped.

"Maybe."

"Then you should know that I can't act until the title cleared. Of course, it won't make any difference now especially since there doesn't seem to be any back taxes."

"Of course," they said at the same time.

Dan gave the two women a dirty look as he jumped from his chair and pretended to open the small safe. "Now what did I do with that file?"

There was no denying the heavy footsteps that pounded across the board walk in front of his office just as someone turned the knob on the front door. The twins' heads snapped around at the same time. Immediately, he tried to distract the intimidating duo. "Liza, Lizzie," he said in an overly loud voice. "I'm having trouble finding the title." Making sure whoever was outside could hear him.

Liza and Lizzie jumped to their feet as they hurried toward the open window. Immediately, the footsteps jumped from the wooden sidewalk into the crowd of people. By the time the twin's made it to the opening and pulled back the curtains it was impossible to tell who'd been standing there watching them, listening. As they continued to scan the crowded street, out of the corner of her eye, Lizzie caught just a faint glimpse of a man with blonde curly hair and broad shoulders as he disappeared behind the livery stable. For a brief moment she had an odd feeling in the pit of her stomach. Then as quickly as the motion came, she dismissed it.

What they really wanted to do was dismiss themselves and go catch the intruder red- handed but the clock was ticking and they both knew beyond the shadow of a doubt that the slippery weasel sitting behind the odd looking desk would throw the metal bar across those hard wooden doors behind them and they would lose the very thing they'd come to save.

As the sister's gave each other a knowing look that said they were pretty sure who they'd seen, they walked proudly back into the clerk's desk nearly knocking him to the floor as he stood inches behind them. The three of them intentionally sat down. Liza gave the irritating man a leading look as his groping eyes followed her long slender fingers as they pulled a small brown bag out of her shirt. Purposely, she left several buttons undone as she diligently counted out several bills, accidentally dropping one or two of them. "Oh, sister, can you help me?"

There was no missing the desire in the bankers wanting eyes. To say that this woman was anything less than pure prime beef would be an understatement. But, when he looked up he swore he stared directly into the face of the devil. "There ain't nothing in there for you!"

Then as though something pulled him back to reality he asked coldly, "To whom will this be deeded?"

"Liza and Lizzie Baxter," Liza said in a professional manner.

"You won't be using your married name of Jones?" he asked surprised at the titled names.

"No," she said respectfully, "my children are Jones. I'm still a Baxter."

Lizzie sat and watched the busy man the way a lion anticipates his next living meal as he studied the document. She didn't like his offhanded mannerism and she didn't like his insinuations either.

"There just one more thing," he said smartly. Complicating the exchange even more. "I need Hattie's signature here," he pointed at a bare line. "Before I can legally sign this over to you." He had a huge smirk on his face. "I don't suppose you have her signature on you?"

Lizzie took in a deep sigh. "No. Sister do you?

"No."

"We've got something better." Intentionally, Liza got up and walked to the door and opened it, "Hattie, can you come in here please." Within minutes the woman made her way into the cold looking office.

She had been waiting in the other room all this time! What an idiot! He'd never taken the time to even look! "I see you've thought of just about everything."

"Just then Dan got a smug look on his face. "I guess this meeting is concluded then."

"Just about."

"Sign here, Mrs. Paul," his tone was like spitting out dirt. He hated being made a fool of.

"Say it nice," Lizzie stated coldly.

"What?"

"Say it nice or I'm going to put a bullet in you left foot."

Dan knew that the cagey outlaw would do exactly what she said. "Please, sign here if you would, Ms. Pauls. Yes, that's perfect. Thank you."

Liza gazed lovingly into the older woman's face, "We'll meet you at the general store in just a few minutes. Go on, we're fine." Within minutes, the room was quiet.

"Thank you for your time, Dan," Liza said politely as she signed her name on the deeded document.

"Gosh, I hope you didn't miss your engagement because of us," Lizzie said in a sarcastic tone as she neatly wrote her name on the deeded document as well.

The clerk was completely taken aback at the skill of their handwriting. Each letter was identical to the others. If he hadn't seen them writing their names individually, he'd of sworn that they were forged. Was there nothing different about these two women? "Not at all, Miss Baxter," he answered back just as sarcastically. Without thinking he reached into his bottom desk drawer as he heard the clicking sound of pistol hammers. When he looked up they were pointed directly at him, held by two black eyed vipers. Carefully, he placed the bottle of whiskey on top of the desk.

Liza gave the pompous man a hard look as she spoke, "I reckon you're going to need a lot more than whiskey to get you out of this one. The document please." It was as though the man had to seal the document in his own blood before he finally handed it over.

"Is that so? What? You're a fortune-teller now?" he scoffed.

"You know, Dan," Lizzie stared at his arrogant face, "I don't much like you. Never have." Her eyes were dark and menacing. "I think you're a two faced liar and you'd sell your own mother for the right price. I also believe that you know exactly who wanted this particular piece of ground and why. You could save yourself a lot of trouble by telling the truth here cuz if we find out differently, we'll be back."

"And it won't be for some foreclosed deed!" Liza added.

"Honestly, I don't care what you might think of me, Lizzie Baxter because I don't think much of you either. Parading around these parts like some crowned princess, actin' all high and mighty," he said back in self-defense. "I know about you and your vicarious ways. Besides, if I did know something, which I don't, I couldn't tell you," his rat-like eyes tried to penetrate those of his intimidator, it wasn't working. "It's against the law!" Like a stuffed sausage he sat back in his chair exhausted at the mental battle.

"What do you know of the law? You can't even keep your land office in order!" Lizzie snapped.

Liza saw the thunder exploding from Lizzie's coal black eyes as she took over the conversation. "Really, Dan, I don't think you know either one of us well enough to know which of us is vicarious." She gave him a half inviting smile. "But, if you give us a minute of your time, we would be more than willing to, you know, accommodate you. What do you think sister?"

"I'm in!"

"I wouldn't let either one of you close enough to me to spit! Why, you'd probably kill me in my sleep! Or worsted!" he countered.

"Probably," they said in unison with no emotion.

Just as both women were ready to leave, Lizzie looked directly into the cowardly man's face, "By the way, tell your mystery buyer that he can come and see us if he's still interested in the land. We'll make the weasel a deal he won't forget." Then just like that both women stepped out into the light of day and disappeared.

The clerk sat trembling in his chair as the two women exited his office. They were a scary sight! No wonder no one wanted to marry them. Why, they'd slit your throat or something worse. "Man!" he said out loud. "How'm I going to explain this one?" Like a broken down old mule he walked to the wooden door and threw the heavy bar across it. Then he picked up the bottle of whiskey and took a good long pull. "I might well be a dead man by morning. Melding Baxter's! Who need's em!"

As Liza and Lizzie nonchalantly strolled down the dusty street they couldn't help but notice the odd stares that seemed to accompany them. Liza kept fidgeting like an old cow swatting flies. The constant motion was irritating to Lizzie as she grumbled at her identical sibling, "What the devil is the matter with you? Got ants in your pants? Stop that!"

"I can't help it," she said in a perplexing tone, "I feel like someone has stuck a thousand cactus needles in my skin!"

"What!" Lizzie exclaimed as she started to notice the strange stares. No one had ever looked at them like this before. It was as though everything around was moving in slow motion. When Lizzie looked at her sister's struggling face she knew she was telling her the truth. Someone was playing with black magic and it wasn't them.

Immediately, Lizzie grabbed her sister by the shoulders and said two words out loud in Flying Eagle's native tongue. Instantly, the pricking sensation stopped and the happy faces of the walking people returned. Like a hawk scanning the open sky Lizzie looked all around her but there was nothing. A gnawing feeling hit the pit of her stomach as she stared into her sister's disturbed face. "C'mon Liza, let's get Hattie, we're going back to the ranch!"

CHAPTER 24

It was a beautiful fall morning on the Baxter ranch and Dancing Bear had come to love the young girl affectionately named Emmy and she showed it at every given opportunity. She had even taught her several words in her native tongue. It was plain to see that the young woman was very bright. Her thinking skills were unique and it amazed everyone at how quickly she had picked up the foreign language. There were times she struggled at speaking it but she definitely knew what Dancing Bear was saying.

Everyone at the ranch was taken aback at what a hand the young woman was and at whatever task she was given. She never complained and when she was happy her voice rang throughout the house like a bird. Not one person that lived within the walls of that old log house missed Abe's open door to his study as her sweet melody replenished his soul. She hadn't only stolen the heart of Matthew Baxter but everyone else on the Lazy AB ranch as well.

It was like the happy mother and daughter duo had been living here for years. Like they had magically injected the whole family with a long overdue dose of happiness. Hattie had proven to be more than a good cook, sharing her skills unconditionally. She was also a very skilled chess player who challenged Abe Baxter on a daily basis. She had a boundless knowledge of numbers and she wasn't very easily tripped up by any amount of sums. On more than one occasion Matthew would ask her advice on this amount of money or some type of yardage. Making sure that he had added the sums correctly.

Everyone loved it when the older woman ran her fingers across the faded ivory keys that had sat dormant in the corner for years. Everyone in the household was horrified the day that Hattie offered to teach Liza and Lizzie. The twins, however, were thrilled. Except when it was time to practice.

"Hattie, we need to help clean out the barn today." Lizzie stated with one foot out the door.

"Me too." Liza added shoving her sister.

"Oh no you don't!" Hattie insisted.

"Father is going to be awful upset, Hattie." Liza stated.

"When your father tells you to go and practice shooting your guns, do you?" she continued plainly.

"Of course," they said in unison.

"When your father tells you to break a new horse, do you?" she asked.

"Yes." They answered in a skeptical tone.

"This is no different. It's time for piano lessons." She said in a demanding tone.

"Begrudgingly they turned around and sat in front of the wooden noise maker just as Abe walked into the main house. With their backs to him he gave Hattie a half grin and a wink. Quietly, he sat down with a cup of hot coffee and a biscuit to listen. It was a painful prelude. He supposed worse than a woman in labor. In good faith they tried to do what Hattie had insisted pounding their fingers across the ivory keys like a cat's claw on a dry window. Their voices blended together like fire and water as the two collided. Abe wasn't sure he'd ever heard a sound quite like that. As the two of them kept time with each other and swayed back and forth on the long bench singing like a strangled rooster everyone else in the house evacuated. But he was proud of their effort and stayed until the ear-piercing noise was over.

"That was so much better!" Abe said enthusiastically as he stood up. A part of Hattie's biscuit stuck in his throat. He needed another cup of coffee, now!

Hattie gave him a horrified look. They were awful!

"Thank you father," they said in unison. It was plain to see that the two of them thought they were grand singers and they adored his praise. That is until one insulted the other. "Father was looking right at me," Liza said with a conceited look on her face.

"Not only does your gun need sighted in so does your eyesight cuz he was looking straight at me!" Lizzie snapped back.

"Was not!"

"Was too!"

"You sound just like the air that comes out of the back end of Charlie's old mule!" snapped Liza. "That's not nothin I wanna listen to!"

"You take that back!" Lizzie said furiously.

"I can't take back the truth!" Liza injected.

Abe gave Hattie a wide smile and handed her a fresh cup of coffee as she walked into the kitchen. "Quite an undertaking don't you think?"

"Emmy was so much easier!" she sighed. "I had no idea!"

"I can't believe you got them to do it," he laughed. "I should give you a raise just for that!"

"I'll probably need it by the time this is over!" she laughed back.

Crash!

"Ouch, Liza, that hurt!" Lizzie yowled.

"Oh my!" Hattie fussed at she started to get to her feet. "What was that?"

Gently Abe put his hand over the top of hers. "My guess. The piano stool."

Hattie wasn't sure how many new piano stools had been built since the twins' interest in the majestic instrument. One constantly blaming the other for the broken furniture. She too had weaseled her way into the hearts of all of those that lived at the Baxter ranch with little more than her straightforward kindness and honesty.

Naomi and Emmy had become quite good friends and enjoyed each other's company on a daily basis. They were an odd sight: one tall, stocky built with brilliant blonde curly hair and dark brown eyes. The other with her berry colored head barely tipping the others shoulder's, slender built and those wildflower circles that just had a way of absorbing you into her boundless arena of energy.

There was no doubt in anyone's mind that Matthew and Emmy would eventually become man and wife. It was plain to see that they were made for each other. So, when they strolled into the occupied kitchen hand-n-hand one morning and announced their intentions at the breakfast table, no one was surprised.

"Mother, Aunt Lizzie, Papa, Hattie," he said with a gleam in his eye, "Emmy and I've decided to get married."

"And when will this wonderful occasion take place," Liza asked in a cheerful voice.

"We don't want to wait," Emmy said through love filled eyes.

"Next weekend if that's all right with everyone else," Matthew said earnestly as he looked into his grandfather's humored face for permission.

"I'll see that the preacher knows the time," Abe said as he stood and congratulated his grandson. "We'll be proud to have Miss Emmy as part of this family."

"Thank you," she breathed through trembling lips. "I feel so safe here."

"You are safe here," Lizzie stated putting any doubts to rest as to the wonderful young woman's acceptance as she walked to where she stood and gave her a hug.

"Emmy, Baxter, Jones. It has a nice ring to it," Liza said as she looked at the flushed face of the young woman.

"Thank you," she smiled warmly through misty eyes.

"No, mother," Matthew stated in an authoritative tone. "It will be Emmy Baxter. You know we decided that a long time ago."

"So be it," Liza said without hesitation. Everyone in the family knew that Matthew didn't prefer his mother's married name. Only Jeffrey chose to do that.

"And," Abe said in a deep voice, "you have talked with her mother?" He gave Hattie a warm smile.

"Yes, sir. I asked her permission this morning." Lovingly he gave Hattie nod of respect.

Lizzie loved the boy's strength and character. As far as she was concerned he was a Baxter. No child as good as Matthew could have an ounce of Jacob's blood in him. "Now, I for one would like to stay and continue this conversation but we have cattle to doctor. C'mon Liza," Lizzie said in a demanding tone.

"Yup," Liza answered as the two women left the large room.

CHAPTER 25

It was going to be a grand affair! Matthew and Emmy had invited the whole valley much to Liza and Lizzie's dismay. As far as they could tell no one had turned down their invitation. As they rode into the small town they nodded their pretty heads in salutations to several curious onlookers as they stepped off of their horses in front of Nelly's dress shop.

At first Nelly was terrified when the twin Baxter women strolled into her shop, looking it over as though there was a plague hidden somewhere within the clothed walls. In reality just the thought of having to be measured for new dresses to the twins was like being led to the gallows. But Abe had insisted that something new was to be made and worn. There would be no getting out of it this time. To them it felt like a hanging.

"Liza, Lizzie," Nelly said in an inviting tone, "what a nice surprise. How may I help you?" It was plain to see that the woman was terrified.

There was no missing the look of dread that followed their doubled gaze as they pinpointed the young seamstress. They both looked like they were getting ready to bolt.. "We are here to talk about getting some," Lizzie hesitated for a brief moment, acting as though she were about to be sick.

"Dresses, made," Liza finished with the same expression. "Father has insisted."

"I couldn't say it," Lizzie whispered to her identical sibling as she pretended to throw up!

"I know. I barely got it out myself!" It was as though the word had some kind of disease. " I'm light headed!"

Nelly smiled to herself as she walked toward several oblong bolts of cloth. "After I saw the two of you at the harvest dance, well, I couldn't stop thinking about you. When I saw this cloth in Cheyenne a month ago I bought it." Like a mother runs her caring hands across a baby's head she gently caressed the lovely fibers. "I was hoping you would feel comfortable enough to come in. I understand the affair at your ranch is going to be grand." She gave them a quick smile as she adoringly ran her fingers across the soft blue fabric again. "I hope you don't think I was too pretentious but the color that's wound within these strands," she let out a slight sigh, "they are beautiful. Just like the two of you. Looking at your eyes, again I can see they will match perfectly."

It was unnerving to see how the young dressmaker got lost in her own world. Then like a sleek otter she glided out of the room and strolled back in with two identically matched dresses draped across two womanly forms. "I'm sure that the sizes aren't exactly right. I have a fairly good eye for measuring but you two are so toned and you have those amazing torsos. I'm sure they will need to be altered.

I took the liberty of dropping the shoulders a bit and making the strap a little thinner which gave the bustline a little more breathing room. Easy in, easy out. I hate being smothered. No sleeves. Your arms are so perfectly muscled and tanned that I believe the lines of the dress will enhance the beauty of your figure. Then I added a little extra fabric on the bottom so it would flow when you move. I bet they will shimmer like stars in the lantern light." Completely at ease, she placed the outline of the pinned dress up to Lizzie's shoulders; it was plain to see that the woman was all business. "Oh my!" she exclaimed. "Breathtaking!" Then she held the fabric up to Liza. "You two are nothing less that amazing. There's not going to be much altering here. Turn around please. Yes, umm, maybe not at all."

Then as though she realized who it was that she was commanding around like some general the small woman got a strange look on her face as she took several steps backward. "Forgive me," she apologized. "I got too carried away!" There was no missing the terror in her eyes.

"You did all of this with just one look from a dance?" Lizzie asked. Completely shocked at the woman's ability.

"Yes," she said simply. "But you don't have to take them! Goodness no! I just was hoping, well, not really hoping. I wanted to tell you, well, not really tell you. I doubt no one tells you..." Finally Nelly just quietly shut her babbling mouth and stared.

"We'll take them both," Liza said in a respectful tone.

"You will?" Nelly answered, shocked at their approval.

"Anyone who would go to this much trouble over a couple of dresses, why how could we turn down such a wonderful honor." Lizzie stated in a genuine tone.

"Honor?" Nelly seemed so shocked.

"Nothing less." They said in unison.

"Thank, thank you," she stuttered.

"Now, that we are out of the way, we'd like to see if you'd be willing to make Emmy's wedding dress. I know it's short notice. There will be no expense spared." Liza stated matter-of-factly as she laid several coins in the dressmaker's hand.

"Me?" she seemed so surprised.

"Only you." They said again in unison.

"I would be delighted." Nelly breathed. "But, this is far too much."

"No expense," Lizzie cocked one arched brow.

"For your, discretion." Liza added with the same cocked brow.

"I will make her stunning," she breathed as though she were sculpting a statue in her mind.

"We're counting on that young lady," Lizzie said in a teasing tone. Then she added, "We'll pick our dresses up when we get Emmy's." Then just like that they disappeared out into the street.

Liza looked at her identical sibling in shock. "Can you believe that?"

"Nope."

In the same motion they mounted their horses. "Mine won't take much fixin'," Liza said soberly. "Don't know what to say about yours." She stated as she pointed her horse out of the small town.

Lizzie was furious with her sister's calloused remark. "What's that supposed to mean? Liza, I'm talking to you! Liza!"

Later that week when Emmy came in for her fitting the young dressmaker was overwhelmingly excited. "You are going to be such a beautiful bride," she gushed. "I'm so jealous."

"Thank you," Emmy said in a hesitant tone. Normally, Nelly was distant and cold acting.

"Oh, don't get me wrong," Nelly rattled on as she took the young woman's measurements. "I think that big burly looking hunk you're about to marry is nothing less than a doll." She gave Emmy a wink. "I'm sure there are a lot of brokenhearted women paddling around this place." She let out a slight laugh. "Oh don't worry I have my sights set on someone, too."

"Really?" Emmy hadn't missed all the dances that she and Charlie had shared at the Harvest dance.

"He's younger than me by several years."

"Oh." Her tone said she was surprised.

"If you want to know the truth, he's the only one that I've ever really cared about." She let out another quick sigh, "I'd sure like to think that maybe someday he might feel the same way about me." She stopped for a few seconds then continued in a much happier tone. "Anyhow, it's just that you two look so in love," she sighed.

When their eyes met, Emmy gave the dressmaker a sincere smile, "I hope that this man that has stolen your heart realizes it someday, too, for you, I mean. You're a very lovely person, Nelly. I'm afraid I might have misjudged you."

It was plain to see that Nelly was completely taken back at the heartfelt compliment. "What a wonderful thing to say. Thank you, Emmy," she half whispered through misty eyes. It was a strange feeling that had come over the dress maker. Typically she was so jealous of the plain wide hipped woman that she couldn't stand it. But not today. Today she saw Emmy in a completely different light. "Me too, I think." No wonder Matthew had fallen for her; she was definitely a diamond in the rough. "Now, that we have all that hogwash out of the way, I just got the prettiest fabric in and it has your name written all over it. Ohh! It's going to make the most gorgeous wedding dress!"

Emmy gently touched the dressmakers trembling hand. "Thank you," she smiled.

"For what? I haven't done anything yet," she giggled.

"For the measurements," she said quietly.

"Oh, don't you even think about that," she said in a knowing manner, "I know how to take several inches off of each one of those hips!" Like a child she grabbed Emmy's hand and drug her into the back room. "You just need to worry about keeping that man's hands off of you until the ceremony is over!"

Several hours of preparation passed when the two women heard someone hollering Nelly's name from the front of the store. When Nelly came waltzing around the corner dragging Emmy wrapped in fabric and pins, as she continued to babble about some dress she'd made in Paris, both women stopped dead in their tracks. "Can I help you," Nelly said in a business-like tone.

"I need to buy a dress," the heavyset man said coyly as he stared into Emmy's terrified eyes.

Nelly didn't miss the uncomfortable encounter as she protectively stepped in front of her client. "You, sir, must not be able to read. The sign says, "closed," or are you blind."

"I like the one I'm seeing now," he said in a leading tone. "Is it for sale?"

But the petite shopkeeper wasn't amused at the man's arrogant remark as she stepped out from behind the counter and walked directly to where he stood. She was furious as she spoke, "Get out of my shop! Not only can't you read, but no one comes into my shop and insults one of my client!"

"Here, here little lady," he said in an amused tone, "there's no need for that. I don't mean no harm." The woman wasn't any bigger than a flea bossing him around like that.

But what the large man hadn't expected was the quickness of the small woman as she pulled a sawed off shotgun from the inside of her skirt and jammed it smack dab into his sagging gut. "Now, maybe you really are deaf but I think you're just ignorant!" she hissed in a threatening tone. "To be truthful about it I honestly don't care! But if you're not out of my shop before I pull this hammer back I'm going to put several little balls of lead right through that soggy pile of skin you got hanging over that belt of yourn and there ain't no one gonna say a word about it!"

Shocked at her fearless display the man turned without saying one more word and exited the small shop. "Witch!" he seethed. "You'll be getting yours someday!"

Instantly, Nelly placed the sawed-off shotgun back into the pocket of her skirt designed just for that particular situation. Then she slammed the heavy board across the door into an iron holder. Mumbled a few words then turned around and faced, Emmy. "I'm sorry, Emmy, where were we? Oh yes, that old hag she was so put out with me, why I just wanted to die on the spot!" she rattled on. After several more pins and a couple of cups of tea Nelly was finally finished with the basics just as Matthew walked into the small quaint shop.

"Are you ready?" he asked.

"Done," Emmy smiled. Then she turned to the kind dressmaker. "Thank you for a perfectly lovely day."

"My pleasure, Emmy," she said earnestly.

"You can pick the dress up on Thursday," she stated matter-of-factly. "Oh and the twins' too."

"We'll be here," Matthew smiled as he pulled a money band out of his pocket.

"Goodness no!" Nelly stated with a giggle. "It's all been taken care of."

"Then consider this a token of my appreciation."

She gave Matthew a knowing smile. "Thank you."

At the ranch, the wedding plans seemed to be going on in a timely manner. Dancing Bear and Hattie had been busy all morning baking and designing their newfound menu. Several of the hands had been busy building a large platform for dancing and the last wagon load of lumber had finally arrived. Liza and Lizzie on the other hand were busy out in the barn setting bags of feathers in the loft for Matthew and Emmy's new bed. A special surprise just for the two of them. And, sipping on their special brew!

"I decided I'm not wearing no stuffy dress to this high-fa-lootin' wedding! I don't care if it was made especially for me! I'm telling father tonight! That's my final decision!" Lizzie stated firmly. "Last time I did that I couldn't walk for a week!"

"Then what are you going to wear? A gunny sack?" Liza asked in an appalled tone.

"Maybe!" Lizzie snapped back. "You'd better tie one more piece of rope on that tatting of feathers Lizzie instead of sippin' on that bottle and fussin' over some stinking dress! If that thing falls it's going to make an awful mess!"

"It ain't gonna fall!" Lizzie stated in a know-it-all tone as she pretended to make one more slip knot. "That will be twice in one year that I've had to put on one of those flouncy rolls of fabric!"

"How do you think I feel?" Liza said in self-defense. "I'm the mother of the groom. Everyone and their dogs gonna be lookin' at me!"

"I think I'd rather look at the dog." Lizzie joked.

"Well, this dog says that when that bag of feathers up there comes loose I sure hope I'm not the one standing under it!" Liza was furious that her sister didn't feel any remorse for her situation.

"Oh, whatever!" Lizzie scolded. "What, you think you're holier than thou or something," she mumbled in a low tone.

"What did you say?"

"Nothing!"

By the end of the week it was plain to see that Liza and Lizzie had had more than enough of the hoop-ala in the house, grounds, and invited neighbors. They were standing on their last nerve and if they had to be nice to one more person today they were both going to shoot someone! So, like two field mice they silently headed for the serenity of the large old barn for one more quick nip from the corn jar hidden neatly within the straw in the last horse stall. Just a little something to settle their nerves and help them make it through the day.

"Mother!" Naomi yelled standing on the boarded porch stomping her foot before the wily twosome made their intended destination. "You need to talk to Jeffrey! He just insulted me again! I'm not going to put up with it mother! I'm not! I swear I'm going to shoot him!"

"Holy cats!" the twins sighed at the same time. "Not again!"

"He's your son, Liza, what cha think, the horse tank?" Lizzie's eyes twinkled.

"How about some cloth to gag that obnoxious mouth and then we tie him to a tree some where's," Liza added as the twosome grudgingly headed back toward the house. "At least until the wedding is over."

"Mother!" Matthew exclaimed in a strained tone as he saw the duo re-enter the house. "It's almost time! Why aren't' you sitting in the chairs?"

"Your brother and cousin appear to have a problem right now. Don't worry, we'll be there shortly," Liza answered in a cool fashion, surprised that her son seemed to be so rattled.

The words had no more than left Liza's lips when they heard a yowl come from the back of the kitchen then the slamming of a door. Instantly, the twins hurried toward the loud ruckus. Dancing Bear stood with a twinkle in her knowing brown eyes as Hattie held the apron to her mouth. "I think she's going to shoot him," Hattie fretted.

"The big gun or the small one," Lizzie asked anxiously.

"Small," Dancing Bear answered unconcerned for Jeffrey's welfare.

"She won't hurt him bad," Liza giggled with a knowing look on her face, "that one's got buckshot in it." Anxiously, the two women gathered up their dresses and hurried toward the barn just as they heard the shotgun blast.

"I swear, Jeffrey," Naomi seethed, "I'm gonna fill your hide full of lead if you call me a heathen one more time!"

"You couldn't hit the broad side of an outhouse you little heathen!" he teased as he ran from rafter to rafter jumping over the newly bagged feathers.

"I'll show you!"

Bang! The gun exploded again sending little particles of straw and wood throughout the air.

"Naomi!" Lizzie hollered. "Put that gun down before you hurt someone!"

"I'm gonna kill him!" she threatened in a frustrated tone. "I am!"

Bang!

The gun went off again just as Jeffrey jumped from the side loft into an outside pile of hay. Like a scared rabbit he felt for holes then brushed himself off and headed for the safety of the crowd of people and his brother.

When Lizzie grabbed the gun from Naomi the young woman had angry tears running down her reddened cheeks. The twins knew how she felt and didn't blame her for wanting to do her cousin bodily harm. "Now, Naomi," Lizzie said in a calm voice, "you have to stop letting him get under your skin like that. Besides, we have a wedding to go to. We'll deal with Mr. Jeffrey when it's over."

"Yes, mother," Naomi said in a frustrated tone as swiped at something on her shoulder. "You just wait, he'll get his someday!" Angrily she stomped her foot as she swiped at the odd feeling ooze on her arm. Once again she brushed it off.

"What is that on the back of your dress, Naomi?" Liza questioned.

"Where?" she squealed stopping dead in her tracks.

"Right here," Liza said as she swiped her hand across the sticky ooze. She took a moment and smelled it. "Why it's honey!" she exclaimed.

"Honey! Why in the world would honey…," Lizzie said as she looked up in the direction that the sticky liquid was coming from just as a pile of the sticky ooze covered the three of them. Within seconds the rope came loose from the large bag of feathers as it followed the course of the golden strands.

"Oh, no!" Liza hollered.

"Run!" Naomi yelled

"Cocko!" Lizzie's shocked voice echoed.

But neither woman was fast enough to escape the feathered avalanche. Within seconds the whole barn had turned into a white feathered fiasco. It was like a blinding blizzard had erupted in the large old building in the middle of summer. Like all of the pods from the surrounding cottonwood trees had opened their escaping silk at the same time. When they came up for air, Liza, Lizzie, and Naomi all three were sputtering!

"I'm gonna kill him!" Lizzie seethed as she grabbed for the gun. "So help me, I'm gonna kill that little rodent!" It was all Liza and Naomi could do to hold her back. "Look! Look at us!" she fumed. "I didn't even want to put this—thing on but now it's ruined! Father is going to kill us!" Then in the midst of the quaking incident she stared at her sister and daughter. It was all Lizzie could do to keep from falling over from the hysterical sight. The fluffy feathers were floating everywhere, like tiny droplets of snow. Drifting aimlessly downward as the wispy wind recklessly caught them and pushed them carelessly aside. "Liza," Lizzie was laughing so hard, "look at your hair!"

"My hair, look at yours!" she countered.

"Mother," Naomi giggled uncontrollably, "you look like a chicken!"

Both women looked at the lovely young woman talking in complete hysterics as they spoke at the same time, "You really do look like a little heathen now!"

"Yeah," Naomi said in a more sober fashion, "that rotten Jeffrey had it planned all along! You wait! I'm gonna get him good before this day is over!"

"After me!" Lizzie seethed.

"No, after me! I am his mother and I get first whack at him!" Liza stated matter-of-factly.

In the distance they could hear the ringing of the bell, it sounded like a startled rooster. The wedding was getting ready to start and they weren't there. They weren't sitting next to their father in their designated seats. Naomi wasn't standing next to Clinton as a part of the wedding party. Abe had already warned them about any of their juvenile conduct earlier today. Now they knew that their father was going to be furious.

A sinking feeling engulfed the three of them as they wiped as many of the sticking feathers away from their reddened faces as they could. It only made them stick even more. It was plain to see that the twins weren't going to get out of this one. That there would be no escaping the questioning stares from their grand appearance. That Naomi would have to face the humiliation right along with them. There wasn't time for any of the three of them to go and change so they brushed as many feathers as they could off of their dresses, which didn't help much either. And, with their heads held high the trio exited the barn as they made their way toward their waiting audience.

"We are in this together!" Lizzie said proudly as she hooked Naomi's arm.

"Together," Liza said as she took Naomi's other arm.

"Together," Naomi echoed.

CHAPTER 26

At first Matthew couldn't believe his eyes as he scanned the threesome walking like queens with plumed dresses across the distance to the middle of the yard. The fabric of their flowing blue dresses combined with the floating feathers gave off the impression that the three women belonged in some high fashioned brothel or expensive saloon, not at a wedding. Automatically, Matthew stared at Emmy who had her gloved hand placed over her giggling mouth. He gave her a look that said he was sorry that they had ruined her special day. But the gaze that he received back told him she didn't care. She loved this family and if their shenanigans were a part of that, then so be it. Relieved, he turned and gave his brother a sympathetic look, knowing that this must have been a part of his secret handiwork.

Jeffrey merely, smiled as he shrugged his shoulders. "They weren't supposed to be there," he said honestly. "Only, Naomi."

"You are so dead!" Matthew whispered just loud enough for Jeffrey's ears only.

"Oh, I know!" he half laughed as he turned and enjoyed the show like everyone else.

The closer the three women got to their destination, the more gasps they heard. There was no sense in throwing any of the small kernels of grain from the pokes that had been handed out in celebration of the bride and groom. That appeared to be a natural happening with every step the threesome took.

When Abe saw his two daughters and granddaughter he shook his grey peppered head and put his large hands over his face. Now he understood the echoing sound of the shotgun. He could only imagine what had taken place in the confines of the barn. "I should have known," he mumbled to himself as he turned and faced Matthew and Emmy. There was no hiding the laughter on their faces.

Naomi graciously peeled off from her two feathered companions and stood quietly next to Clinton. Trying desperately to become invisible with little success. "Sorry I'm late," she whispered in an apologetic tone.

"I just love those two!" Clinton said to Naomi in a cheerful voice as he proudly took her feathered arm and joined the wedding party.

Naomi gave him an odd look. "What?" she murmured in a low shocked tone. She couldn't believe that he wasn't mad or embarrassed for that matter. But more than that she couldn't believe what he said next.

"You look beautiful with feathers in your hair. It's a natural look." His love-filled eyes twinkled as he stared into her disbelieving face. "That's why I love you," he said plainly "you're who you are every day."

Liza and Lizzie could see Jeffrey making fun of them by mimicking the sound of a silent chicken as they slowly walked arm-n-arm down the middle of the small group. "Bock, bock, bock," he whispered to his Aunt and mother. He knew that he was in trouble and that he had better be ready to hightail it out of there when everything was said and done.

There was no missing the intent to kill that exploded from the twins' dark black eyes like an invading thunderstorm as the two of them gave the mischief maker a dark warning. If he could have ran he would have. But he'd promised Matthew that he would stand up with him. Now that he was there, it would be necessary for him to plan his escape as soon as the vows were recited. He knew that the twins were hell bent on paying him back for embarrassing them in front of the whole valley. But how was he supposed to know that the bag of feathers would fly open like that! Someone didn't use a double knot! Besides, they weren't supposed to be there! The trick was to be played on Naomi, not his Aunt Lizzie and especially not on his mother!

Liza and Lizzie smiled at their inquisitive guests as they walked past them arm in arm. Like two proud swans they sat to either side of their father, capturing him in the mist of their predicted ambience. Acting as though nothing out of the normal had happened. It was all Abe could do to keep from laughing out loud at the comedic site. They reminded him of two plucked chickens! And to make matters worse every time a soft breeze would blow in their direction, the rebellious feathers seemed to float right into his face. On more than one occasion he had to sputter the wayward feathers from out of his mouth. Before long Abe was covered in the masses of filtering white just like his twin daughters.

Luke was sitting to Lizzie's left and Charlie to the right of Liza. "Nice look for you," Luke said to Lizzie with a chuckle.

"Shut up!" she seethed through smiling lips, "or I'll stuff you in the bag!"

"Mighty big words for a woman that looks like she's all ready been plucked!" he countered quietly.

Within seconds of his cutting remark Lizzie stomped on his foot, "How do you like that!" she fumed in a haughty voice.

Luke let out an unexpected yowl as Abe leaned over the two of them, "Don't make me separate you two!" he said in a warning tone.

"He started it!" Lizzie said insulted that he had gotten out of the blame.

"I did not!"

"Charlie," Abe whispered, "you and Luke change sides."

The two men casually did as they were asked smiling at the curious guests behind them. But as Luke graciously sat down, Liza intentionally stomped on his other foot. "Oh, I'm sorry," she foolheartedly apologized, "was that your foot?"

But before Luke had a chance to reply there was a slight tap on his shoulder as a smaller, handsome man with round glasses politely injected his presence next to Liza. In one casual movement, he placed her hand in his as he gave her a cheerful smile. Liza gave him a completely baffled look.

The ceremony was nearly ready to start when Abe came to his feet. The preacher gave him an odd stare as he walked to the back of the crowded platform and escorted Dancing Bear to the front of the benches. Matthew gave him a look that said it was about time that someone escorted her to the front, after all she was an important part of this family too and she being left out didn't sit well with him.

She looked beautiful in her soft doeskin dress and dark brown skin and he was proud to have her sitting with the rest of the family. Politely Abe sat her next to Albert. The smaller man affectionately placed her hand in his as he gave her a warm inviting smile. It was a wonderfully heart-felt gesture. One that no one in the Baxter family missed. Then Abe walked to where Hattie sat all alone dabbing at her tears on the opposite side from where they sat. Like the gentleman that he was Abe held out his arm, and then walked her to the opposite side of his chair. There they were. The Baxter family. Luke, Liza, Albert, Dancing Bear, Abe, Hattie, Charlie, and Lizzie. Abe smiled broadly now that everything was in its rightful place he gave Preacher Prichard the go ahead once again to start the ceremony.

The preacher gave Abe Baxter a quick nod. But he hesitated for just a few moments before he started again. Waiting for the next unscheduled delay. When there was none he continued.

For a brief passage in time the twins sat back and submerged themselves in the wonder of it all. A sainted moment that connected one sister to the other. It passed like a vision between them, Lizzie, who'd never gotten to experience the matrimonial connection of wife to mother. And Liza, who swore on her sister's life that her footsteps would never breach that threshold again.

It was a beautiful, breathtaking moment to watch the adorable young couple exchange their vows of love. Emmy didn't look like the tattered doll that had lain broken like a set of fine China from months ago. No, today she stood straight and tall as her persona shined like an enchanted princess. She was stunning as she stood within the lighted beams of the suns radiant rays. Like a whisper her long curly hair floated within the fingertips of the afternoon breeze. Her finely laced dress that had been designed just for her was flawless just like the look of adoration on her comely face. There was nothing less than the complete sanctuary of love in Emmy's warm brown eyes for the young man that she was about to marry. It was an awe-inspiring sight.

And then there was Matthew. He was such a handsome young man with his coal black hair and brilliant blue eyes. Sitting there looking at him the twin's knew that he was the epitome of a Baxter. He had the best traits of his mother and grandfather. The son who never got rattled. The one who stood for truth and right. The one whose loyalty of family never wavered. The valley's handsome prince.

Today was no exception as he stood with his white cowboy hat, soft brown trousers, white starched shirt, and matching boa tie. There was no missing the feelings of complete love and dedication that he had for the elegant young woman that stood like a wholesome flower in front of him. It was as though an explosion of golden sunbeams and starry-eyed comets met when he took her hand in his and placed the large diamond on her long trembling finger.

Liza and Lizzie's cool blue eyes misted like a fog across a lost forgotten lake as their barren lips, one mystically in synch with the other, breathed the same elaborate words, 'I do' when the young couple accepted each other's love. There was no missing the honest compassion as the bride and groom's waiting lips met, then parted with enamored respect one for the other.

The twins could feel the hurt of their own two empty hearts tied securely within one another as their closed eyes crossed the distance and let the honesty of those haunting words spark a light that had been dead for years deep within them. Somehow within the enchanted moment of those brumal words a warm wind of forgiveness caressed the finely honed cracks breaking the tempered chain of bad blood so that life could begin once again inside the abandoned chambers. It was an oddly wonderful feeling of liberation.

The twins sat quietly for several minutes, sharing the pivotal moment, accepting the truth of it. And when they opened their eyes there was no doubt they had been carried back to a dark place only to be ejected like an exploding bullet, back, to this place in time. "So be it." They whispered within each other's mind. And within that minds picture, before either sister could gather their wits about them they saw Charlie's hand was comfortably resting in Lizzie's and Albert's was comfortably placed in Liza's. They had no idea when the exchange had taken place but it seemed like such a natural state of being that neither one offered to remove it. The two enamored women gazed into both men's' smiling faces just as several feathers floated from their hair onto the two men's unexpected noses.

Like smitten school girls they let out a soft giggle as they stood up and joined in on the congratulations of the young couple. In fact the identical siblings got so caught up in the emotional feeling from the captivating ceremony they forgot all about killing Jeffrey. Well, at least for the time being.

When Liza walked up to her son to give him and his new wife a hug, Matthew couldn't help but grin. "Quite an entrance mother," he laughed as he plucked at one of the wayward feathers.

"Wasn't it," she smiled. Then she looked into Emmy's kind face, "I'm sorry, we didn't mean to ruin your day."

Emmy gave Liza a huge hug as she spoke, "You two could never ruin anything for me. You're the ones that gave me my life back. How could a bag of feathers match that?"

"Aunt Lizzie, you're lovely as usual," Matthew said happily.

"Quite," she smiled as her eagle eye's searched for Jeffrey.

"Naomi, that's a different look for you," he teased as he pulled her up into his large arms and swung her in a circle. "I thought I was going to bust a gut when I saw you three!"

"Well, your brother is in big trouble because your new bed is lying on the floor of the barn!" Lizzie stated in a huff.

"I'm sorry, Aunt Lizzie, but I'm so happy," Matthew said earnestly, "that it doesn't matter where I sleep as long as I have Emmy lying right next to me!"

"Matthew!" Emmy swooned embarrassed at his bold remark.

"Jeffrey completely ruined my hair!" Naomi seethed.

"Well, I think you're all lovely," Clinton concluded sincerely. "It would take a lot more than a bunch of feathers to make any of you ugly."

"Amen!" Charlie said as he squeezed Lizzie's hand. Together the small group headed toward the food and music.

CHAPTER 27

It was a grand day with all of the merriment and laughter. There were thank you's galore and enough good lucks to go around for a life time. Matthew and Emmy embraced each congratulation with heartfelt enthusiasm. It was hard not to be proud of the newly wedded couple.

Several hours came and went as the azure blue sky gave way to a dimming sun as the men folk started lighting the torches to either corner of the oversized platform. It was such a joyful event. Even the sound of the fiddles and guitars seemed to have a new twist on such old melodies. No one wanted to leave.

Lizzie had kept a close watch on Jeffrey's whereabouts as she danced from one end of the wooden platform to the other. On every given opportunity she would unsuccessfully try to snatch the young varmint out of the lovely dressmaker's arms, but he was slippery like a fox in a hen house and would purposely dance the other direction and she'd miss him completely. "If I get my hands on you!" she hissed as he waltzed by. At one point she was nearly to where she could grab the back of his collar when she felt a tap on her elbow. When she looked up, there stood Abe and Liza.

"Come on," he said cheerfully, "this is our dance, just like when you two were little girls." There was no missing the delight in his happy face. "We'll show them how us Baxter's do it."

"My pleasure, father," she smiled proudly. The thought of Jeffrey completely disappeared.

The three Baxter's stood in the middle of the platform with two fathers holding hands with two young daughters to either side and two mothers with two young sons to either side. Liza and Lizzie gave the children adoring looks.

When the music began, they politely bowed to the other dancers. Like they were humbly showing their respect for being invited to share in the dance. They in turn did the same. It was a moving sight. Liza and Lizzie stood like two identical shadows swaying to the melody of the musician's music like two warrior princesses. Abe was such a dignified looking man in his white starched shirt and brown pants. His silver peppered hair contrasting with the softness of their blue dresses which seemed to accentuate every curve of their toned bodies. One two three, sway two three, one two three, back two three, swing, side two three, circle, circle. Liza and Lizzie joined hands like two perfectly matched swans as they surrounded their father. Then the whole pattern started all over as they switched partners until they made their way back to their father.

From one end of the platform to the other the threesome's danced. It was like watching a sage grosses elaborate mating call. Every footstep, every movement of their silhouettes, every matched motion was perfection. Abe was the stem that stood solid and strong rooted deep within his ruling domain. His sense of integrity and pride showed in the circles of those deep brown eyes. Liza and Lizzie were the two pedaled blossoms that melded within the blood of that stem giving them the strength that pumped the red liquid from one velvet petal to the other.

There was no missing the fact they were Abe Baxter's daughters. They stood like him, straight and proud. They smiled like him through pearly white teeth that looked like a freshly painted picket fence. They had his determined features and mannerisms. They even had that same devilish twinkle in their adoring eyes, just like him when they laughed. The twins loved their father. It was so apparent on their attentive faces that it made the silent onlookers sigh. All eyes were on the breathtaking trio.

Clinton and Naomi leaned against the rail and watched like two school children seeing candy for the first time as the twins' long dark hair floated in the breeze like feathers clinging to their slender bodies. Luke stood with a mist in his eyes as he remembered back to the first time that Abe had taught them this silly little dance. It was the only one he knew that both girls could participate in at the same time. Leaving one or the other out of the fun never occurred to the man. He always had a dark-haired, dark-eyed daughter on each foot.

Matthew wrapped Emmy in his large arms as he held her firmly against him as they stood like two doves watching the amazing picture unfold right in front of them. The whole performance had a way of solidifying his god-given state of being and her placement of family.

Charlie stood just inside the darkness watching the faces of the many suitors that would have enjoyed being where Abe Baxter was standing. He saw the lust in their greedy eyes for the two women that swayed like a matched set of colorful plumes. Not one man standing there would've hesitated to invade the sacred bud of the two lovely flowers. They would have savagely sucked every ounce of the sweet nectar from the two matched petals. All of them knowing they'd never have that chance. If he was only a younger man.

Then the music slowed as Abe looked into Naomi's enamored face. With one gentle motion from his hand he instructed the young woman to come to him. Without hesitation she stood within the protective arms of her grandfather. Then he turned and did the same thing to, Emmy. She too stood within the protective arms of Abe Baxter. The twins motioned for Clinton and Matthew to come to them. They stood to either side of their partners as the music started its rhythmic motion once again.

As the crowd stood there watching there was no doubt that the broad shouldered dignified looking man was the leader. He had settled this savage land. Digging his roots deep within the soil of the Lazy AB Ranch. He was the stem of his creation and they were the petals of the wildflower. The wedding party looked like a wagon wheel as they turned then joined back together. The whole display was mesmerizing.

When the music finally stopped everyone clapped and gave hurrahs of approval. Liza, Lizzie, and Abe gave each of their partners a thankful bow as they breathlessly headed to step down from the crowded platform. The laughing trio was quite winded.

"Mother," Naomi said breathlessly, "that was wonderful."

Lizzie gave her adoring daughter a big hug. "I forgot father had even taught us that little dance." Her cool blue eyes gave away her remembrance. "We were very young then. It was past time to teach it to you my beautiful daughter." She gave Naomi a huge hug. "Just make sure you teach it to your children."

"I will mother."

Clinton couldn't keep from staring at the alluring woman standing in front of him. Not a day went by that she didn't just amaze him at some higher level. "Lizzie," he said with the utmost respect, "I've never met a woman like you in my life. Thank you for giving me this unbelievable opportunity," he said through misty eyes. Then he walked to where she stood and gave her the most heartfelt hug she'd ever had. "I just love you two." The twins stood completely baffled. She knew she liked that boy. Then he spun on a dime as he turned and smiled at Nomi, "If you're not too winded, this is our dance, darlin." Just as Clinton whisked her away, Emmy joined them.

There was no missing the adoration in her misty eyes. She had such a sense of belonging here. "Thank you," she whispered through trembling lips, "I've never felt more beautiful than today."

"Good," Lizzie said teasingly, "cause we got us a hard week planned." Once again she looked around for that scoundrel Jeffrey but he was nowhere to be seen. He had made a mockery out of his brother's wedding and she was determined to settle the score. "Where did you go now you stinkin' weasel?" As she glanced through the crowd, she didn't see the lovely dressmaker either. "That sounds about right, get all liquored up and take advantage of some poor innocent woman!"

Abe couldn't help but laugh when he saw his daughter's determined look as she hunted for her nephew. He felt sorry for Jeffrey cause he knew just what would happen if Lizzie caught up with him. Then, out of the corner of his eye he saw Liza talking to the minister as they waved Lizzie over.

"Are you sure this is what you want?" the preacher asked.

"Yes," they said in unison.

"It's very generous." He stated.

"There's no one else to trust it with right now. Besides, your silence will earn every penny of it."

"So, no one is to know?" he seemed so shocked.

"Not till the end." They said in unison.

"Not even, him?" Nonchalantly he looked across the room at the dignified baron. "No." Their tone was final.

"Then that's how it will be. I'll be there." He stated matter-of-factly.

"Thanks," they said in unison as they each shook his hand.

Abe couldn't tell what they were saying but it looked pretty serious. He was about to walk over when Hattie touched his elbow.

"Emmy doesn't have a father to show what a lovely bride she is tonight to the townsfolk. So—I--."

Without hesitation and before the older woman could finish her sentence, he said, "It would be my pleasure, Hattie." Intentionally, he walked toward the perfectly matched couple. He saw the fear in her eyes when he walked up. She was such a lovely young girl. "Emmy Baxter, may I escort you to the floor?"

"Yes, sir." Her hand was trembling.

"You need not ever fear me, Emmy. You're one of us now. You hold that chin up high and look these people straight in the face. You're a good god-fearing woman, no man could ask for more." Abe stopped directly in the middle of the dance floor as he waved for the musicians to stop and the floor to clear. Everyone was having so much fun that no one paid any attention to his request. Several times he asked for silence.

Bang!

"What was that?" Jeffrey said as he jumped to his feet, dragging Nelly out of the bed of straw with him.

"I don't know!" she stuttered.

"C'mon. We've got to get out of here before someone finds us!" Anxiously, Jeffrey pulled the dressmaker to her feet.

The crowd jumped to attention as Abe gave the twins a curious look. Immediately, they pointed at each other. Neither one taking the blame. Then in unison they said, "Now, shut up!"

All Abe could do was shake his head and laugh. "Ladies and gentlemen, now that my two beautiful daughters have your attention. It is my great pleasure and honor to introduce you to the wife of my grandson Matthew Baxter and my newest daughter, Mrs. Emmy Baxter." He gave the band a nod as he waltzed her across the floor with the greatest of ease as gentleman after gentleman politely tapped each other on the shoulder as they swept the blushing young bride across the floor. The song was nearly over as the last gentleman tapped out the one before him as Emmy took in a deep breath.

"What? I couldn't very well relinquish my responsibilities as best man by not dancing with the bride now could I?" Jeffrey's green eyes had the devil in them and his breath smelled like sour whiskey.

"Of course," Emmy whispered as she stared bravely into Jeffrey's troublemaking face.

"I see that look on your face. You're not going to hold what I said about your large ass against me forever are you?" he smirked.

"No more than you're going to hold the fact that I think you have a big fat mouth against me," she smirked.

"Touché!" he threw his head backward and laughed. "What now that needs you're a bonified Baxter you think you can insult me in front of all of these fine folks?"

"These fines folks don't care spit about you."

"Man it didn't take you long to become all high and mighty. Uh, let me think, I seem to remember a time when you didn't think you were so full of yourself."

Emmy wanted to run. Run so fast, so far away that no one would ever find her but instead she stood her ground. "It doesn't take much of a man to sour a woman's reputation. Only a coward would do that." She gave him a half smirk, "I'm pretty sure I'm looking at one of those."

Emmy's face was white as a sheet when Lizzie noticed that her obnoxious nephew was dancing with the young bride. "Damn!" she said out loud before she thought. Hell bent on destruction; she walked toward the dancing couple.

"What?" Liza said when her eyes followed her sister's path. Like a panther, Liza walked from the back dipping in and out of the crowd. But, before they could get there, Clinton had taken Jeffrey's place. Once again the hoodlum disappeared like a ghost.

"Emmy," Clinton said in a concerned state, "are you alright? What did he say? Did he hurt you?"

Emmy gazed into Clinton's kind face, "Men like Jeffrey, will never hurt me again."

"Atta girl!" he said with conviction.

Several more dances came and went as the early evening hours turned later and later. It was finally time for the last dance of the evening when Charlie and Lizzie made their way to the open floor. No one seemed to notice the odd pairing. For once everyone was too caught up in their own lives to notice one old cowhand and a beautiful barren maiden.

As their cheeks pressed against each other that feeling of lightning invaded her soul again. The rhythmic beat of one silhouette was magical as they swayed across the wooden floor. It was like no one else existed. Watching them dance together, no one would have ever guessed that Charlie was twenty years her senior.

"Charlie," Lizzie whispered in his ear, "would you like to go swimming with me later on this beautiful moonlit evening?"

Charlie squeezed his strong fingers into her muscled back, "Why, Miss Baxter," he teased, appearing to be taken off guard, "is that an invitation to see me naked?"

"No," she answered with a twinkle in her blue eyes, "it's an invitation to see me naked."

Charlie threw his head back and laughed out loud as they danced across the wooden floor. "Checkmate," he concluded.

Once the last song was played it was time for the festivities to end. Matthew and Emmy had been the perfect hosts. Staying until the last song had been played. But now it was time for the evening to be over. It wouldn't be long before the sun would be popping up. Regrettably, everyone waved good-bye as the last guest exited the large open gate. They'd all had such a wonderful time.

Liza and Lizzie gave the young couple safe passage to Matthew's newly decorated room. They both stood with their hands on their hips as they gave fair warning to anyone that decided to disturb their honeymoon night. There was no missing the look of terror on the hired hands' faces as Liza explicitly explained what part of their anatomy would be missing in the morning if they did. And, there would be no sense in lying about it because they always found out. As far as she knew, no one dared to enter the main house.

When she and Liza walked out onto the wooded porch, Lizzie looked into her father's exhausted face, "It's too crowded in here tonight, I can't breathe. I'll be around come morning." Gently, she touched his kind face. "It was a wonderful evening father. I forgot what it felt like to be your little girl."

"You'll aways be my little girl." He whispered.

"What would I do without you." Lovingly she gave him a soft kiss on his cheek. Then, she gave her sister a quick nod as they headed down the steps. "Kind of a long way to be riding home all alone on such a beautiful night don't you think, Liza?" Lizzie said in a knowing tone as she watched Albert step into the small buckboard.

"Yes, I do," she said honestly as she hurriedly waved him to a stop as Lizzie and Charlie mounted their horses and rode out the back way.

CHAPTER 28

It seemed natural to Lizzie riding along side Charlie beneath the golden moons soft inviting rays. There was just something about the man Lizzie couldn't put her finger on. He was so kind and yet had a mysterious side to him as well. He was wild and untamed like a rouge stallion. A side that intrigued her inner core.

"It won't be long now," she smiled warmly.

"Good," he said nonchalantly, acting as though he'd done this a thousand times as he stared at the lone rider coming towards them.

"Charlie?"

"Yes," he smiled.

"Lizzie?"

"Yes sir."

"For the brand." Charlie stated.

"For the brand." Lizzie countered.

As the two riders entered the small hidden meadow Lizzie had an old feeling wash over her. As though there were a set of eyes watching their arrival. With the vision of an eagle she did an one eighty as she scanned the golden meadow. She didn't see anything out of the ordinary so she consciously blew the feeling off as she stepped down from her horse.

"Wow!" Charlie stated in awe. "Lizzie, this is ghostly! Are you sure you want to spend the night here?"

"I know," she breathed as she un-cinched her horse and laid the saddle across the bare fallen tree. "There's no safer place than here. This meadow and I, we're connected."

"Really?" he said soberly. "How so?"

"The water is magic," she said as though she were the only living organism within ten miles. "I believe that it has a heart of its own that beats within the rhythm of the water. And within that heart lays forgiveness, strength, courage, and healing. That it knows when someone's soul is broken. When they are beyond repair and there is no hope left. I believe it has special healing powers that it gives unconditionally from within itself. And, it knows how to fix even the most broken of hearts. It doesn't know how to do anything else but show you comfort and love."

Her blue eyes were crystal clear like moon drops on a lost forgotten lake as she turned and gazed into Charlie's mesmerized face. "Look around you," she whispered, "it's like some sacred place that knows your name without being told. It cradles you the way the wind brushes the bottom of a leaf. Listen to the sweet harmony of the singing birds, and the joining in of the chirping frogs. Listen to the sound of the willows as the soft night air swishes its long feathery fingers across the tops of their waiting heads like a loving mother's hand to a child. Listen to the constant humming of the crickets. It's like an enchanting melody being played just for you and me, Charlie." Her crystal blue eyes were misty. "It doesn't judge and it doesn't condemn. It's the only place for our special night," she sighed as she faced him. "I've waited my whole life for you Charlie Redbone."

Charlie stared at the woman that stood before him. There could never have been a time that he had been more intrigued by her unselfish nature than tonight. Her wisdom reached so much farther than any woman he'd ever met. Why she had chosen his company was a complete mystery to him. Especially, when there were so many younger, more eligible men than he in this valley. Ready to be her stallion. Yet here she was happy to be in his company. "Lizzie," Charlie said in a soft tone as he walked to her side, "I've never met anyone like you."

Lizzie gazed into his kind steely eyes. "Nor I you, Charlie," she whispered as she began to disrobe.

Charlie stepped into the warm liquid and took in a refreshing sigh. The soothing water felt good on his tired muscles as he submerged himself to his chest. For several minutes he stood and watched as Lizzie dove back and forth under the protection of the water. She reminded Charlie of a young otter, carelessly dipping and diving. When she finally surfaced for the last time, she stood inches away from his long muscled torso. She was mesmerizing in her naked state. Her cool blue eyes penetrated his soul as his steely circles surrounded her heart. Like the very feathers that had covered her body, his soft fingers pulled her gently into his waiting arms. Lizzie offered him no resistance.

Her long raven colored hair hung to her waist with a few rebellious strands draped over her slender shoulder. Her crystal blue eyes stared adoringly into his steely circles as droplets of water slid from her long black lashes when she blinked. She stood still as a statue for several minutes as she slid even closer to his naked form.

There in the middle of the warm water their burning flesh bonded them together as one. The broken down cowhand that had appeared out of nowhere and the self-made sorceress who'd been condemned because of her sister's blood. They were a perfect match. Like two wild horses. Neither broken to lead waiting for the ideal rider.

Charlie gently placed his hand in the small of her back. It was as though he was breaking a wild colt gently gaining its confidence. Their breathing became united as she bathed in the silhouette of his quiet being as his wanting lips covered hers. She melded against him like the droplets of water that clung to her wet tanned body.

When he finally released her she smiled through trembling lips as she led him to a hollowed out stone in the middle of the pond. "You sit here," she instructed, "the water will feel good on that sore ole back."

As far as he could tell the warm water appeared to be coming from a small opening several rocks above where he sat. The soothing warmth felt like massaging fingers on his back. Maybe the water was magic.

Lizzie made herself comfortable on a rock by his knees as she leaned her head against Charlie's thigh. There was no reason for words. All that would have done was spoil the moment, like rotting fruit. So, they sat silently like two muskrats just enjoying each others company and the warmth of the inviting water. After a passage of time had come and gone, Charlie slid down next to Lizzie.

There were no words to describe the way she made him feel as she placed her long tanned arms around his muscled neck. Like a champion with his prize, he carried her wet body to where their blanket lay beneath the large weeping willow. As though she were a piece of fine china he laid her down on the soft offering.

Lizzie's heart felt like it was going to explode out of her wanting chest as she lay cuddled within Charlie's strong muscled arms. He was exceptionally handsome on this warm moonlit night with his silver flecked hair pushed back away from his rugged looking face. His long torso was hard and solid for an older man. But on this particular night he acted anything but old. His cool steely eyes absorbed every square inch of her lying here within the magical beams of the silver moonlight. His typically rough hands felt like softly tanned leather against her skin as he ran his fingers down the middle of her wet back. The warmth of it gave her goose bumps. It was an odd sensation, as though those broken fingers had belonged there from the beginning of time. Almost like they had a way of branding his name on her skin. Lizzie hadn't felt this alive in years.

"We've changed everything tonight, you know," he whispered in a husky voice.

"I know," she answered breathlessly as his warm lips kissed the side of her long slender neck.

"No regrets, Lizzie?" he asked in a whisper.

"Not one, Charlie," Lizzie swooned.

"Nor I you, Lizzie Baxter," he whispered as his wanting lips gently touched hers.

"But, Charlie, I've never..."

Now he understood.

Liza took her sister's advice and was on a dead run to catch up with Albert's wagon. "Albert," she yelled several times.

When he realized that it was her calling his name he brought his horse up with a quick start. "Liza!" he said red faced. "I didn't see you! Are you all right? Why, I nearly ran you over!"

"Oh, yes, quite," she stammered, unaffected by the dust in her face. "Listen, it's awful late, would you like to stay here for the night?"

"I don't know," he stated soberly. "Is that decent?"

"Decent? I think so. Unless you plan on running around the yard naked!" she laughed. "If you're worried about it you can stay in Lizzie's room if you'd like," Liza offered. "She won't be home till morning. Or we have an extra room in the barn that's quite nice that no one uses." She gave him an adoring smile, "Maybe we could go for a moonlit walk later."

The handsome man gave Liza an understanding smile. He hadn't been sure of her affections until now. He hadn't been sure that she felt about him the way he felt about her at all. So, he graciously accepted her invitation. "I think I'd better stay in the barn though," he laughed. "Lizzie's room a might too close!"

"Why, Albert!" Liza giggled as the two of them unhitched the wagon and put his horse in one of the stalls with plenty of grain and hay. "It's just back here,' she offered cheerfully as she opened the door to a clean, neatly kept room. "For our special guests."

"Thank you, Liza," he said genuinely as he turned and faced the beautiful woman.

"No, thank you, Albert," she sighed as she closed and locked the door behind them.

"Liza Baxter!," he said through shocked lips. "I had no idea."

"Well, now you do!"

CHAPTER 29

Charlie and Lizzie lay sleeping like two quiet stones beneath the beams of the moonlight when something woke Lizzie with a start. An old familiar feeling had found its way into her mind warning her of an intruder. She sat up for several seconds and stared at her surroundings but she couldn't see or smell anything within the light of the shining moon. Satisfied that it was nothing she nudged the man lying next to her. "Charlie," she whispered, "I'm cold." When she turned and looked into his sleepy face she saw a completely different Charlie.

With a sparkle in his eye he held up the edge of the blanket and eagerly welcomed her warm body inside. But, when she glimpsed one more time over her shoulder, Lizzie jumped like a cat to her feet! She swore she saw a very familiar pair of sea green eyes in the darkness.

"Lizzie?" Charlie said as he scouted the darkness. "What is it?"

"Ghosts I guess." She whispered. "Nothing but ghosts."

"There's no ghosts here, Lizzie only you, me, and the moon. Hurry up and scooch in here now I'm cold."

Within seconds of hearing the sound of his heartbeat, Lizzie fell sound asleep.

But in the darkness just past the ripple of the tall wispy reeds a pair of angry sea green eyes crossed the distance to where the beautiful seductress lay within the arms of the contented cowhand.

Dripping wet the silent invader hid within the shelter of the darkened shadows. "One more second and I'd have slit your disloyal throat you two-timing harlot! One more! That's all I needed!" Back and forth the hidden bandit stomped like a rutting bull on the soft marshy grass. "Then he'd of been dead, you nothing less than a murderer, tried, convicted, and hung! You're high and mighty rein would be over! Finished! You'd never be able to bring forth another suckling prairie rat like the heathen you raised! The one that acts just like you! " Hidden in the timber he looked across the steaming pond.

"Like a slick snake you slip through my fingers, escape my grasp! You're in my way! Holding up progress! But not this time!" He placed his shaking hand over the small bag that hung with a thick black braided twine around the bandits neck. "This time I will finish what I've started." He let out a wicked laugh. "So, you sleep tight my little prairie witch! Stay snuggled against the skin of your spurious cowboy! But know this, you two she-devils are about to learn a valuable lesson the hard way! I'll see to it personally!" he seethed as he exited the opposite side of the timber. Frustrated he mounted his horse and disappeared into the night.

CHAPTER 30

Three months had come and gone since the marital union of Emmy and Matthew. They were such a happy couple. And the love that they felt for each other became magnetically contagious in the Baxter household.

It had taken longer than Liza and Lizzie thought it would for all the paperwork to clear the main filing in Cheyenne but when it did there were tears galore when the deed to Hattie's property was given to the young couple for a wedding present. Their souls could rest knowing no one outside the Baxter family would ever own the rights to that particular piece of ground again. It would connect with the far West side of the Baxter Ranch.

Jeffrey was furious the morning they gave the document to the young couple. When they left the room his attention turned immediately to the lovely woman on the other side of the table. "Well, once again you have outdone yourself—mother," he said in an insolent manner as he stared at her through reddened eyes across the breakfast table. "What, did good ole Aunt Lizzie talk you into this one, too? You don't seem to be able to do anything without her permission!"

Liza stared into the angry face of her troubled son. She couldn't help but wonder what in the world had happened to him. Why was he always so hateful? She'd tried hard to keep everything equal between the two boys but Jeffrey made it hard. "No," she said in a determined tone as her eyes lightly filled with water.

"Oh now what, you gonna cry?" There was no remorse in his face, "Why, because I told the truth? Because, I know that you've always loved Matthew more than me?" He sat like a rooster on a fence post. "I'm not afraid to call you on your stupidity, mother!"

But, Jeffrey had no more than gotten the words out of his ugly mouth when Lizzie rounded the corner of the kitchen and kicked his chair to the floor. Within seconds the loud mouthed hoodlum lay sprawled out like a spider with nothing but broken lumber beneath him. "When you're in this house you worthless weasel, you will address everyone with respect," her words were like ice.

"You stinking, witch!" he hollered as he tried to get back up.

Within seconds he lay back on the floor with Lizzie's face inches away from his own. He knew if she could have killed him right then, she would have. The woman was frightening! He never saw her pull the knife like a sixth finger from its hiding place but he knew it was there and he knew what her intentions were as he felt the tip of the metal blade burning a hole in his throat. "Listen you pile of cow dung!" she seethed as she held the front of his shirt with her knee purposely gouging his abdomen. "I will gut you like a fish if you ever talk to me that way again!" She was lightning quick and it was all Jeffrey could do keep from staining his pants as he tried to slide across the floor, doing everything he could to get away from her. And her eyes, they were black as coal! She reminded him of a coiled rattlesnake! "Mother!" he whined.

"You'd better call for your, mother!" Lizzie hissed. "Cause she's the only thing that's kept you alive this long!" Then, like the boy's flesh burned her hands, Lizzie released her grasp and walked over and poured herself a cup of coffee, never taking her eyes off of the younger Baxter.

Liza sat at the table shaking her dark head. "This conversation is over, Jeffrey," she said soberly.

"You have no idea how over it really is—mother!" Jeffrey stated in a huff as he hurried out the door just as Abe walked in.

"What did I miss?" he asked suspiciously.

"Nothing," they said in unison just as Hattie placed a fresh plate of butter biscuits on the table.

Hattie had become quite a hand at the Baxter ranch both in the kitchen and in the garden. Her meals were nothing less than spectacular and no one was willing to give her up. Especially, Abe. Why, according to him the angels themselves had landed smack dab in his kitchen and he was willing to do battle with the devil himself to keep her.

"Morning," she said in a light tone. After all of the hideous remarks that the lying scoundrel had made about her dear sweet Emmy, she couldn't help but enjoy the show when Lizzie reprimanded the nasty tongued outlaw. She had been watching the inevitable disturbance from a safe distance and as far as she was concerned the dark eyed vixen gave him everything that he deserved. "I believe someone just rode up to the yard, Liza," she teased as she gave her a warm smile.

Liza had been seeing Albert on a regular basis since Matthew and Emmy's wedding. They seemed like an odd match and yet they were perfect for each other. There was no missing the affection he felt for the blue-eyed twin when she would come into view. He saw Jeffrey hurry across the wide open yard just as Liza stepped out on the wooded porch.

"Morning," she said with a wide smile.

"Morning, beautiful," he answered.

"Coffee?" it was plain to see that the sentiment between the two was mutual.

When he stepped up onto the platform he gently kissed her cheek, "I told Luke I'd help him out for a minute or two, then I'll be in."

"All right," she said as she watched him walk toward the barn. "Hattie made biscuits." She couldn't help but smile as he waved his hand behind his head.

CHAPTER 31

Albert had taken the time on more than one occasion to show Luke the many shortcuts to setting a good pair of shoes on any horse, tame or ornery. How to gently restrain a raunchy colt so you didn't get your head kicked off. He'd shown Matthew how to make sure that his grain didn't get wet and his secret way of storing it. When Albert walked into the dimly lit barn his first encounter was with the one person he didn't want to have any dealings with. "Morning, Jeffrey," he said politely.

Jeffrey openly opposed his mother's so-called choice of a boyfriend and he refused to be a part of it. The hatred he felt for the blacksmith was very evident. He had a way of constantly, throwing in sly dirty little remarks whenever he could. He'd told his mother on more than one occasion that the man was nothing more than a gold digger after their family fortune. He made a big stink every time the man showed up, embarrassing his mother with his blunt outbursts. Obviously, today would be no different.

"So, you out smellin' the dog?" he asked in a filthy tone. "My mom in heat?"

Albert wanted nothing less than to take the punk kid and rattle his head a good one against one of the heavy wooden planks. Maybe the blow would put his brain back into a normal condition. But, instead he simply said, "That's no way to talk about your, mother. Pretty disrespectful don't you think?"

"What I think don't seem to matter round here," he said in a dejected tone. "But you, you're the main dog. Come around here acting like you know so much. Trying to impress my mother right out of her money with your so-called knowledge!" He let out an arrogant laugh, "That won't be hard, she's not that bright." Jeffrey saw the heated flame in the man's eyes. "What, I hit a nerve? You want to hit me Mr. Blacksmith man? You want to hurt me?" Jeffrey stood there full of himself knowing that Albert would never lay a hand on him. "What, you think my mother will want a man what beat her son?" Then he took a step closer. "Just so's you know, I'm not afraid of you so come on you stinking money grubber let's do it!

Let's see how tough you really are! I'm gonna...," he never got to finish his sentence.

"What in the devil's gate is the matter with you?" Abe hollered as he grabbed Jeffrey by the back of his shirt and pants. Like a mountain the man stood over the boy shaking him hard. "I've told you time and time again never to talk about your mother like that! Have you no conscience? Decency boy? What is it going to take with you? Do you hear me?" Abe was furious. "Now, you will face the consequences." Within seconds, Abe and Jeffrey disappeared from sight.

"I'm sorry, Papa, I didn't mean it!" Jeffrey begged. "Besides, Aunt Lizzie started it! She's always getting me in trouble!"

Albert heard the young man squeal as they faded from sight. "There's a lot of hate in that boy," the blacksmith said as he walked toward the back of the barn.

Lizzie and Charlie sat horseback in the open yard as they watched Abe drag the young man into the timber and out of sight. "Something's not right with that boy," Lizzie sighed. "In his head. Something just ain't right." Together they lopped out the wooden arch.

The twosome slipped off at every given opportunity but offered no explanation as to the depth of their involvement. They made it very plain that their relationship was no one's business but their own. But Lizzie had a glow about her that no one had seen in years. The soft-spoken cowhand and the beautiful enchantress. They seemed to make the perfect pair.

After Abe had taken Jeffrey for a little stroll in the woods life seemed to settle down a bit. Especially, since Abe gave the young man an unpleasant ultimatum to his inheritance and the promise from the back of his hand if he didn't straighten up. But, that didn't stop him from telling everyone he knew that he didn't agree with his brother's choice in a bride.

He would boast how there were several beautiful women in the small town that would have better suited for their prestige. Especially, the pretty young dressmaker. After all their family had tamed this land single handedly. They certainly didn't need some large, hipped heifer to ruin their bloodline.

He also let everyone know how much he disliked the livery man that had taken such a shine to his mother, trying to convince them that all he was after was her money. His and Matthew's inheritance. But more than that he told anyone that would listen how much he hated his Aunt Lizzie. How badly she treated her own flesh and blood. That she'd just a soon kill him as look at him. That someday she would be sorry for his mistreatment.

The people in the small town were sick of hearing about how badly Jeffrey was treated by the rest of his family and for the most part ignored his constant whining and lies. All he did was feel sorry for himself and complain about how much work was expected of him on a daily basis, which in fact he did very little. How hard his life had become, which he did nothing to change. How he never had any money and everyone else seemed to have more than their fair share, which he never once attempted to earn. He was sullen and jealous over his mother and his brother, which made every morning that he decided to grace his family with his arrogant presence explosive.

Today wasn't about to be any different! As usual Jeffery was being a pain where he sat down! And as usual he had been out drinking all night with his new found buddies. Lizzie chose to ignore the arrogance of the younger Baxter as she gave instructions to the rest of the family for the day's workload. Fall was coming on fast and they needed to get some late calves branded and check the outlying perimeter for strays one more time before the snow fell.

"Charlie, Emmy, you two will bring out the food and other supplies in the wagon. Naomi, you, and Clinton finish up doctoring that young heifer and her calf in the corral and then come out and join us. We'll all eat lunch together at the crooked branch."

"All right mother," Naomi said as she smiled at Emmy. Within minutes the two women disappeared out the door of the old log house.

"I'll expect you'll be next," Matthew kidded to Clinton as they each grabbed one more biscuit, gave Dancing Bear a quick hug and exited the door of the kitchen.

Jeffrey gave the pretty Indian woman a disgusted look as though the two men would have picked up some kind of a disease hugging her like that.

Then Lizzie stared at Jeffrey. She had a glint in her eye that he hadn't seen before. "You can ride with me today, nephew," she said bluntly knowing that the man would have nothing to do with it.

"Why, so you can make up some excuse to shoot me in the back and leave my dead body rotting on the prairie?" he was very leery of the look on her face.

"Maybe," she half laughed as she gave Liza a knowing look.

"You wish," he said in a disdainful tone.

"Then what do you plan on doing all day? Sleeping off another one of your drunken stupors? Encase you haven't noticed; this is a working ranch." Her voice had an icy edge to it.

"Like I don't know that," he countered, "you shove it down my throat every stinking day!"

"I'll shove something else down your throat you little weasel if you don't get that lazy thing you're sitting on out that door and get going with the rest of them!"

"I hate you!" he screamed.

"I'm sure you do," she answered with little emotion.

"Someday, you won't be able to boss me! You just wait! Someday, you'll be sorry!" he yelled red faced.

"Yeah, well not today," her dark eyes snapped at him. "So git!"

Within seconds, Jeffrey was out the door and hurrying to catch up with the others.

"Lazy brat!" she seethed.

"Amen," Liza agreed.

CHAPTER 32

It had taken a little longer than Charlie and Emmy had expected to get everything loaded into the wagon. "We're late," Emmy hollered through laughing lips as the twosome waved at Clinton and Naomi as they went past.

"We'll catch you in a bit, I think this horse has a stone in its foot," Charlie said in an unaffected tone.

"I can help," Clinton hollered as he started to pull up his horse.

"Nah, I got Emmy, she can help me." He gave the glowing woman a quick smile. "Don't worry, we'll be along."

"All right," Clinton said as he kicked his horse into a soft lope to catch up with Naomi.

Charlie loved Emmy. She was a wonderful young woman. And he too was glad that she and Matt were husband and wife. In fact lately, he had been wondering what was taking himself so long to let them know about, him and Lizzie. "So, you think that boy is worth it?" he asked the lovely woman sitting next to him teasingly as he watched the pride wash across her face.

"I don't know, but I'll make him believe that I am," she grinned.

"I bet you will," Charlie laughed out loud. "I bet you will!"

The twosome had traveled about two hours when Charlie noticed a small dust cloud to the East of them. He didn't know of anyone that was working cattle off in that direction so he handed Emmy the reins and cocked his rifle.

"What?" Emmy questioned in a worried tone. She saw the dust cloud too as her mind raced back to another terrifying time.

When Charlie saw the horrified look on her ashen face he gently patted her hand. "Probably nothing," he said in a voice that told the young woman he wasn't taking any chances. If Lizzie said watch your back, that's exactly what he intended to do. So, nonchalantly, he had Emmy cluck the horses up to a quicker pace. Their intended party couldn't have been more than a mile away. Just over the next ridge according to his rough calculations. "Now, if for some unknown reason, not saying that it will be, but if there is, and I tell you to make these horses blow outta here like dynamite, you do it ya hear?"

"Of course, Charlie," she said in a scared tone as she gripped the reins even tighter.

It wasn't a matter of being sharper or more in tune with the prairie it was just a stroke of luck that Charlie saw the shiny reflection from the rife barrel as he spotted a man hidden like a mole in a hole within the timbered trees. "What the hell are you doing way out here?" Instantly, he turned and laid his rifle against his shoulder and fired. Emmy jumped a foot. "Go, Emmy!" Charlie yelled.

Within seconds a shot was returned as Charlie slumped over the back of the seat. Emmy let out a high-pitched scream as she pounded the backs of the startled horses. From that point on everything happened in slow motion as Emmy continued to slap the backsides of the sweating team. They gave her all of the power that she asked for but Emmy had no idea where she was and when she made the startling discovery that she was too close to one of the small ravines, it was too late. "Mother!" she yelled as one horse slid over the edge of the steep slope pulling the other down the hillside like a skipping stone. There was no way to stop the inevitable; they were going over the edge. The wagon was going to roll!

Emmy couldn't believe her eyes as the wagon flew into the air like a rider being ejected from a green broke horse. She could hear the shrill sound of the horse's strangled squeals as one animal toppled over the other like two small children wrestling. She tried to hang on to Charlie's body but he was too heavy as the swirling force pulled him from her arms like a spinning top. Emmy's own body sailed across the distance like a bird scanning the horizon floating like a feather sliding like a piece of ice off the cliff into the fast moving water. "Matthew!" she whispered.

It took all of the strength that Charlie had to drag himself to where Emmy had slid over the edge of the tall ravine. He knew no one could have survived a fall like that. He could hear his own sobbing in his ears. "No!" he cried. "Not Emmy!" Within seconds, Charlie passed out.

When he came to there was a shadow standing over him like a large old tree. His face was shaded from the sun standing within inches of his head when he woke. Like a mule the shadow kicked Charlie as hard as he could in the ribs. "Dirty cow punching thief!" he yelled furiously. "What did you think an old worn out pile of cow dung like you could kill me? You should have listened!" He took pleasure in listening to Charlie let out a deep moan as the green-eyed marauder held him up close to his angry face as he spoke, "You're not man enough to be mixed with a Baxter you old cowpuncher! I told you that I'd get even with you!" With one quick kick the masked man shoved Charlie off of the steep ravine.

Charlie lay like a broken doll curled up in a pile of rocks just shy of the rolling water below the small cliff. The crazed man let out a low menacing laugh as he turned and mounted his pacing horse. Intentionally he rode past the point where Emmy had disappeared into the rolling water. He spit into the open void. "Not much of mule now, are ya?" Then he kicked his horse into a full out lope as he headed toward the safety of the thicket of trees. He knew it wouldn't be long before someone would come looking for the missing duo.

CHAPTER 33

It had been a good hour and Matthew was starting to get worried about where Emmy and Charlie were. They should have been here by now, even if the wagon was heavy with fencing and branding supplies. Naomi and Clinton hadn't been that far ahead of them. As he branded the larger heifers he constantly watched the horizon for the dust from the moving wagon and the team. Finally he walked to his horse and stepped aboard. "I'll be back in a bit," he said in a worried tone.

Lizzie looked up from the fire, "Where you going? We're not done yet."

"They should have been here by now. Something's happened. I can feel it."

"They probably had a problem getting that stone out is all," she concluded. "Do you want me to go with?" Lizzie asked as she came to her feet with a worried scowl on her dirty face.

"No, the wagon probably broke down or something. I'll be back before too long. Side's, she's got lunch!" he smiled.

As Matthew rode in the assumed direction that he thought the wagon would travel, his heart was in his stomach. It wasn't like Emmy and Charlie to be late. If either one said that they'd be somewhere they were there. But as his worried eyes scanned the distance he couldn't see any wagon. He was just about ready to turn back when his horse let out a loud nicker. In the distance the exact sound was returned. Trying to figure out where the sound was coming from, he kicked his horse into a soft lope. Once again the animal made the high pitched squeal, anxiously waiting for an answer. There was something familiar in the air and the horse knew it, so Matthew let him have his head as he loped over a hill and down a small ravine.

Matthew's heart stopped dead in his chest when he saw the turned over wagon sitting at the bottom of the small knoll. There was food and supplies strewn everywhere. Like the wagon had rolled several times before it came to rest on its side. "No!" he screamed out loud as he pounded the sides of his horse. Like a maniac he dismounted on the run.

Frantically, he looked for Emmy's broken body but she was nowhere to be seen. Like a scared pup receiving a bad scolding, he hesitantly looked over the edge of the watery ravine. His heart sank in his gut as he picked up a piece of her blue cotton shirt stuck on one of the jagged rocks. There was no doubt in his mind where Emmy was. The tall woman that was afraid of the water. The one that couldn't swim. His wife. His Emmy had been thrown into a watery grave. Matthew fell to his knees sobbing like a young child.

As he started to gather his senses about him he noticed that one of the other horses had a broken leg and was turning in circles around the edge of the rigging. The other stood still as a stone wrapped within the leather bands, seemingly afraid to move. As he held the shredded blue cloth in his hand he walked to where the hurting horse stood. His large oval eyes told Matthew that he didn't understand the pain. With one shot the animal lay lifeless on the hard grassy ground.

"What was that?" Lizzie said with a start as her head snapped upward at the sound of the echoing blast. In one quick stride she was aboard her horse and on a full out run in the same direction that Matthew had gone. Liza was hot on her heels.

For a brief moment, Matthew thought he heard a moan. When he turned around he couldn't see anyone. Then he heard it again. As he looked over the edge of the small ravine, praying that it might be Emmy, there lay Charlie on a long odd, shaped ledge that reminded him of a broken finger. "My god!" he yelled. "Charlie! Charlie are you all right?" There was no response from the devoted cowhand.

Like a gazelle Matthew ran to where his horse stood and grabbed his rope. Anxiously, he tied one end to the wheel of the wagon as he fully intended to climb to the bottom. But as soon as he flipped his rope down the side of the rocky cliff, Matthew stopped dead. Not more than two feet from where Charlie lay still as a stone was a huge diamond back rattler. As he studied the lay of things, there were several rattlers. Charlie had landed directly in the reptiles den. "Don't move!" he hollered. "My god!" he yelled. "This can't be happening! It can't!" he ranted, not knowing what to do.

Just as the last words left his mouth over the hill Lizzie came flying like the wings of an eagle. She dismounted on the run with her gun drawn. It only took a second for her to size up the unbelievable situation. Instantly, she put her gun back in the holster just as Liza flew over the ridge in the same fashion as her sister.

"Lizzie!" Matthew all but screamed. "Char, Charlie's down in the ravine!" He rubbed his hands through his black wavy hair like he couldn't believe what was taking place. His eyes were wild with fear and his face was ashen white. "He's in their den! He's lying there in the rattler's den!" Like a madman he let out an anguished scream that nearly deafened everyone.

Instantly, Lizzie grabbed him and slapped him hard across the face. As though the sting brought back a moment of reality, Matthew walked to where the last known remains of his beautiful young bride entered the rolling water, sobbing like a lost child.

"Charlie," Lizzie breathed in an emotional state as she glanced at her sister. Her whole life lay at the bottom of that ravine. "I'll go," Lizzie said in a collected tone as her heartbroken eyes followed the dangerous trail downward. "He's my man. It's my responsibility. I'll go."

"I can't allow you to have all the fun sister," Liza stated matter-of-factly as she took off her gun belt. "He might be your man, but I love Charlie, too."

"I have more immunity than you," Lizzie said matter-of-factly. "We both know that." Her cool blue eyes told her sister that she didn't believe her. "We both know the bite will come. Besides, the ledge might not hold us both."

"I don't care what comes!" Liza snapped. "You're not going alone!"

"Don't be a fool Liza," Lizzie said in a cold tone. "There's no since in us both being sick! It's all I'm going to be able to do just to get him out alive!"

"We'll go together," she said sternly, "we've always gone together. We'll share the bite; we'll share the fall."

"Who will pull us up?" Lizzie asked as she stared at Matthew's sobbing image. "The three of us? Who?"

Within seconds of her bold announcement Naomi and Clinton flew over the ridge at the same time, at breakneck speed. "Mother!" Naomi yelled breathlessly.

"Oh, no Mighty One!" Clinton stated under his breath as he saw Matthew rocking like a blind child at the side of the cliff. "What happened?"

"They, will pull us up," Liza smiled knowing she'd gotten her way.

"No," Lizzie said, "only you will know what I need from up here. If the rock breaks, then you come."

"So be it," Liza said in a concerned tone as Lizzie reached for her rope.

"Are you crazy?" Clinton yelled in disbelief. "You can't go down there! They're everywhere! No! Let's shoot them first! Even up the odds!" he said in a panicked tone as he paced the ledge.

"We could never fear our brothers," the twins said to Clinton as though it were from the same breath.

"You make sure and pull Charlie up when I tell you to," Lizzie stated through black trusting eyes as a nauseated feeling engulfed her senses. "Not one minute before."

Naomi walked to where the edge of the cliff started to fall off. Without speaking she sat in the tall grass and folded her legs. In a hypnotic state she started clucking. Clinton stared at the lovely young woman as though he were standing on some foreign ground. When she didn't acknowledge his presence, he sat next to her. As though her fingers were made of feathers she took his hand in hers. When he looked into her freckled face her wildflower eyes were completely dark. This was not the Naomi he knew. This was Chief Mad Dog's granddaughter, Chief Flying Eagle's daughter, this was the Mighty Princess, Little Feather.

She continued to cluck softly. Her eyes told him to do the same. At first it felt odd for Clinton sitting in the dirt with his legs crossed, clucking against the restraints of the blowing wind. But after he had done it for a while the pattern became constant and comforting. His whole body relaxed like a wet leaf as his wondering eyes looked forward and watched the amazing theatrical display unfolding in front of him.

Lizzie looked like a black widow spider as her long legs countered every water soaked rock that she came in contact with. Her movements were perfectly timed and in complete rhythm with her hands. When she did slip, Liza held her tight like a worm on the end of a fishing line.

"Liza," Lizzie said in a warning tone, "whatever you do don't drop me. There are at least six of them right under my feet." Her worried crystals wound within the answering circles of her sister.

"Don't drop you!" Liza grunted with a wet brow as she let go of the rope a little at a time. "What have you been eating lately? Lord, Lizzie! I pray the rope doesn't break!"

"Shut up!" Lizzie seethed from below her in a quiet put out voice. as she could "I'm the same as I've always been!"

"Yeah, tell that to my bleeding palms!" Liza hissed back.

"What? Are you saying that I'm fat, Liza?" she said angrily arguing with her sister.

"I never said that you were fat, Lizzie, just that this rope only holds so much weight!"

"I swear to heaven when I get back up there you and I are going to the dirt!" she threatened through tight lips.

"Oh, I'm scared now!" Liza said through clenched teeth.

"All right." Lizzie's voice changed completely as the anger became a whispered urgency. "Nice and easy, Liza," Lizzie whispered as her feet touched the rocks like a velvet cloak.

CHAPTER 34

In the distance Lizzie heard Naomi and Clinton clucking. No wonder the scaly reptiles were so dormant. It was the sleeping chant that Chief Mad Dog had taught them when they were young and now they were both grateful that Naomi had learned it too. "Don't stop now," she whispered to herself, "or neither one of us will live through this."

Liza laid across the top of the rough ravine, holding the rope like it was Lizzie's only lifeline. She watched in silent horror as twin looked like she was doing some exotic dance stepping over one snake's scaly back and then another. Carefully placing each footstep so she didn't disturb the poisonous serpents.

It had been years since Liza had seen so many rattlers's this size in one place. As though they'd been beckoned here by some unforeseen force.

After several minutes of holding her breath, Lizzie finally reached her destination.

"Charlie," she whispered with breathless emotion. There was no response. "Charlie," she said again as she rolled him over. Lizzie's heart began to pound in her chest as she saw the blood trickle from the side of his mouth. She knew he was barely holding on. Her heartbroken eyes followed the invisible beacon to where her sister laid waiting. For a brief passing in time their souls bound as one and Liza felt the beat of her sister's shattered heart. Her saddened eyes said it all.

"Please," Liza whimpered completely distraught, "not again." Tears of frustration etched their way down her tanned cheeks. "I beg you, don't let it be."

As Lizzie sat Charlie upright there was no missing the ache in his steely eyes or the bullet hole in his chest. She gave him a weak knowing smile as her heart sank like a hidden treasure. It was very obvious that the downed man wasn't going to be able to help her. So, she took in a deep breath as she tied the rope securely under his arms and knotted it over the hole in his chest. It took all of the strength that she had to drape his body across her back like a sack of wet grain. Lizzie let out a deep grunt as she came to her unsteady feet.

For a brief moment her mind traveled back in time to warm moonlit nights when his body covered hers like a soft blanket. She loved the touch of his hands as they traveled every inch of her body. The smell of his skin. The feel of his wanting lips that matched her own desire. The warmth within those steely eyes hungered only for her. She'd fallen heart and soul in love with Charlie Redbone.

Today, Charlie was a lot heavier than she remembered on those warm moonlit nights. "I'll save you, Charlie," she whispered through strained lips. "If it's the last thing I do! I've waited my whole lifetime for you, damnit! I love you Charlie Redbone and, and I don't love no one!" she sobbed. "You can't just appear out of the blue one day and die on the next! I won't allow it! Do you hear me, Charlie! Don't you die on me! Please Charlie, hold on!"

Tears of anguish ran down Lizzie's tanned cheeks as they splattered like rain in a red mud puddle. She took in a deep breath as she readied herself for the journey back to the bottom of the rocky ledge. She wasn't even sure she could get him there. "If it's the last thing I do, I'll save you Charlie." She whimpered. So like the soldier that she was, and through nothing less than pure grit and determination, step by step, she put one foot in front of the other.

It was a long tedious process as she made her way to the life line that her sister patiently held. "I'm coming, Liza," she whispered through strained lips. "I've got him, I'm coming." It didn't make any difference what or how long it took, Lizzie was determined to save the one person that made her whole.

When Lizzie fell face first landing on her skinned hands and bloodied knees she held her breath as she looked directly into the lifeless pools of the scaly reptiles. Their tails rattled high like a hundred beating drums. Their long clammy necks stretched to the limit of their boundaries, waiting.

Not all of the snakes were completely dormant but with Naomi's constant chanting most of them were paralyzed. Some of the larger snakes pretended to be frozen in a circle on the red ground. They acted like guards giving her safe passage never offering to block her path or bite. On several occasions one of the larger reptiles would slowly advance toward her, tongue snapping, tail shaking. She knew the attacking vermin would willingly pierce her skin over and over if they could slither close enough to invade the circle. They never made it that far. Protecting their princess the sleeping giants came to life. The bigger, heavier snakes hissed, coiled, attacked, and killed any serpent that came close to their guarded domain. It was an oddity neither twin had ever seen before.

"Thank you, Mighty One," Lizzie whimpered.

"Thank you, Mighty One," Liza whimpered within the same breath. .

Again and again Lizzie fell as she struggled from her bleeding knees to her unsteady feet as she stared at the braided lifeline like a compass. It seemed like an endless journey. When Lizzie finally made it to her destination she was weak, out of breath and physically exhausted.

"All right, Liza," she whispered breathlessly. "Give me a minute then pull him up." Like her fingers were made of lightning, Lizzie made a makeshift harness as she leaned Charlie up against the crumbling wall. Gently, she place a kiss on his warm bloody lips. "Don't leave me, Charlie. We've got lots of ridin' left to do."

Naomi and Clinton kept clucking.

"Clinton," Liza said in a soft urging tone. "I need you to come and help me. He's too heavy. I can't lift him."

As though the man was hypnotized from the constant echoing lullaby he started to his feet. But Matthew put his heavy hand on his broad shoulder and walked to where his mother lay on the top of the ravine. "I'll do it," he whispered in a broken voice.

Together, the two of them slowly pulled the broken cowboy to the top of the rocky plateau. Matthew couldn't believe Charlie was still alive with the blood trail he'd left behind him on the rocks below. As though his broken body was made of glass Matthew carried Charlie's battered body to safety and gently laid him down on the red dirt.

"Emmy?" the cowboy could barely speak.

All Matthew could do was shake his head as tears rolled down his reddened face. He was in shock.

Lizzie stood still as a stone at the bottom of the crooked fingered shelf with Charlie's thick sticky blood dripping down her muscled back like rain. Her hair and forehead soaked in salty sweat and red mud.

By the time Liza and Matthew looked over the edge of the crumbling ravine, there were at least thirty snakes gathered at the bottom of Lizzie's feet. One especially large black intruder. Where had this one come from? It was nothing like the rest of them. Lizzie could feel the heavy bodies of the waking assassins as they joined their newly acquired leader.

As Liza and Matthew looked down at the unthinkable sight it reminded them both of a well-schooled band of moving sticks. They continued to watch in complete horror as Liza started to cry from terrified frustration. He'd only seen his mother cry once in her life, and that was when Maria died.

"Mother," Matthew whispered completely distraught at her unexplainable condition. She was his rock and rocks don't cry.

Liza knew that her identical sibling was in deep trouble as she studied the unthinkable mess she was in. If she stayed where she was, her sister would die. There were too many of the sidewinding devils. She also knew if she went into the serpent's den to save her twin they would probably both die.

Lizzie was too far away for Liza to reach and Liza was too far away for Lizzie to reach. Both sisters were too far away to salvage the bite. Both sisters were too far away to save each other.

Liza looked down just as Lizzie's large blue agonizing eyes looked up. Both women had the impending look of death on their dirty grief-stricken faces. They knew if one died they'd both die. One heart. One Soul. One breath. Liza could feel her sister's confused pain; Lizzie could feel her sisters.

Lizzie knew the birth-born devotion they held for each other and the selfless choice her sister was about to make. Those devastated circles begged her sister not to come but Liza ignored her sister's silent request.

Matthew watched in complete awe as a lone teardrop fell from his mother's tortured eyes. Just as the very same droplet fell from his aunt Lizzie's tortured eyes. Both pods of icy blue water cascaded downward to certain death. His mind swore the lone teardrop seemed motionless...was it even falling? Once again he shook his head in disbelief. None of this was real! It couldn't be! Then, from out of nowhere he swore he saw a cloud of eagle feathers cascading downward cradling but not touching the lone teardrop as both women silently wept.

"Forgive me," she whispered emotionally to her son. "She can't fight them alone and I can't let her." Today her allegiance was for their survival, within seconds Liza slipped over the edge of the deep ravine.

"Mother!" Matthew yelled in complete shock. "No!" he howled just as the parallel beads of blue water collided then exploded like lit dynamite! Matthew fell backward from the impact of the blow like a startled cat holding the life line to his mother's fate! The blast was loud like high-pitched thunder as it echoed across a deep endless canyon! Once again he shook his head trying to gain some semblance of reality!

Anxiously, he scrambled to the edge of the rocky ravine. The sight below was unimaginable! "What in the name of all that's real is going on here?" he asked himself as he watched every entrecote movement his mother made trying desperately to reach her sister.

"Water?" he questioned his eyesight for at the bottom of Lizzie's feet was a large blue pool of water. It stood out like a yellow moon on a dark night. "Where did the...? How did the...?" All he could do was hold his breath and watch!

Matthew was shocked at how the scaly serpents shied away from the pool of icy blue water. Hissing their way back to dry land just as his mother's feet lightly touched the red ground. For a brief moment he only saw one person. Not two. In his minds-eye that was impossible yet here he sat stunned by the undeniable scene. Watching as the watery protection gave the two hearts a moment to breathe, to share this unthinkable heartache. To share the unfathomable destruction.

He'd heard his Papa say when he was a boy, over and over how their battles were one and the same. He'd told him how good always devoured evil. But, how was this good! For who? Charlie? Lizzie, Emmy? Brokenhearted he listened to Naomi and Clinton's constant clucking.

There they stood. The two of them. Like one huge immoveable force. Determined to save each other. Denying the death serpent's angry quest. One breath, one heart, one soul, the same blood.

"Are you some kind of idiot?" Lizzie whispered, totally putout with her identical sibling for climbing down the rope.

"You're welcome," Liza whispered back through clenched teeth.

"Well, now that you're down here what's your great escape plan?" Lizzie asked with one arched brow as she felt the water subsiding.

"I don't know, I think I must have been out of my mind," Liza lied.

"That is so typical of you!" Lizzie seethed through tight lips knowing she would have done the same thing.

"If you're so upset, why am I standing here risking my life?" she accused. There was no hiding the relief in both sisters' resigned faces. The placate that lingered within those dark circles told them both this was an unimaginable situation. That the love they shared for each other had selfishly put them in harm's way.

Like two old Weeping Willows they waited for the sound of the whispering wind to give them direction as they stood perfectly quiet. Then, Liza began to cluck. Lizzie did the same. As the water subsided it gave the twins just enough time to regain their strength.

Liza and Lizzie had no idea how long they had stood in the midst of the lions den. An hour. A minute. Two or five. All they saw when they opened their eyes were hundreds of waking reptiles! Hissing and rattling when one scorned objector came too close to another. Drying red rocks! And, one large black serpent his only intent was their demise!

Like two sleek cats they each grabbed the waiting rope and started climbing.

"It must have been your singing," Lizzie chided. "They died of boredom."

"My singing!" Liza snapped back at her sister, "how can you even say that? Do you think this is a joke! Singing is the least of our problems!"

Then as though the insult from her identical sibling finally sunk in she retorted, "Besides, have you listened to your own voice lately? Even that old rooster in the barn can't compete with that! Shoot! He'd probably croak just trying to match it!" Bickering, that's what they did when they were scared. And right now, they were both terrified.

"Liza, Liza, Liza," Lizzie scoffed. "We all know that I got mother's..." Lizzie froze in her tracks. "Liza," Lizzie whispered barely moving her lips, "with the Mighty One as my judge don't move."

The tone of Lizzie's voice made Liza freeze like a prairie dog hiding from a hungry predator. Lying on the back of her pant leg like a scaly leprous leach was a huge black rattler. As though he were an eight-legged centipede climbing a rock he slid up Liza's back like the bullet of a stone-cold killer.

She could feel the weight of its clammy body as it draped itself over the edge of her shoulder. Her breathing became sporadic and slow. She'd had encounters with snakes since she'd been a child, but she'd never been close enough to smell their breath. The fearless encounter didn't unnerve Liza in the least as she stared at his large square head. Like a King on his throne, he rested there for several minutes as though he were on the top of the world. Taunting her, waiting for the perfect moment to strike, paralyze and kill his prey. He was big, wily, and angry.

Lizzie knew that her attack would have to be precisely timed and perfectly executed. But more than that she knew the bite would be intense. That the slimy serpent would slide its long needle-like fangs deep into her tanned flesh like a fishhook. That it would be harsh in the coming and scolding in the going. That she would take the punishment from this designated King for intruding in his sanctioned paradise! No matter how unintentional it had been.

Lizzie spoke to the slithering snake in a calm soothing tone. But the scaly reptile refused her message as he continued to climb. Fearlessly she stared into his dark clammy eyes. Something was different and it made the hair on the back of her neck stand up. She spoke to the snake again only this time in Chief Mad Dog's native tongue. Lizzie saw the words had confused the serpent for a brief moment as a clarity washed across those beady dark eyes, then just as quickly it reverted back to its mutated state giving Lizzie just enough time to wrap her strong hand around the back of the fighting snakes massive head.

The reptile fought its startled restraints! It jumped, squirmed, slapped, and tried to bite like a rabid dog. A characteristic they had never dealt with. He was so heavy and his slippery body made him hard hold! Something was definitely a miss here. A hidden force that Lizzie couldn't identify had been placed deep within the scaly serpent, just like the one Liza had dealt with in the small place called Crocker. Like an eagle's talon she clung to the massive hunk of flesh knowing better than to let him go. "Hurry, Liza, get to the top, I can't hold him much longer!"

"But, he's going to bite you!" she argued, scared for her sister's life. "Let me take him!"

It had been a long time since Lizzie had experienced the pain of those poisonous crystals. And, its determined persistence somewhat surprised her when she felt the honed sard penetrate her skin. "He already has," she said through a pained look as she clung to his wiggling flesh. She didn't want to kill the wily serpent. On more than one occasion these very reptiles had provided the main ingredient to their medical medicinal potions. She couldn't disrespect the one that had taught them those secret remedies even if it had been dosed with bad magic, sent on an unthinkable journey.

"Get rid of him, Lizzie!" Liza shouted. "Hit his head against the rocks and throw him! Throw him hard! He's evil!"

But, instead she held her breath as she gave the scaly rattler a hard throw into the wild blue yonder! But the reptile was having none of it! As though the wily deceiver sprouted wings he purposely jumped at Liza. As she threw herself away from the intended bite, the rope, her lifeline snapped like a dry twig.

Lizzie grabbed her falling sister by the back of her pants. "Hold on, Liza!" Lizzie demanded frantically as she wrapped her arm several times around the tightened rope that bound them together. "Hold on to my leg!" Liza hung upside down like a bat! "This isn't a good position, sister. From here, your butt looks huge!" Lizzie said. "I hope he didn't bite you there!"

"Shut up! There's nothing wrong with my butt!" she countered as she clung upside down to her sister's leg. "Quit babbling up there and get us out of here!"

"Don't pull my leg out of the socket!" Lizzie argued. "I'll never walk again!"

"Clinton!" Matthew yelled. "Help me! I can't hold both of them!"

Like a bullet, Clinton hurried to where Matthew sat, holding the dangling duo. When the two women finally reached the top of the ravine, Clinton and Matthew had droplets of sweat pouring from their brow.

"My word!" Clinton exclaimed, "What were you two arguing about? That was no place to argue!"

"My butt!" Liza stated in an insulted tone.

"Your what?" Clinton stood there completely baffled at her reply. "You could have both been killed! That's no place to argue about your butt! Did it bite either one of you? The snake! Did he bite you?"

"Yes," Lizzie stated with no emotion as she ran to where Charlie lay.

Then he stared at Liza. "Yes," Liza stated as she stared at her sister with regret as she sympathetically joined her.

"Where did he bite you?" Clinton asked in a furious tone. "Where blast it?" He looked like a coyote standing in front of a firing squad! "Where!"

The two women were taken aback at the younger man's rattled demeanor. It wasn't like him to get so shook up. "It's all right, Clinton. We will take care of it," Liza whispered.

Brokenhearted, Lizzie knelt down beside the faithful cowhand. His typically wind burned face was ashen and his shirt was drenched with blood. Lizzie couldn't believe her eyes. "Charlie," she whispered. Her heart was in her throat. "What happened, Charlie?" she said through a barely audible voice as Naomi wrapped part of her shirt around the bite on the back of her mother's arm. "Can you hear me?"

She knew her cowboy was dying. That today he'd taken his last ride beneath the azure blue western sky; his last lope across this forsaken open prairie. That by nightfall him and ole Redbone would be gathering strays hidden behind those sparkling stars they shared on so many moonlit nights. Driving them cattle toward the Mighty One's opened gates. Lizzie dropped her head. There was nothing that she could do to stop it. No medicine to cure it or, magic strong enough to save, Charlie.

"Lizzie," he mumbled just as the last color of life faded from his steely eyes, "for the brand." Then, Charlie placed a small black bag in her trembling hand as he took in his last breath.

"No!" Lizzie screamed. "Don't leave me, Charlie Redbone!" she screamed. "I can't do this! I can't!" Lizzie hung her head as she took her sister's hand in hers. Together they shook their fists toward the heavens and chanted words that neither Clinton nor Matthew understood.

Instantly, a huge whirlwind swirled around them like a tornado. The dirt and the blowing sand was blinding. It was as though they had scolded the heavens for pulling the life from this empyreal man.

When the wind finally subsided, Lizzie laid her head on Charlie's bloody chest and wept in a fashion that no one had ever seen. It was like her heart had been turned inside out flooding the drowning chamber with her own blood. Filling the fading vessel with debris from the aftermath of an unexpected fate. A sweet whisper of love that had allowed the sunlight to flow back down the passageway to her dying soul. The ripped violently away. Within seconds Lizzie was throwing up.

"We need to get you two home!" Clinton exclaimed completely shocked at what had just happened.

"No!" Lizzie screamed. "I won't leave him! I can't!"

"There's nothing we can't do for him now! We have to go!" Clinton practically threw the two women onto the backs of their waiting horses. He gave them no time to retrieve their own reins as he raced for the safety of the Baxter ranch.

When they got to the house Abe was just mounting his horse to come and find them. Charlie's horse had come back to the barn alone. "What in the world!" Abe exclaimed as he dismounted.

"They're bit!" Clinton hollered. "Help me!"

"Who's bit?" Abe asked.

"Liza and Lizzie, the snakes bit them bad!"

Abe knew that the two women were immune to the reptile's horrendous bite but he also knew that they would be very sick. "It's all right, Clinton, calm down. They will be fine."

"What's alright? Nothing is alright! None of this... I don't' even know what to call what's alright!" he shouted uncontrollably.

Quickly, they helped the twins up the stairs toward their rooms. "Stop!" Lizzie insisted. "Liza has to come to my room! Our room!" she screamed.

"Why your room?" Liza asked offended at her sister's insistent request. "Why not my room?"

"Because we have to be together! This has always been our room! Our room!" she seethed through angry heartbroken tears. "If you..! If...you... die! You're not dying without me!" she screamed at the top of her lungs. "Not without me!"

Even Liza was shocked at her sister's outburst. "Alright, Lizzie." She conceded. "I won't die without you. I promise." Then she made a face and crossed her eyes.

"I saw that!" Lizzie snipped.

Like a scurrying squirrel Naomi started the process of extracting the venom from her mother's shoulder. "Mom, this is going to hurt," she said sympathetically.

"I've been hurt worse...!" But Lizzie let out a yowl that rattled the windows as Naomi opened the swelling wound. Like a well-schooled physician she placed the special powder in the opening as the poison started to bubble out.

"Whatever you do Clinton don't touch that if you have an open cut on your hand." Naomi instructed in a direct manner. "Hand me that yellow moss right there." She directed. "Thanks. This will absorb anything that the venom comes in contact with." She saw the worry on Clintons pale face. "It's all right. I'm immune, too." Carefully, Naomi bandaged her mother's shoulder as she turned and gave Liza a weak smile. "Same for you Auntie." Naomi instructed with tears in her eyes as Clinton walked Lizzie toward the large feather bed.

Liza patted Naomi's warm hand and gave her a reassuring smile. "I'm much stronger than, Lizzie. She's always been a chickens butt! Why, I've had...!" Liza let out a high-pitched earthshattering yowl! "Devils gate, Naomi! Did you cut my shoulder off?"

"Ahh-huh! Chickens butt am I?" Lizzie snipped at her identical twin as one boot then the other dropped on the floor.

Just then Abe stuck his head around the bedroom door. "What in the name of corn-jar whiskey is going on here?" Immediately, he gave Clinton a hard stare. His face said he needed answers.

"We ran into a bit of trouble, Abe." He stated matter-of-factly.

"I see that. Where's, Matthew?" Abe's voice was stern.

"I don't know." He answered plainly. "I don't know."

As quickly as Abe appeared, he disappeared.

"I don't think we should talk about it right now, sir. Not here." But, when he turned around no one was standing next to him. "Where'd he go?"

"Talk about what?" Lizzie questioned. "We're not dead ya know! We're right here! Tell em sister!"

"Yeah!" Liza added. "We're right in the room for crying-out-loud!"

"Naomi," Lizzie said in a pathic tone, "don't be concerned, we will have high fevers for several days, maybe even a week. Just watch for the yellowing ooze."

"Yes, the yellowing ooze." Liza repeated.

"If it comes then you'll know what to do." Her demeanor was so dramatic.

"Who? Who's coming sister?" Liza asked in a confused tone.

"There may be some sleep talking. Even mystery dreams." She said truthfully as she scowled at her sister.

As the twin sister's sat quietly with their fevered heads against the full feather pillows it was plain to see the effects of Naomi's sleeping tea and harrowing incidences of the day had started to invade their exhausted conscience. They both had the start of slight glazing over their bloodshot eyes. Silent tears drifted down Naomi's tanned cheeks as she laid her head on Clintons shoulder.

In the distance the small group heard the distinct echo of horse's hooves as the jangle of riggings rattled like death in the open yard. It sounded like a hollow tomb in Lizzie's aching heart. The two identical women heard every hoofbeat as their large hooves pounded the dry dirt. The sound startled their slumbered senses to a honed remembrance as the two women took in a deep breath. The familiar sound jolted them both to life the way a cranky ole rooster wakes a sleeping household.

CHAPTER 35

Matthew was in shock when he rode into the grounds of the Lazy AB Ranch with Charlie's dead body like a slain deer tied to the back of one of the horses from the shattered wagon. Mechanically, he handed Abe the reins to the sweating animal as he stepped down. But, his feet had no more than touched the sacred earth when the most ear-piercing, high-pitched scream came from the upper floor of the old log house.

Like a rocket Abe started running. "Lizzie!"

Matthew fell to his knees! "Emmy!" he sobbed in the openness of the quiet yard as he stared at the stars above him.

It was complete ciaos when Abe slammed open the door to Lizzie's bedroom. Naomi had a hog tied hold on Liza and Clinton was doing his best to hold his own with Lizzie! Both women were hell-bent on destruction.

"Let me go!" Lizzie screamed. "He's waiting for me! You stinking skunks hind end! I heard him! I heard him!" Her eyes were full of fever. "No!" she screamed. By now Liza had escaped Naomi's wrestling move. The two of them stood shoulder to shoulder on the far side of the room. Their dark eyes snapped. Daring anyone to come close. They looked like two ghosts in their long white nightgowns.

Clinton had never seen anything like it! They were terrifying! No reasonable force to be reckoned with! "Naomi, are you hurt?" he asked as he held her close.

"No." she answered. "Liza would never hurt me."

Abe stated matter-of-factly. "You need to know that's not Liza and that's not Lizzie." His tone made the hair on her arms stand up. "This is Warrior Walks the Night. And, this is Warrior Stalking Moon."

"What?" Naomi whispered in disbelief. "Back away slowly. I'll handle this from here. Clinton!"

Clinton was completely rattled! He'd never encountered anything like this in his life! "Abe, we had some…! Not me so much but Liza and Lizzie…! It was horrible! We…, me and Naomi clucked and clucked…! I didn't know what—to—do…! Snakes!" He shouted.

"Hundreds of them! Where'd they come from?" He gave Abe an odd look. "Emmy!" he wept. "Holy heavens! Sweet, Emmy! We can't find her! Couldn't find her! The water! Too much water!" Immediately, Clinton rubbed his hands through his black curly hair. "There was trouble Abe! Too much trouble!"

Instantly, Abe wacked Clinton hard in the face. "Stop it!" he demanded.

Clinton stood there in shock. "Yes sir." He said as he shook his head. What had just happened? Did he get kicked in the face by a mule?

Then Abe turned around slowly as he cautiously walked to where the twins stood ready to do battle with this stranger who had dared enter their spiritual domain. Their eyes followed every movement he made like a hunting mountain lion ready to pounce on its prey! He'd only witnessed this behavior one other time when they were young. He knew what they were capable of then. He could only imagine what they could do now!

"Warrior Walks the Night, Warrior Stalking Moon," his tone was direct with authority. No pity. He couldn't show them any pity. "Chief Mad Dog say you do good today. He's very proud of the way you handled the danger!"

Their eyes scanned up and down his silhouette like a crawling spider. Neither twin moved a muscle. "So say you." They said together in a distrusting toneless voice.

They looked ridiculous standing there in identical white nightgowns. Holding their hands out like they both held a loaded pistol.

"He tells me he knows about the battle. He knows!" he stated with authority as he stared at their dirty faces. "I know. I know about the battle! You saved many!"

"Saved? Who are you to tell me, saved. And who is this that stands behind you like a shaking rabbit. Does she feel saved?" her tone was menacing.

"This is Flaming Sun, Chief Flying Eagles daughter!" he stated sternly. "You will speak of her with respect!"

"We do not know this daughter! How do we know this is true?" Like cats they slid closer. Their eyes were dark. "Our Chief will peel away your hide for what you did today!" they hissed as they spoke the same words at the same time.

"Give her to us! We will tell you of her worth!" they hissed.

This was a situation that Abe had never been in with the twins. He wasn't sure he could trust their intentions. "How do you know about the battle…in…here?" She placed her hand over her heart.

"How do you know save this battle?" they questioned looking like they were ready to pounce. "In here!" they demanded, their sharp eyes were cold and threatening.

"Because I am the one that taught you to fight the evil one! Me! You don't back down! You don't hide in the bushes like mice!" his tone was loud and demanding. "Me! Abe Baxter! I am the one that said, "Stand Tall!"

"And who tells her stand tall?" Liza accused.

"I will!" Demanded Naomi as she stood directly in front of them both. "I fight!" her eyes were dark and threatening. "Know that I am Little Feather daughter of Chief Flying Eagle and my mother Sunless Flame! I do not know you! I do not hide in the bushes like a scared mouse! I do not run like a chicken from a coyote! I stand! Beside you, Warrior Walks the Night! And with you Warrior Stalking Moon! I am not afraid!"

Together, the three women stood there, nose to nose, heartbeat to heartbeat! Naomi refused to be afraid of either one of them! Then she slowly backed away, her haunting eyes never left theirs. Immediately, the twins put their guns away.

"Come my princess warriors." Abe demanded. "It is time to rest from your battle. Your day has been long. You have done well!" his heart was pounding out of control.

"And you?" they stared at Naomi in a haunted gaze. "What will you be done?"

"I will stand watch!" she stated in a knowing tone. "I will shoot my arrows at the evil one! I will defend my birthright!"

"It will be." They said together.

"Come," Abe instructed. "We will discuss this thing!"

"Yes, father." They said in unison as though the spell they were under broke. Knowingly, they crawled under the cover's in the large feather bed. "Thank you, father. For saving us. Take many cares of our Little Feather, she is our sister's daughter."

Abe took in a deep breath as he pulled the covers securely around them. "Sleep now my wounded princesses. Sleep." When

Abe finished tucking them in and turned to face Clinton his features were pale white. "You come with me!" he demanded.

"Yes, sir." He said without hesitation.

"Naomi, you stay right here! Ya hear me?" he demanded.

"Yes, papa." Then she asked. "Was that real?"

"As it gets!" he answered as the two men hurried down the stairway through the front door of the old log house and out into the yard. Breathlessly Abe demanded Clinton. "Go help Luke!" Then he grabbed his grandson by the shoulders and pulled him to his unstable feet.

The heartache that sat within Matthew's disbelieving eyes ripped his heart out. The shaken circles told his grandfather that he didn't understand any of it. "She's really dead," he said plainly with no emotion.

"Dead?" Abe questioned.

"Emmy," Matthew stated in a hollow tone as he held the blue cloth from her shirt in his trembling hands. "She fell into the river, papa," he said sadly, "she can't swim. Charlie, too. He's lying dead on the horse."

"No!" Abe said completely speechless as he pulled his grandson into his large arms.

"She never hurt anybody," he wept. "Why would someone want to do such a terrible thing?"

"I don't know," Abe said compassionately hoping that the young man didn't collapse where he stood.

"Hadn't she been through enough, papa?" he struggled to say. "Battled enough?" His face was so full of pain and misunderstanding! "Can we bury her memory next to mother and Maria?" he asked in a compassionate tone. "Can we papa? No one will ever hurt her there."

"Of course," Abe said through tear-filled eyes just as Jeffrey rode into the open yard.

"Thank you, Papa," Matthew whispered as he walked toward the barn. He never acknowledged his brother. He never saw him.

There was no missing the cagey look on Jeffrey's face as he walked to where Abe stood holding one of the crippled horses. "What's wrong with Charlie?" Jeffrey questioned. "Too much whiskey for the old codger!"

"Charlie, and Emmy are both dead," Abe said in a barely audible voice.

"What?" Jeffrey shouted. He couldn't believe his ears! He acted like he was being strangled! "Dead? How? When? Who would have done such a terrible thing!"

Abe gave the young Baxter a curious look. "Tell me you know nothing about any of this," he said in a sober manner.

"I don't," he said in a threatened tone. "Why would you say such a thing?"

"Jeffrey," Abe stated, "you haven't been the same boy since you've started hanging around those hooligans that you're so found of. Drinking, carousing around. Making a complete horses butt of yourself. I pray for your sake that you're not lying to me, son, because if you are the consequences will be far worse than a walk to the timber. I will kill you myself!" With that being said, Abe turned and led the broken animal toward the barn to tend to Charlie's body.

"Why are you blaming me!" Jeffrey screamed. "I don't know nothing! I didn't do nothing!" Like a madman he jumped on his startled horse and flew out of the arched gate like the devil himself was on his tail! "Damn you!" he yowled. "Damn you all to…!" Like a fleeing coyote his words faded behind him as he disappeared with a cloud of dust through the arched gate.

"Have mercy on us all Mighty One," Abe said out loud, "this is going to be a vicious battle start to finish."

www.ingramcontent.com/pod-product-compliance
Lightning Source LLC
LaVergne TN
LVHW010200070526
838199LV00062B/4438